Hooked Into Murder

A Yarn Genie Crochet Mystery

Celeste Bennett

Island City Publishing LLC

ISBN-10: 1-946890-02-2
ISBN-13: 978-1-946890-02-3

DEDICATION

This book is dedicated to Beasley, my stubborn Scottish Terrier, and Dreampuff, a friend's adorable Pomeranian.

CHAPTER 1

Tears stung my eyes as I watched Mr. Twerk grab an industrial-sized pair of scissors from his desk and reduce my credit cards to a colorful pile of plastic pieces. He used one unscathed card to gather all the little pieces up into a mound that he shoved off into a wastebasket at the edge of his desk. The bits all cascaded into the trash, making little plinking sounds as they hit the metal. All gone. Without my cards, how was I going to buy that lovely Christo yarn I'd been dying to try?

"Was that necessary?" I asked my financial advisor.

"Imogene Warren, you signed legal papers for me to negotiate your financial matters and get your bills in order. I've been trying to do just that, but since we've talked last, you have made sixteen more credit purchases. Your inheritance share of the royalties from your aunt's mystery series will just about cover the expenses for the colonial in Winnetka. However, her being dead, she can't very well write any new novels, can she? As time goes on, that revenue source will dry up. If you intend to keep her mansion, you have got to get your spending habits under control."

I reached into my pants pocket to finger the ball of Shesay yarn I'd secreted there, gray with little silver sparkles and metallic threads already woven in, a little stiff and scratchy. I should have brought the swatch of Cashmerino yarn

I'd knitted up as a gauge for the scarf I made Frank. Frank is the undercover FBI agent who declared he loved me—just before I foolishly told him to leave me alone. That little knit square would have been much softer, more soothing to my nerves.

"Of course I want to keep the house," I told Mr. Twerk. "I've lived in that house with my Aunt Tilly since I was six years old. Now that she's dead, I miss her so much that I get distressed easily. I was only trying to brighten my spirits when I bought a few of the new Red Thread yarns. I didn't think it would hurt to make a few small purchases."

Mr. Twerk sighed a deep-down sigh. "Spending a hundred dollars ten times is the same as spending a thousand dollars. Even the small purchases add up. If you insist on keeping the mansion and its household staff, then I recommend you eliminate everything that isn't essential for your survival, cut your expenses to the bone, and sell all your other assets."

"Which assets are you referring to? My financial portfolio? That was only a fabrication made up by Jorgji to steal my wealth. My jewelry? That was all taken by Jorgji, too. The paintings and art collections? The house in the Cayman Islands? I had to sell that house, the paintings, and the art collections to give my half-sister her share of the inheritance from our aunt. All I have left, besides the mansion, are my clothes and my yarns."

"Too bad there aren't any additional manuscripts of your aunt's that you could sell. Those would fetch a mint now that she's dead."

I blew out a puff of air through pursed lips so my hair would blow away from my eyes and I could let off steam. "You sound just like Rosenthal and Gildenstein."

Mr. Twerk raised his eyebrows at me. "Who?"

"Rosenthal and Gildenstein. They were my aunt's literary agent and publicist. If I have to tell them one more time that the last two manuscripts I have are unfinished and of no value to them, I'll scream."

The eyebrows went up farther before they settled back to their unemotional level above each beady eye. "You do still have the Bentley and the Rolls. They'd fetch a good price," he said, shifting in his chair. "Might keep the wolf from the door a few more months. It's a shame your husband was killed before the FBI could discover where he hid the billions he absconded with."

"He was not my husband!" I shot up out of my chair and began to pace the room. I didn't want to talk about Jorgji, the man who plotted with his wife, Karine, to get my money—and succeeded. "The lawyers have assured me that since he was already married in Albania, our marriage wasn't legal."

"Legal or no, until the FBI recovers your missing funds, you are without two dimes to rub together." Mr. Twerk tidied up the pencils, pens and other objects on his desk then slid the scissors back into the top drawer.

"They haven't recovered any of the money yet, have they?" he asked me, eyes averted to the stack of overdue household bills that I'd brought for him to deal with.

I stopped my pacing for a brief moment to glower at him. He continued to avoid my stare by shuffling the bills around a bit more before placing them in the file folder with my married name, Imogene Dalmat, neatly penciled on the tab.

"No. The electric company wouldn't be threatening to shut off my lights, and I wouldn't be here talking to you if I had my money back. I've called the FBI Financial Crimes Investigation Unit every day, sometimes two or three times a day. Mr. Stevens, the agent assigned to my case, told me to stop calling him. He'll call me when he has news to share."

Mr. Twerk harrumphed. He slid the one lone unscathed credit card across the top of his desk towards me. "I'll contact the utility companies to negotiate delays in payment. I've already consolidated all your cards to this one account with the lowest interest rate. You'll have just one credit card bill to pay each month, but it'll be a whopper."

He took a pencil out of its wooden stand, stuck it in the electric pencil sharpener where it whirled around to sharpen its already sharp point. He removed the pencil to test the point against the tip of his index finger. Satisfied, he hunched over his desk and began making tiny sharp pencil notes in my file.

I paused my pacing to pick up the lone white rectangle with the holographic bird in the corner. I smiled a knowing smile. I was not alone. I still had my Select Rewards Visa. We headed towards the office door.

Mr. Twerk looked up from his folder scribbling in time to catch sight of my expression, the glint in my eye, and the tight grip I had on my credit card. He said to me, before he hunched back over his desk, "You won't be able to use the card for any more purchases. It was maxed out after I put my service fee on it."

Darn. I hadn't counted on my financial advisor charging me to cut up my cards.

CHAPTER 2

"We'll take good care of her and find her a lovely home." The man in the crisp black suit lightly patted my slumped shoulder through the open door of my Bentley, more a spurious reassurance than a genuine promise. When I didn't get out from behind the wheel, he placed his fat fingered hand on my car door and said, "If you could please leave the vehicle, Mrs. Dalmat, we've got a man at the ready to detail it before we put it on the showroom floor."

"I told you, my name is not Mrs. Dalmat. I just have to sign my name that way on legal papers until my lawyers can get my marital status straightened out." I stared out the windshield at the man in the gray uniform with the name "Stanley" embroidered in red on his left chest. He had stationed himself near the Bentley dealership's door after I signed the sales papers. He was keeping a watchful eye on my Bentley, now their Bentley. As I sat, he continued to stare. I let him look all he wanted. He could take a picture for all I cared. I was going to remain seated in my car, holding the crummy check they'd issued me until I was ready to leave.

Pulling my coat tighter to my chest, I adjusted the knit cable cashmere scarf around my neck so it wasn't cinched so tightly and hunched my shoulders closer together. Letting go was harder than I thought it would be.

I hadn't approached the Bentley dealership in Chicago to sell my car because they were too close to home. It would be devastating to catch sight of a stranger driving my Bentley. Almost as devastating as having to turn my baby over to Stanley.

I thought in Troy, Michigan I could make a clean break, and that's what I was doing—breaking. I wondered if it would do me any good to get a hold of Agent Stevens again? I guessed not. Four times in one day was the limit, even for me.

Mr. Black Suit said to me, "Mrs…Miss Warren, you can always come back and visit her whenever you like—until she's sold, of course."

He removed his hand from the door when I gave him a scalding, scathing look.

"I understand how difficult your *circumstances* must be…" He began, talking softly, cajolingly like I was one slice shy of a full loaf. Maybe I was more than one slice short after spending time in a jail cell accused of using my knitting needle to murder Jorgji.

"Cab's here," shouted Stanley at his lookout point near the dealership's door. Stan-the-man visibly relaxed as the yellow cab pulled up and parked near us. Both Bentley men had been jittery when I insisted on getting into the front seat of my vehicle for a last parting good-bye before the suited man had the embroidered man take my Bentley to wherever men named Stanley, dressed in service uniforms, take cars to 'detail' them. I hoped he'd be gentle with her.

The cab driver rolled down his window. "Someone here call a cab?"

"Yes," both men said in unison, nodding in my direction.

I had to be going. Recently, I'd learned that cabbies keep their meters running even while parked. I needed to go while the day was still bright, light and young. I had already scheduled an appointment at the Chevy dealership and was eager to stop off after that to see Frank's sister, Janey, and her new baby while I was in the area. I patted the Bentley's dashboard lovingly and ran my hand over the heated black leather seat cushions one last time. I slipped the check into my purse, pulled my knitted beret onto my head, adjusted my scarf again, buttoned my coat, picked up the package I'd brought with me, and stepped out into Michigan's brisk November air.

"You look great," I said to Janey. "No one would ever suspect you had a baby five weeks ago."

"Ya think?" she asked twirling around in her living room while placing a hand on her flat abdomen. "I've been working out trying to get back into shape for work."

I looked around, searching for signs of Frank, wondering if he'd been there recently. The last time I was in Janey's living room there wasn't a baby swing clicking away like a neophyte's metronome; the pint-sized baby bed and changing table weren't in the corner. I was sleeping in the room designated for the baby's nursery, and Frank was sleeping on the couch.

"Have you seen or heard from Frank?" I asked, still surreptitiously looking around, trying to sound casual.

"No," she responded. "He went on special assignment the minute the prosecutor dropped the murder charges against you and your name was cleared. I know he'll get in touch with me as soon as he can, but since I'm off work, I'm out of the loop and have no way of knowing when that will be."

"Oh." I tried not to sound disappointed, but I was.

She seemed to sense it. "Do you want me to have him call you when I hear from him?"

"No. I don't want you to do that," I lied. "He's got my number." Boy, did he ever. When he said he loved me, I'm the one who wanted time to sort my feelings out. I was still sorting; it would just have been nice if he had been there to sort with me.

I forced my mouth into a smile that I feared had become

more of a grimace and said, brightening my tone, "I made the baby a gift." I pulled out the package that I had wrapped myself and handed the box to Janey. While I fidgeted in my chair, she gently removed the haphazardly placed tape, pulled away the Sunday comics that I had used for wrapping paper, and pulled the lid off the box.

Janey opened the newsprint inside the box that served as replacement tissue paper.

I explained, "Sorry about the wrapping. I saw this article on Pinterest about how chic it is to use newspaper for gift wrapping."

She held up the paper wrapping and read the headline out loud. "Murder in Deep Tunnel?"

I quickly grabbed the paper from her hand. "Well, maybe I should have been more choosy about the sections of the paper I used. It's probably a good thing babies don't read. I wouldn't want that unsolved murder of the man with a smashed-in head to keep the baby up at night."

"Are unsolved murders keeping you up at night?" Janey asked me, a little too intuitive.

"I was disturbed by the reporter's descriptions of how vicious the attack was on that worker. I try not to think about the fact that the man's coworker, who was suspected of the murder, wasn't charged for lack of evidence. I have to keep reminding myself that my home has a state-of-the-art security system that Gordon sets every night, and that the murder was underneath downtown Chicago—miles away from me. When would I ever be in downtown Chicago?"

"That's great that you've found a way to use logic to help overcome your fear of being murdered," Janey said to me, knowing in the past more than one person had desired to see me dead.

She smoothed her hand over the blanket. "It was so sweet of you to bring the baby this blanket; I know how much you abhor leaving home. It means a lot to me that you came here to see us." Janey smiled a knowing smile at me, and I relaxed. It was good to be with someone I liked and trusted after so many betrayals.

I glanced around the room, reliving the brief time I spent there with Frank. "I'm doing my best to overcome my phobias, but I'm afraid I still spend a lot of time at home, reading magazines and the novels my Aunt Tilly wrote and doing my yarn crafting."

Janey held up the blanket and examined the pattern closely. It was my first attempt at crochet, and it turned out a little unconventional. I didn't have any baby yarns, and thanks to Mr. Twerk, couldn't buy any, so I used sock yarns doubled up and tied together. Some of the yarn ends had come untucked and were sticking out haphazardly.

"This blanket is...em...lovely. Thank you so much."

"I'm so glad you like it. Mandy stopped over as I was wrapping it and she thought it was hideous and told me not to bring it. I almost didn't bring it after her comments."

"I'm so glad you didn't listen to her. It's wonderful to see you. Frank will be pleased to hear you're doing so well." Janey ran her hand over the surface of the blanket again. Before I could turn the conversation to the direction she started in with Frank, she asked me, "Did you knit this?"

"Oh my, no. I don't knit anymore, not since my knitting needle was used to murder Jorgji. I've taken up crochet. No one can ever accuse me of murdering anyone with a crochet hook."

While Janey refolded the blanket onto her lap, I continued to glance around the room until I spied what I was hoping to see. I walked over and took the gold gilded frame off the stand by the sofa and studied the eight by ten picture of Janey and her twin brother, Frank. Dressed in black suits and ties, each held up their FBI badges for the camera. On either side of them was a silver-haired bookend parent. If that picture had been small enough to slip unseen into my purse, I would have.

"Isn't that a great picture of all of us? Samantha Simpson took that at our FBI graduation in Virginia. Dad and Mom were so proud of us," Janey said. "I wanted to name the baby after

Dad and Frank, but my husband didn't want to saddle him with a first name like 'Frances,' so we settled on 'Jonathan,' Frank's middle name."

I continued to look at and commit to memory that Windsor-knotted tie, the short, smooth, neatly combed dark brown hair, the clean-shaven face, the brown eyes flecked with blue that stared back at me from the confines of the frame.

I wondered why Samantha had been at their FBI Academy graduation; she was a criminal defense attorney, not a photographer. "Samantha was at your graduation? You two are friends?"

"Not really. She was there because she and Frank were engaged at the time."

I almost dropped the frame. Frank had never mentioned this little fact to me. "When did they break their engagement off?" I asked, trying to sound nonchalant.

"About a year ago. They were engaged for a couple of years before they both realized they wanted different things in life." Janey walked the short distance to the kitchen. "How about a snack?"

I did some fast calculations in my head. Frank hadn't been broken up with Samantha for long when I'd crawled into the back seat of his FBI undercover car to hide from hired killers. I wanted to know more about their break-up but was uncertain of how to broach the subject without finding out more than my heart could handle. If I had been only a mild attraction, a short dalliance until he could patch things up with Samantha, my spirit would have been crushed, and all my efforts to fight my agoraphobia to have a normal life with Frank would be for nothing.

Janey began making a clatter as she took plates, cups, and saucers out of her cupboards. I was all ears as she resumed her chatter, but I could feel myself shriveling inside as she continued to talk about the love of her life—her baby. She failed to elucidate further on the love of my life and what had separated him from Samantha.

14

I kept my ears open while she talked, but clamped my mouth shut. I had to let the matter of Frank's previous love interest drop, for my own good.

Janey went about her tasks, unaware that her casual statements about Frank and Samantha being an item had caused a severe blow to my fragile ego.

Frank had hired Samantha to clear me of the erroneous charge of murdering my pseudo-husband. Frank and Samantha worked together tirelessly to secure my freedom. I found it strange Frank never once mentioned their previous connection, not even after he and I developed a fondness for each other. I looked at that handsome face behind the glass.

What other details of his life was he keeping from me?

"Would you like to hold him?" Janey asked me.

"I sure would," I said, running my fingers along the set of his firm square jaw line in the picture.

She set the cups and plates on the table and said, "He's over there in his swing. I just got through feeding him before you got here."

Darn it. She was referring to the baby.

Janey headed to the corner of the living room where she fished an obscured blob of baby, arms and legs dangling, out from his mechanically swinging seat. The clicking noise immediately stopped as the seat stilled.

The baby she was holding had a giant's round head, and there was a bit of curdled drool at the corner of his mouth. He looked at me cross-eyed. He didn't have any hair, and there was a double chin hidden in the folds of his neck. His little pastel blue shirt had spittle on it.

"What a cute little guy," I lied. *Mistake.* She handed the baby to me. I held him out at arm's length, a hand under each little baby armpit, not knowing what I should be doing. He smelled funny, like sour milk. *Weren't babies supposed to smell sweet?* And his head was wobbly on his shoulders.

"Here," she said, positioning him up on my chest and placing my hand so it cradled his head. My other hand she put on his diapered bottom. "You need to support his head and keep him stable. He's not old enough to support his head very well."

Yeah, a head that big must be heavy.

The warm little bundle I held snuggled in close to my chest and gave a little cooing noise. I missed Frank more every minute.

We went into the kitchen where I sat at the kitchen table and told Janey all about my money situation while she fixed us tea and got out a tin of cookies. Little Frankie—Johnny—fell asleep in my arms.

"I'm so broke I don't even know how I'm going to pay Gordon and Keiko their wages next month." I grabbed the edge of the burp cloth that was under Johnny's head to wipe up the few tears that insisted on rolling down my cheeks. When Johnny's head tilted to the side awkwardly, I put the flat of my hand against the side of his head and shoved it back into its original position.

Janey jumped up unexpectedly, startling me and almost waking Johnny. She looked at his peaceful sleeping face and then looked around, bewildered as to what she had jumped up for. "Until the guys at the FCIU can identify the overseas banks where your money went to, it sounds like you need to find a job."

I eyed the red tin she'd brought out of her cupboard, but I politely waited until she arranged the cookies nicely on a serving plate and properly offered them to me before I re-juggled her sleeping baby to grab a few.

"A job? I hadn't thought of that. What kind of job do you think I could do?" Cookie crumbs scattered on Johnny's head. I brushed them off. His head wobbled a bit again.

"I don't know. What are you good at?" Janey bounced up again and hovered near me. She fluttered around me before setting a paper napkin next to my cookie plate. Rather than retake her seat, she remained standing next to me. Still hovering.

I pondered her question while chewing. *Just what was I good at? Spending money? Knitting? Hiding from hired killers?*

"I don't think I'm good at anything—except I did type my aunt's manuscripts and handled her correspondence up until the time of her death." I reached for another cookie or two. Johnny's head tipped back as I leaned forward, but I managed to catch it before it went too far and clunked the table.

"Well, there you go." Janey whisked her sleeping baby out of my arms, strode across the room and laid him down in the bassinet next to the baby swing. "Maybe you can get a job as a secretary or administrative assistant or something like that."

Her house phone rang. I was hoping it was Frank.

It wasn't Frank. The caller was Janey's neighbor. She was attempting to clear her yard of its leaf accumulation and was having some trouble with her leaf mulcher. I guess she wanted Janey to come over and give the man a pep talk or something.

"Do you mind keeping an eye on Johnny for me while I run over to help my neighbor start her mulcher? I'll only be gone a few minutes."

Watch a baby? Panic began to set in. My breathing became shallow and quick. I could feel the sheen of sweat starting on my forehead. The shakes would soon follow. I wiped my already perspiring hands on my skirt. "What if he needs something? I've never diapered a baby before, and I don't have working feeding equipment or anything like that."

"I doubt he'll need diapering, but if he does, there are clean cloth diapers on a shelf under the changing table. He shouldn't need to feed for at least another couple of hours. I'll only be gone a minute or two." She looked at me and then back at the bassinetted baby. "Uhhh, maybe I should bundle him up and take him with me."

While she got her coat on, I tiptoed over to the bassinet and peeked in. The baby was sleeping quietly in this little oval bed. In his sleep, with his little arms stretched up over his head, he resembled his uncle the first time I saw him sleeping. Only the baby was chubbier, and he had on clothes. Janey would only be gone for a minute or two. I'd heard babies sleep a lot. *How hard could it be to watch a sleeping baby? Wasn't that what I was already doing?*

The second that front door closed, there was a gas explosion sound coming from the baby's bed, closely followed by little Johnny's wailing his round head off.

I picked him up, remembering to hold his head and his bottom, which now felt a lot squishier than it did before. He was stinky, and it wasn't from sour milk. I laid him on the pad of the changing table to examine his Velcro fastened diaper. I pulled one tab loose and peeked inside.

P.U. I held my breath while removing his diaper. It looked like he squirted out a Sneakers bar in that thing. Gagging, I rummaged around trying to find something to wipe that residue off his bottom.

My search was interrupted by a stream of liquid that arced up from him like a lawn sprinkler to spray his little blue shirt. I did my best to take his soaked wet shirt off him without breaking his arms. He was not very cooperative, and his screaming was not helping my nerves.

I managed to wrestle a clean shirt on him, despite his hollering. As I knelt at the changing table to return to my baby toilet paper search, another stream of water issued forth to sprinkle the clean shirt I had just put on him.

"That's a pretty neat trick there, Bub," I told him. "I bet you could get a job choreographing the fountains at the Bellagio in Vegas."

He stopped crying. His crossed eyes uncrossed and focused on my face. He blew little saliva bubbles out of his mouth and made a little cheery baby sound, waving his arms and legs in obvious delight.

I smiled at him and made a few spit bubbles myself.

I pulled out another shirt from the stack and got busy wrestling again. It wasn't easy, but I managed to get his bubbling, squirming, kicking body into a fresh, clean shirt—just in time for him to squirt it again. *Darn.* I had thought that fountain had run dry.

Janey returned a few minutes later to a mound of soiled baby clothes, a waste can filled with gooey baby wipes, and

Johnny and me rocking in the rocking chair. Johnny's sweet breath tickled the crook of my neck; the smell of baby powder and butt wipes surrounded us. My homemade baby blanket was tucked around him; he was snuggled close to my heart, sleeping soundly, naked except for his oddly-shaped hourglass cloth diaper that kept velcroing itself to my wool sweater.

Having gained experience with babies, I figured I was a shoe-in for a babysitting job.

CHAPTER 3

The sun had weakened its stance and steeped the sky into darkness by the time I started out for home. Winnetka was a long way off, and I'd only traveled a few miles when I became aware of a pair of headlights mirroring my every move. I turned right. They turned right. I stopped. They stopped. I shrugged off their shadow movements, attributing my paranoia to the fact that I was always hyper-aware of my surroundings when out in public. Phobias do that to me.

As I got closer to the highway, I found the lights continued to show in my rear view and side mirrors. Frightened, I sped up; the van sped up. I drove faster, turning the radio louder and refusing to look into any of my car's mirrors.

I traveled for several miles along the interstate corridor with my squinting eyes focused only on the painted lines on the road. When I did relax enough to take notice of my surroundings again, my dashboard caught my eye.

How long had that blinking red light been there?

I didn't know if there was a phobia for the fear of flashing red dash lights or not, but if there was, I developed it then.

I slammed on the brakes and yanked my vehicle over to the expressway shoulder. Something green sped past me. It was too dark to get a good look at the van or the two men in

20

the front, but I recognized the headlights.

I breathed a sigh of relief upon their passing. They hadn't stopped when I stopped, so I concluded that I wasn't being followed; it was my paranoia about being followed that led me to believe I was being followed.

I opened the glove box and dragged out the padded folder that held my insurance rider, vehicle registration, and the owner's manual. I hastily flipped through the thick booklet, but I couldn't find the proper page number for dashboards. There was an obscure section marked "Warning Lights, Gauges, and Indicators." These six pages declared that 'warning lights can signal that something is wrong' and for me to pay attention to them to 'prevent costly repairs or injury.' However, those pages had absolutely no information about what the lights were or what it meant when they flashed on.

Thank you, Dilbert engineers for writing a manual that non-engineers needed a manual to understand.

I shifted into park and turned the heater up to high while I studied the booklet, page by page.

While engrossed in my reading, I was startled by a sharp rap on my window. I clutched the manual and its padded folio to my chest to still my heart or deflect bullets, whichever was appropriate.

A man knelt down, and his round brown face filled my window's view. The Michigan state logo, the two cute little deer holding hands around a shield, was on the navy blue cap of the state trooper looking in through my car window. He knelt down as I rolled the window down to talk to him.

"Yes, officer?" My hands had started to sweat, and I was trembling, a little hold-over from being arrested and incarcerated by the police earlier in the year.

"Good evening, Ma'am," he began, tipping his shiny hat visor a little in greeting. "I need to see your license and registration, please."

I wiped my hands on the unheated cloth car seat before pulling my wallet out of my teddy bear print diaper bag that I used as a purse. I fumbled nervously but managed to hand him my license promptly. The car registration soon followed from its pocketed spot in the padded folio.

In my rearview mirror, I watched in the glare of his headlights as he strode to his blue cruiser—carrying the identification for me and the car I had recently purchased.

A semi barreled past, and my car rocked with the updraft, too close for my comfort. I watched a string of vehicles, like a necklace made of odd-shaped beads, switch lanes to maneuver safely around the cruiser's flashing lights: a candy apple red sports car, an azure blue sedan, a black truck with a green camouflage cap, a golden caddy, a solar flare orange Lamborghini—all passed me, the drivers craning their necks, looking at me like I was the highway criminal I felt myself to be.

When I saw a green Caravan tucked in between a silver PT cruiser and a daisy yellow Volkswagen, I wiped my hands again and mentally reminded myself, "You're stopped on the expressway, but this time you are not on the run. No one is trying to kill you—that you know of."

The officer started to walk back to my vehicle. To my relief, he didn't have his gun drawn or his handcuffs out. He also wasn't carrying a ticket booklet, only my papers.

His form was outlined in my headlights as he walked around to the front of my vehicle and then to the passenger side before coming back to my window and asking me, "Ma'am, was there a reason you stopped? Your vehicle and you both appear in good shape. The tires are all inflated. Are you having an emergency situation of some kind?"

"I don't know for sure, officer. There's a red light flashing on and off on the dash that wasn't there when I bought this vehicle today. I stopped so I could look up what that light means." I held up the open manual so he could see the proof of my claim.

He shoved his cap back to expose a head of closely cropped curly black hair. When he moved his head closer to my window, I got a whiff of the lavender and lilac shampoo he'd used.

"You mean the low fuel light?" He pointed to the light in question.

"Is that what that light is?"

"Yes, Ma'am." He pulled his head back from my vehicle and put his hat back in place. The curls and scent hidden, he stared hard at me with a look of disbelief.

"Do you think I can make it home? If I can get that far, my butler can put gas in the car." I had never fueled a vehicle in my life. The thought of being in the vicinity of a gasoline dispenser filled me with a new terror. I wished I had brought my knit swatch of Frank fabric to use as a 'worry' cloth. I vowed never to leave home without that patch again.

"Uh, don't you live in Illinois?" he asked looking at the driver's license he held in his hand.

"Yes. I live in Winnetka; it's north of Chicago."

He handed me my license and papers, steadied himself by placing both glove-encased hands on the frame of my open window. His face a mask of concern, he said, "Ma'am, you're not going to make it that far. Chicago is over 150 miles from here. You'd better get off at the next exit and fuel up."

I thanked him for the advice, but when he didn't head back to his multi-lighted vehicle as I expected, my arms grew weak and fell to my sides. I waited for the handcuffs to appear and the voice command that would tell me to step out of the car.

He tipped his hat back a little on his beautiful black hair, he leaned in a bit towards me again and said with a serious expression and soft voice, "Next time, ma'am, remember it's against the law to stop on the expressway unless it is an actual emergency."

He walked back to his cruiser leaving me with my mouth open.

Just what did he think a blinking red light on the dash was?

It was full scary dark by the time I hit the next exit. At the end of the off ramp I stopped. My fear of the dark waged war with my fear of strangers. The officer had said I didn't have enough gas to make it home so I had to figure out the refueling thing so I could be on my way.

I debated the merits of staying locked in my vehicle with all the doors locked until dawn's light, but the chilly weather made that impractical and Gordon and Keiko would be worried when I didn't arrive home. All debating with myself stopped when a green van came up to my back bumper, too green and too close behind me to be a coincidence.

The Van's passenger door swung open; a tennis-shoed foot came out and touched the pavement.

I forced aside my phobias, gunned my engine, and cranked the steering wheel hard to the right.

The van door closed. I could hear the van's engine rev up behind me. A quick check in the rearview mirror confirmed the van had turned in my direction.

Car horns blared as I did a U-Turn in the middle of the street and crossed in front of several vehicles to head in the opposite direction. I was prepared to make as many evasive maneuvers and anger as many drivers as needed to prevent the green van from catching up to me on the way home.

The van slowed but kept on going, no U-turn. I took my foot off the accelerator and my vehicle's speed dropped dramatically. It took a little longer for my heart rate to do the same.

After I turned down several side streets and was sure I'd given the van the slip, I chose a well-lit station with big green sunbursts on its sign, canopy, building, and pumps. It looked friendly enough.

Inching through the cars and trucks whizzing in and out of the station, I selected an unclaimed dispenser.

The car on the other side of the pump contained a load of teenagers with their faces painted maroon on one side, white on the other, waving little maroon and white flags, shouting and hooting. I noticed several of the cars around the station had similar flags attached to antennas and door casings. Very disconcerting and distracting.

I read the instructions printed on the pump face. Seemed

easy enough. I pulled a sturdy blue paper towel from a convenient dispenser near the pump, and using that to cover the pump gun handle's deadly germs; I pulled the pump gun out.

A green Dodge van rolled slowly by the station, but it didn't pull in. I tried to ignore the feeling of déjà vu that kept pricking me.

The gas nozzle didn't reach around to the filler port side of the car. As I struggled, a green color stirred in my peripheral vision again.

I stopped my struggles with the hose to get a closer look at the van. *Was that the same van and men as before?* At least the driver's drooping mustache seemed familiar, but before I could get a good view the van was gone.

"Get a grip. On the pump handle and yourself. Green is just a favorite color for Dodge vans in Michigan. Michigan College fans and all that," I muttered to myself. No matter how much I told myself to stop it, my hands still continued to shake.

With renewed urgency, I struggled to loop the hose up and over the car, to no avail. It was like I was trying to jump rope with an elephant.

"Hey lady," yelled the station attendant through the window he opened on his kiosk. "You gotta pull up closer to the pump or turn your car around. The hose isn't that long."

I looked at the pump. Looked at my car. I had given the pump too wide a berth when I pulled up. I got back behind the wheel to maneuver my vehicle into proper position. I felt perspiration began to dot my forehead as more cars pulling into the station forced me to select a dispenser farther away from the safety of the kiosk.

I stood in the cooling night air, proud of having gotten close enough to the dispenser to put the nozzle easily into the fueling spot. Shivering, I waited patiently for the flow of gasoline to start.

Another green van drove by, or maybe it was the same one. I chose to ignore it.

After a few minutes of standing there, the attendant slid his window open again, stuck his head completely out and yelled at me. Again.

"Hey, lady. You gotta select the grade you want and depress the trigger. You want I come out and show ya?" Everyone at the station turned to stare at me.

How humiliating. That attendant had on bigger earrings on than I did. "No. I've got it now. Thanks." Feeling foolish, and mortified that everyone was looking at me, I pushed the yellow button that had the highest black number on it.

I shut my eyes tight and squeezed the trigger. I felt a thrum in the nozzle as a heady odor assailed my nostrils; it was intoxicating.

Gasoline "92" filled my tank at a rapid rate with the help of that rubber hose and my tight grip. I opened my eyes. The gasoline was pouring into my car, sight unseen. I inhaled deeply of the strong aroma.

A few seconds of that and I got light-headed, so I held my head away from the fumes and glanced around at the others to see who was still watching me, noticing my accomplishment.

Everyone was either cleaning windshields, high-fiving each other, yelling at painted faces, airing their tires or filling their cars with dangerous liquid. They had lost interest in me. Even the attendant had shut his window.

My chest swelled with pride nevertheless. I was a kindred spirit with my fellow travelers; we were all pumping our gasoline. I was even undisturbed by what looked like the front edge of a green vehicle showing from behind a corner of the station.

I heard a "click" and the surge was gone.

I squeezed the nozzle back on. It clicked off. I clicked it on. It clicked off. According to the pump display, I'd pumped in fifteen point two gallons. That sounded like enough to get home on, so I stopped. I could always have Gordon put the rest of the gasoline in the next day.

"First time pumping gas?" Mr. Big Earrings asked me as I

grabbed a couple of packages of "Grandma's Best Cookies" off the display stand and put the requested amount of money on the counter.

"No. I've just got a lot on my mind," I lied. I had hoped lying wouldn't get to be a habit.

The attendant handed me my change. My hand was on the door, pushing out to leave when the attendant popped out from behind the counter and grabbed my arm.

"Lady. Wait," he implored me. "Don't go out there. I just saw a man get into your car. "

I squinted out to where my car was on the far side of the farthest pump. There was definitely a man leaning into the front seat of my car scrounging around.

While Mr. Big Earrings called the police, I staved off cardiac arrest by opening up one of the cookie packages and eating the contents.

I opened the second package of cookies and began eating them when Mr. Big Earrings told me the police were only a few minutes away.

Before the police got there, a man with a hooded sweatshirt obscuring his face, scurried out from the front seat of my car and dashed across the parking lot, carrying something in his hand. He hopped aboard the green van that came around the back corner of the building, and they sped off.

The curly-haired trooper from my earlier stop listened patiently to my story as I explained that I still had my purse; the only thing the thief had taken was the folio with the car registration and owner's manual. Having just bought the car, I had nothing else in the vehicle.

I could smell the herbal shampoo when he shook his head in disbelief at my rotten luck.

"The high school football team just won district finals. This was probably just a celebration prank," he reassured me. "I'll make out a report, but I doubt we'll see your papers again. You should just request duplicates."

I gave credence to his words, but my eye began a nervous

twitch when he said, "You be sure and keep your cell phone handy in case you have any more trouble. If you're still in Michigan, you call 911 and ask for me, Officer Sawney."

He handed me his business card. I took it in silence, too ashamed to admit that I didn't have a cell phone with me. Mr. Twerk had canceled my carrier contract to save money.

CHAPTER 4

I crept along at the lowest non-ticketing expressway speed allowed, steadfastly ignoring the one finger gestures of the other drivers. Adjusting all my mirrors, I carefully monitored the other vehicles surrounding me. I felt certain I was going to toss Grandma's Best Cookies the next 100 miles of my journey, but when no green vans appeared in any of my mirrors, my stomach settled. I rounded the corner to my driveway, certain that the ominous predators seeking my doom had been left behind in Oshtemo, Michigan.

I avoided the garage with its empty Bentley parking spot and left the Bentley replacement in the driveway. At the front door, I scrounged through my purse for my house keys, trying to remember the last time I had them. I'd not needed to use them for months. Having no luck finding them, I returned to the car to get the garage door remote so I could enter through the garage—sans keys.

I searched the entire front seat and flipped both visors down. No remote.

Had I forgotten to pull my garage door clicker opener from the Bentley before I left Troy?

It was too late in the evening, or rather too early in the morning, to awaken Gordon or Keiko to answer the doorbell, so I re-examined my bag hoping the keys were in there somewhere. Moving the small balls of yarn aside, I found loose change, a tube of lip balm, a small gray mottled stone and a silver crochet hook in the bottom of my bag. No keys.

There was a spare key under the loose step at the back porch of the house. As I walked in the shadows, the decorative shrubs edging the front of the house rustled in the dark breezes. Somewhere in the distance, an owl hooted. My ankle brushed the marigolds edging the side of the house, netting an unpleasant, deterring odor. The second screech of the owl had me hastening back to the light of the front porch where I sank my hand deeper into my oversized purse, groped the bottom again, and checked all the side pockets.

I had learned how to pump gasoline and buy little pre-packaged cookies at gas stations, yet I couldn't open my front door. Not wanting to remain outside so late at night, even with all my potential killers jailed, I surrendered my key search. I would just use Gordon's house key and garage door opener until he could make me a new set of keys and get my opener back from the dealership.

I pushed the doorbell, jumped up off the top step, and cleared the two lower steps and bounded into the bushes when I heard a blood-curdling scream echo from inside the house.

When the door wasn't answered immediately, shadows from the trees lining the drive began to take on a life of their own, their branches mocking my phobias. I returned to the spot in front of the door and rang the bell again as I looked distrustfully around me. I was prepared this time for the shrill door bell scream that pulsed through the night air, but it still unsettled me. Gordon was going to have to reprogram that doorbell to a different sound. Anything was better than that screaming.

There in the blackness, illuminated by the glow of the entryway light, waiting for someone to open those solid oak doors, I wondered why I was hanging on to that enormous old house so tightly. I'd sold almost everything I owned, except my yarns, to make things square with my sister so I could maintain that mansion for her and me to live in together. I loved that house, but did I love it more than Gordon and Keiko? Mr. Twerk had urged me to sell the mansion. He said I would get enough from the sale of the estate to pay Mandy for her share of the house plus have enough money left over to pay Gordon's and Keiko's wages for several years.

Without the mansion, would Gordon and Keiko even want to stay with me?

Keiko opened the door just as I was bracing myself to generate another doorbell scream. She, in her oversized red Chicago Bulls tee shirt and red bull slippers, yawned me inside.

I said, "konnichi wa" to her, hoping I'd said, "hello" correctly.

She said, "okaerinasai" to me.

"Huh?" I had no idea what she had said. I was grateful to be home. I just I hoped she hadn't just said that there were green van men waiting for me inside the house.

Seeing my confusion, she said, in recently learned and heavily practiced English, "Welcome home, Missy Imogreen." Then she smiled and asked, "Do I do good?"

"Yes. Very good. Thank you, Keiko." She was taking an "English As a Second Language" class at night school and learning English faster than I could pick up Japanese.

"That new car?" she asked me, opening the door wider to look out at the car I had parked in the drive.

"Yes. It's new." I looked back out at that hideous silver sedan box.

"I like."

My only response was to give Keiko a weak smile. I couldn't speak more than two words of Japanese, and she didn't understand enough English for me to begin to explain how unlikeable I found that dash-lighted, gas guzzling, unheated-seat car, and how tired I was. I only wanted one of Gordon's homemade sugar cookies, and the warmth of my bed.

The crinkling sound of plastic being pulled off the cookie plate in the kitchen drew Gordon from out of nowhere.

"Those have been waiting quite a while for your return. Do you want me to warm them?" Seeing my anguished look, he pulled out a chair for me. "Miss Imogene, what's wrong?"

I started to blubber about babies, cars, gas pumps, Frank not calling, meanie financial advisors, green vans, shrunken bank accounts and my lack of employable skills. Somewhere in the midst of my inane babble, I found myself with a warm sugar cookie in one hand and a tall glass of cold milk sitting on the table in front of me.

Gordon stood at the ready with a hankie.

I took the hankie. "Sit down, Gordon. I have to talk to you." I sniffled, hiccupped loudly, and set the uneaten cookie down, dabbing my eyes with his handkerchief. There was no point in delaying 'the talk.' I needed to cut his and Keiko's employment.

"I need to talk to you, also. May I speak first?" he asked.

I glanced up. He had taken the time to dress in his black suit, white shirt, and tie—even though it was very early in the morning. His coffee-and-cream brown eyes were looking to me for consent to speak. His face, marred only by a few small scars along his jaw line, remained expressionless, but his eyebrows were knit close together—his butler way of showing concern.

How much concern would he have for me when he learned he was being given the boot for all his years of service?

"Of course." I let him speak first—welcoming the delay in his pending dismissal.

"As you know, I was in your aunt's employ for almost 20 years. I have loved every minute of my time here with you and your aunt, but she's gone now, and you have grown into a beautiful young woman, capable of being on her own. There is a man I once knew facing charges for a crime he did not commit. It is a very complicated case, and I believe he'll need my help and lots of it. If you think you can manage without me, I should like to retire before I am too feeble from these old wounds to be of any help in clearing his name of these false charges." He clapped a hand on his left thigh and let it rest there for emphasis.

I felt tasered, my body taking 12000 volts all at once. All I could do was stare at him, and then at his crippled leg hidden beneath his dark pants. Gordon had been a member of my aunt's household almost as long as I had. After my staying with my cousins hadn't worked out, my aunt hired Gordon, a wounded vet, to help with me and the house so she could continue her writing career. He'd always had those facial scars and leg wound. He walked with a limp that sometimes slowed him down a bit, but he was a long way from feeble. He was my mentor, confidant, protector, sugar cookie maker. *What was I going to do without him?*

I looked into those sincere brown eyes and felt reality rear up and smack me full in the face. The FBI had yet to find my missing billions. Unless I discovered money secreted away somewhere in this old house or could discover how to grow money on trees, I couldn't afford to pay Gordon; I would have to learn to live without him.

A tender smile saddened his face as he patted my hand. "I have the 401K your aunt set me up with for my retirement. If it's all right with you, I'd like to keep the third-floor apartment as a home to come back to when I've resolved these old issues for my friend. I will send you money to help with the household expenses in exchange for allowing my occupancy upon my return."

"I would love for you to stay here. The third-floor apartment was renovated specially for you; it has always been yours. You don't have to exchange anything for it."

I suspected he'd made this retirement decision while I was carrying on about losing my Bentley, but with his and Keiko's wages out of the picture I was hopeful of being able to keep the lights turned on.

I stayed up a while longer pondering my plight and eating cookies. *The Morning Herald*, the previous day's paper, lay folded and undisturbed at my spot at the table, begging for my attention.

I spread the paper out on the table near my empty

cookie plate. I perused the front-page headliner of spies and government double agent espionage briefly before moving on. Those stories were too far beyond my comprehension to hold my interest.

The secondary stories of murder and mayhem weren't any better. Too depressing. I did take the time to skim the news about the man bludgeoned in a city tunnel to see if the suspected murderer had been arrested. He hadn't.

I flipped through the remaining pages until I got to the help wanted ads. I scanned the lengthy list and immediately found one that looked promising.

> Downtown Chicago start-up magazine business seeks receptionist to handle incoming calls, clients, and visitors during peak business hours. Some nights and evenings required.

That sounded like something I could do. I dashed to the den and typed up my resume. Then I had to scrounge up a stamp and envelope to mail it because my internet service had been sacrificed to Mr. Twerk's cutting.

Yawning, satisfied I'd done what I could for the time being, I headed off to bed. My situation had started to look up.

Well, maybe not so much. Before I could get all the way up the sweeping front stairs, the doorbell screamed. I peered out to see my look-a-like half-sister, Mandy. She is also my cousin thanks to the pre-marital affair my father had with my mother's sister. I opened the door before it screamed again and re-woke Keiko and Gordon.

Mandy waltzed in, dressed in new ZZenga blue jeans, an Italian wool blend sweater, radiating excitement. Her hair was cut and highlighted in an artistic style that only an experienced and expensive hair stylist could pull off. A white diamond sparkled at each ear lobe.

"Do you know how late it is?" I asked her. She ignored my question, not putting that Rolex watch on her wrist to proper use.

"Wait 'til you see what I got with my inher'tence." Mandy bounced up and down. I was glad Frank wasn't there for her theatrics because she obviously hadn't bought a new bra along with her other purchases.

"I can see. New jeans, new sweater, new watch—."

"No. Come outside and see. It's sorta in the shadows; I had to park a ways down the drive 'cause some idiot left their stupid Malibu up near the door." She grabbed me by the arm and pulled so had no choice but to follow her to the front door.

I was speechless. There in the driveway, behind that stupid silver thing I had driven home, was a shiny black Bentley. My heart skipped a beat, and I choked up.

Mandy bought my Bentley back for me? But how? When? I'd sold the car only that morning in Michigan.

"Ain't it a beaut? It's just like yours, same color and ever' thing—only mine's newer. Now we can both drive a Bentley." She was beaming a smile from sparkled diamond earring to sparkled diamond earring.

I was glad I had cried all my tears out with Gordon before Mandy got there so I wouldn't begrudge my sister this bit of happiness.

I gave her a big hug. Her gaze never left her Bentley, so it was easy to conceal my tears from her. "It's a beaut alright," I said. "Congratulations."

"Guess what else?" she asked me, ballerina-ing herself up on tiptoe and then back down again several times. Her smile was about to crack her face in two.

I couldn't begin to guess. "You bought a Rolls with a swimming pool in it?"

"No," she said. A frown flitted across her face. "They have those?"

The frown instantly dissipated as she laughed, waved her ringed hand at me, easily dismissing my sarcasm. "You silly. I bought me that penthouse apartment on Chicago Ave. The one that I, as a realtor, have been showcasing to all those rich executives for the past six months. It's got five bedrooms and a workout gym, sauna and an all-glass windowed corner view of the Chicago skyline."

I clutched my abdomen, but it plunged to the ground anyway. My acrophobia kept it there while my sister talked about the skyline view in her high-rise apartment.

"But I've already added your name to the deed here. You own half of this house. I thought you were going to live here, with me, in our home."

"I was going to, but Martin is out on bail now. He needs a place to stay before he goes to trial for attempted murder. I didn't think you'd want him to come here and live—what with you being the potential murderee and all."

"I think I need to go in and lie down," I said, walking away from my sister and her misplaced devotion to her brother from another father. Heading for the security of the house, I left my sister standing there alone.

CHAPTER 5

I should have read those newspaper headlines, and then that phone call from a tenacious reporter early the next morning wouldn't have caught me off guard.

"Miss Warren. Did you have any idea your father was a spy for the Russian government?" asked a man whose phone call woke me up at 6 a.m..

I'm not very agreeable with only three hours sleep. I hung up. The phone rang again.

"Miss Warren?" It was the same male voice. "I'm with the Washington Review."

"What do you want? How did you get this number? It's supposed to be unlisted."

"Please," he said. "Don't hang up. Just hear me out. I'm sure you must have a statement for the press about the allegations against your father. I want to help you tell your side of the story."

"What allegations? You've got the wrong number." I was ready to hang up again when I heard him say my father's name. I froze, the receiver in my hand.

"Wasn't your father Edward Timothy Warren?"

I put the phone back up to my ear. "Yes, but he he's been dead for 20 years."

"Wasn't he working for the CIA at the time of his death?"

"No! He was a Back and Becker tool salesman at the time of his death. You've got the wrong number." I held my breath and the phone, unable to hang up.

"You may have thought he was a traveling salesman, but news has been leaked that Edward Timothy Warren worked for the CIA and was recently discovered to have been a double agent spy for the Russian government. An unnamed source within the Department of Defense let it leak that newly uncovered documents show your father was carrying stolen top-secret stealth missile plans when he boarded a plane bound for Asia. The Russian informant who was part of a delegation that met with him has just requested asylum in the U.S. He says your father contacted the Russian government and offered to sell them the missile plans. When your father was killed in a car crash soon after his arrival in Nepal, it was uncertain what became of the plans he was carrying—until now. This informant is alleging Russia has found the plans and is building these undetectable missiles to use them as part of their military intervention in the Ukraine. Some political advisors believe Russia won't stop there."

I listened. Uncomprehending. My meek and mild father could not be the same man this reporter was talking about.

At that moment, the sun chose to come blasting in through the open blinds of my window. Clutching the phone, I crossed the room to the window and yanked the curtains shut. The room plunged into darkness as I groped for the bedside lamp to switch it on.

"I'm willing to work with you to get your side of the story out," he said again to my silence.

"I was only six years old. I don't have a side to this story." I slammed the receiver down, clicked the light back off and snuggled into my bed hoping that was all a bad dream.

The phone rang again. I covered my head with my pillow, wishing self-smothering was a possibility.

Where was Gordon? Why hadn't he answered the blasted phone like he always did? Where was Keiko? They couldn't both be unavailable.

38

I continued to hear persistent rings despite my best pillow efforts.

Keiko knocked on my door a few minutes later. "Many calls," she told me through my closed bedroom door.

I pulled the pillow down and away from my head. "Tell them they've got the wrong number."

"Right-o, boss." I could hear her skipping down the hall, more cheery than anyone has a right to be when I am not allowed my sleep.

I kept the blinds and curtains closed and dragged myself out of bed. I groped around for my robe before going downstairs, seeking yesterday's paper from where I'd left it on the kitchen table.

Seems the whole world panicked overnight at the thought of an aggressive Putin being given American plans for a 'ghost' bomb capable of wiping out thousands of people indiscriminately. The Russian informant alleged he had been privy to the American double agent bringing the plans to the Russian government and now that the plans had been found, he had come forward altruistically to prevent the loss of innocent lives. The informant, fearing for his life for sharing this information, was seeking asylum and money from the American government so he could live out his life comfortably here in exchange for his good deed.

My father's name was not mentioned in that article. Nor was the name of the Russian informant requesting asylum.

I ran and opened the front door to retrieve the morning paper for the latest news. A series of flashes blinded me. People dotted my front lawn. Microphones were shoved in my face. Everyone was shouting over the sound of their neighbor to get my attention for a statement. The ones that weren't shouting where shouldering heavy video cameras aimed at me.

I scrambled inside with my paper and shakily locked the door, muffling the shouts.

The morning paper gave the name of the suspected document thief. Seems my lying, wife-cheating father was also a double agent at the time of his death. The father I loved, the man who cuddled me on his lap and read me stories, the man who had baked my favorite cookies, was now branded a traitor. I read the article in disbelief.

> **Washington, D.C.** New information has been released by the US Department of Defense regarding the death of special agent Edward Warren 20 years ago. Agent Warren was in the Megheri mountain range in southern Asia with his wife when his vehicle went over the edge of a mountain, killing them both.

I paused to grab the hem of my robe and wipe my stinging eyes before continuing.

> A member of the former Russian KGB team that worked with Warren to secure the American plans for a stealth missile has come forward seeking asylum under the protection of anonymity. He says Warren was paid a huge sum of money by the Russian government to secure secret U.S. government documents alleged to be related to the development of a long-range missile system. The plans were for a weapon that could elude detection when launched and could remain undetectable until the missile was too close to its target to be stopped by conventional anti-missile systems. DOD has stated they are carefully reviewing the allegations against Warren and the implications this new information brings. They refuse to comment on the type of missile the Russian agent is alleging or if these missiles were ever developed or if they are in use today.

Wonderful.

Keiko handed me a cup of freshly brewed coffee and asked, "What I fix you for breakfast, Imogreen san?"

"How about an order of deception to go with my double-agent father?"

"Eh?"

"Nothing. Nothing for me. I've had enough already." I flung the paper on the table face down. I took a big gulp of coffee and then regretted it when I scorched my mouth. I felt the burn all the way down. I preferred tea. It was Gordon who always drank the pot of coffee Keiko made every morning. *Where was he?* It wasn't like him not to answer the phone.

"Where is Gordon?"

"Gordon san gone. He take bags. He leave note to you." Keiko handed me a sealed envelope.

After we had talked last night, Gordon let no grass grow under his feet once he decided to retire. I hadn't expected him to be gone so soon. I felt a keen sense of loss and aloneness when I broke the seal on the envelope, unfolded the single piece of stationary and read his note.

> *My dearest Imogene,*
> *After I had worked on the doorbell as you asked, I checked the air flights last night and found a flight to my destination that was leaving at 5:30 this morning. I hated to leave without saying good-bye, but it was very late when you retired to bed. I felt it best to let you sleep. I'll be in touch.*
> *Yours truly,*
> *Gordon*

The smeared, blotchy scratchy printing was out of character for fastidiously fussy Gordon. I carefully folded the single piece of paper and slipped it into its envelope. I set it on my dresser when I went upstairs to get dressed, intending to file it with my other important letters and notes—after my search for a brick wall to bang my head against.

Knowing there were no brick walls on the premises, I opened the blinds a crack to let some light in, but I refused to get dressed. I intended to stay in my room all day—processing. I had lost my parents, my aunt, my husband, my money and one of my best friends—my recently retired butler. He, at least, had the possibility of returning to me—if I could hang on to the house until he got back.

I had Keiko shut the incessant ringers on the house phones off. After a proper amount of lollygagging, I began to develop a list of things I needed to do to set my life in order. First, I had to pay the bills and keep the house. Second, I wanted to hire someone to investigate what had really happened to my father. The man I had known as a child would not sell out his country for money. It went against everything I understood or remembered about him.

I had no funding to do any of this, so I either had to get the money my pseudo-husband had stolen from me or find a way to get money. Setting things right with the investors Jorgji had cheated, getting to know my half-sister, Mandy, better, and finding out why Frank hadn't contacted me all were shoved to the bottom of my to do list. Some tanked out more than others.

Mandy would have remained on the bottom permanently, except that she got elevated to a higher level when she got the spare key out from the loose corner of the back step and came storming into the kitchen via the back door. Interrupting my buttered toast breakfast.

"Why hasn't anyone answered your phone? And, do you know your doorbell out back doesn't work? I couldn't go to the front door because you have a bunch of reporters hanging around outside there."

That explained the silent doorbell. I looked out the back door. Her Bentley was parked just beyond the back hedges. I could see a blond head slumped down in the front seat.

"Is that Martin in your car?" I asked her, peering out trying to get a better look at the face partially obscured by the hedges.

She bristled. "What if it is? He can't just hang around the apartment all day. It's not healthy."

"He is under house arrest. He has a tether on! And a restraining order against him!"

"He's in my car. That's sorta like an extension of my apartment, and I'm sure he's more than 500 yards away from you. Stop getting so snotty. You always were so whiny."

I slammed and locked the back door, pulling down the shade. "How could he leave your apartment when he's supposed to have an ankle tether?"

She grinned sheepishly. "It's dangling from the ceiling fan. We left the fan running on low. The probation people prob'bly think he's walking around like a caged tiger, and that's what he was doing before he got outta that thing. I couldn't just leave him there. He was going crazy."

I ignored the reference to the obvious. "Yes. You could have. He's supposed to be there! I don't want him here. I don't want him anywhere near me. That's what a restraining order is all about."

"Look. Let's forget about Martin for a minute. What are you going to do about your father? His name is all over the papers. He's public enemy number one now. I'm so glad no one knows he and I are related." Her ringed fingers twisted around each other. "Now I know why your aunt Tilly paid momma to be quiet about the affair she had with your father and why she told me to keep quiet about it, too."

"MY father? He's your father, too." I looked at my sister-cousin in a new light. "Are you disowning him now that everyone is making him out to be a bad guy?"

"Well..." She turned away from me and opened the cupboard to take out a cup for coffee.

"If you are, you can forget about getting your share of the money he left me when he died—money that I was going to share with you." I didn't have any of that money left, Jorgji got it all, but I wasn't about to let her know that.

"I'm not sayin' I'm disownin' him exactly." She was intent on filling the mug half-way, the rest of the space being

43

reserved for the sugar and cream she dumped in. "I only came to ask you not to mention me to the papers. Let's just let the fact that we're sisters stay our little secret. Okay?"

I peeked under the window shade to look out and make sure Martin's head was still visible in the front seat of the Bentley; I didn't trust him any farther than Keiko could swing a broom. He had slumped down further in the seat, but I could still see some blond sprigs of hair sticking up. My hand came up instinctively to my throat remembering the grip of his hands there. "I'm willing to keep my silence if you are willing to make sure Martin stays away from me."

She gave me a sour look, but we shook on it. I returned to my buttered toast, and she returned to her car to take Martin back to her apartment, promising me she would keep him there.

Keiko and I kept the phones turned off and refused to answer the knocking on the door the rest of the day. Eventually, the reporters gave up trying to enlarge the story of my father's duplicity and moved on to the next media blitz.

Moving on for me wasn't as easy, but I was determined to forge ahead with my life. I would get a private investigator to clear my father's name. I would do what I could to negate and then forget about the horrible allegations in the paper. I was going to return my father to his previous state when I was six—my flawless hero.

I just had no idea of how hard that was going to be.

CHAPTER 6

I found over thirty private investigators listed in the Yellow Pages. I chose the one that had the easiest address to drive to and who gave free consultations. Chilton Detective Agency, advertised as Chicago's finest, was located on the north side of Chicago in Evanston. Mr. M. Chilton wasn't in when I got to the office located on a small side street next to a discount tire store.

"I'm sorry. Mr. Chilton just stepped out for lunch," his secretary told me when I advised her I had an appointment. She had the fingertips of one hand soaking in a small bowl of pink liquid at the edge of her desk.

"Will he be gone long? I'm sure he said I could come in at 12:30." I looked at my watch. It was 12:31.

"He usually takes a long lunch on Wednesdays. Can you come back tomorrow?" She looked at her watch and swished the liquid in the bowl around a little.

"No. I can't come back tomorrow. I want to talk to him today. I don't understand why he'd set me up for an initial consultation if he wasn't going to be here."

"Oh, well. If it's an initial consultation you're after, I've heard that spiel enough times I could recite it in my sleep." She pulled her hand out of the liquid and rubbed the ends of her fingers on a small tea towel as she began rattling off in a rapid, clipped tone, "We're 100% confidential. Chilton

Detective Agency is dedicated to solving cases using tried and true methods. Our clients find us discreet, confidential, professional and internationally renowned. We're small enough to be personal and large enough to service the entire greater Chicago area. We keep you in direct communication at all stages of the investigation. Got a cheater spouse? We'll find 'em. Runaway teenager? We'll find 'em. Embezzler employee? We'll find 'em. Deadbeat Dad? We'll find 'em. The quality of our work is well known by our competitors. Let us do you..." Here she paused her one long exhalation to take a breath before beginning again. "A service. With over 15 years in the business, our experienced private detectives are eagerly waiting to assist you with all you investigative needs. We need two grand up front and $600 a day plus expenses." She sat back down at her desk. "Shall I sign you up?"

"That's the initial consultation?" I asked her.

"Yeah, pretty much give or take a cheat or two."

"But you haven't asked me anything about my case or discussed how you or rather, the agency is going to handle it."

"Oh, Honey, to do that you'd need to pay the $2,000 deposit." She pulled an emery board from her pencil holder and began buffing her recently soaked nails.

My dream of clearing my father's name was being filed down, one fingernail at a time.

"This is ludicrous. I was supposed to get a free consultation. This is false advertising. I want to speak to the owner of this agency."

"Sure." She looked up at me, hazel eyes as monotone as her voice. "He's down the street at the Tequila bar having lunch."

I wasn't crazy about going into a bar to talk business. "Is there someone else I can speak to? Perhaps one of the agency's other investigators is in?"

She resumed her grooming. "We don't got no other investigators—just Melton."

The minute I stepped into the Tequila Bar I had no difficulty determining which patron Melton Chilton was. Aside from the bartender, he was the only other person in the bar. He was saddled up to the bar on a tall stool drinking his lunch. A rumpled coat lay on the bar stool next to him. The cuffs of his dress slacks, as well as his shoes, had seen better days and so had his no-longer-white shirt. The quintessential retired cop private investigator. Or so I thought.

"Hey, Mel. Looks like you got a client." The bartender went down to the far end of the bar and began wiping off the glasses sitting on a rack.

I walked over to the man on the stool with his back to me; I cleared my throat and held out my right hand. "Mr. Chilton, I'm Imogene Warren. We have a 12:30 consultation appointment."

"Oh yeah." He didn't turn to face me when he spoke, so I pulled back my unseen outstretched hand. Without glancing once in my direction, he reached over, pulled his jacket off the stool, and motioned for me to sit down—which I did.

Still not facing me, he took a deep breath and began, talking to the drink on the bar in front of him. "Chilton Detective Agency is 100% confidential. We're dedicated to solving cases using tried and true methods. Our clients find us discreet, confidential, profession..."

I held up a hand to stop him and slid onto the coat-vacated bar stool next to him. "Your secretary has already told me all that."

"She did?" When he turned to face me, I could see my earlier assessment of his former profession was correct—it was the age I had misjudged. He was obviously cop material. The set of the mouth, the hard look of the eyes, but he was young, about mid-thirties. Retirement was not what ended this man's career with a police force.

"Well, what you need an investigator for? Got a cheater spouse?"

"Not anymore. He's dead."

He looked a little miffed. "Got an embezzler?

"Not anymore. He's in jail."

More miffing. "Deadbeat dad?"

"Close," I said and began to tell him my story of how my dead father was being accused of being a double agent. The bartender kept wiping down the bar, coming closer and closer to where we were seated. So much for 100% confidential.

"Is there someplace we could go to talk?" I asked Mr. Chilton.

"Here's as good a place as any. Andy won't tell no one your secrets. Will ya Andy?"

Andy continued to wipe the bar, making like he couldn't hear.

"Look. I just want to know if you can help me clear my father's name or not."

"Sure. You got $2,000?"

I thought about the two dimes Mr. Twerk said I didn't have. "I don't have it now, but the FBI is working on getting my money back."

"That the embezzler?"

"No. The dead spouse."

"That why he's dead?"

"It's complicated."

Melton tipped up his glass and gulped down what liquid was left then held the empty glass up, aimed at Andy. "When you get it uncomplicated and can get your deposit, come back and see me. High-quality companies like Chilton Detective Agency can't stay in business very long without getting paid."

I heard the bartender cover his laugh with a cough.

CHAPTER 7

Those first few nights without Gordon in the house, I slept sporadically with invisible missiles shooting through my nightmares. Every bump, creak, squeak and gurgle sound the house made in its alleged silence woke me up. I told myself those were all normal household noises, just pipes rattling, walls settling, traffic vibrations, fault lines shifting and benevolent ghosts walking, but nevertheless I stayed huddled in my bed until dawn's light, fearful of what might await me if I went to check out the noises.

The third evening without Gordon, exhaustion overtook me just in time for me to be startled awake by a phone call at 3 a.m. I was going to give that reporter a stern talking to.

"I know you have them and I want them." A mechanical Vader sounding voice wheezed into the phone. My heart rate went from 60 to 160 in three seconds.

"Who is this?" I asked the phone.

The labored in and out breathing unnerved me while I waited for the mechanical voice to answer.

"Just do as I tell you…"

I pounded my bedside stand with the receiver hoping the sound would break an eardrum at the other end of the line.

"Not very smart…" I heard just before I disconnected the call. I wrapped my arms around my stomach as tremors took over my body. This couldn't be happening. There was nothing that I had that anyone would want so I couldn't figure out why this person chose to call me. It had to be a prank or a wrong number.

When the phone rang again, and the mechanical voice started in, I hung up and called the phone company to see if there was a way to trace the call. They took my complaint and said someone would get back to me. When the phone man called me back an hour later, he said the call had originated from a pre-paid cell phone purchased with cash and they had no way of making the connection to who owned the cell.

I dug officer Sawney's card out of my purse. He answered on the second ring. I explained to him that I'd gotten a threatening phone call and told him what the caller had said.

"Mrs. Dalmat," he began. "I'd like to help you, but there is no way my jurisdiction extends to complaints originating in Illinois—unless you have evidence the caller resides in Michigan."

"I don't know where the calls came from. They were made from one of those disposable cell phones."

"If you get any more calls, the phone company should be able to tell you what cell tower the calls are coming through on. That might help pinpoint the area where the caller is."

He also suggested that I contact the Illinois State Police Department if I got any more calls. I didn't know anyone in the Illinois Police Department and didn't care to make their acquaintance.

At 6 a.m. I gave up trying to sleep, took a quick shower, and dressed for my job interview. I drove into Chicago's crowded downtown business section, unable to shake that spooky feeling that my every move was being dissected for some nefarious purpose. No green vans mysteriously reappeared to plague me, so I chalked the hair-on-the-back-of-the-neck-standing up sensation to my not getting enough sleep, eating too skimpy a breakfast, and having to adjust the seat forward to reach the peddles when I got into my car—not how I had left it last.

The doorbell had been screaming just fine and my car seat properly adjusted before Gordon left. He must have found time to not only work on the doorbell but to check over my car as well before going to the airport. To think anything else was unthinkable.

Locking my vehicle in a self-parking garage, I noticed the skies had darkened, so I grabbed my lucky umbrella from the trunk. The umbrella was a little bent from where Gordon had used it as a weapon to save me from being killed, but that was why I considered it lucky.

Those dark laden clouds began releasing their load just as I was leaving the shelter of the parking structure. Squinting at the mixture of street signs and traffic lights surrounding the garage, I headed towards the sign that said LaSalle Street, thankful to have recognized that sign through the torrential rains.

The business district was chocked full of buildings, all of them skyscrapers with elevators and lots of people—three of my strongest fears are heights, elevators, and people.

Rainwater ran down the faces and sides of the buildings, poured onto the sidewalks and flowed into the streets where it rushed into the storm drains to be taken wherever the rainwater goes in Chicago.

As the rain began sheeting, I took off at a run to find my destination. In my haste to be on time for my interview, I overlooked the traffic 'do not walk' sign.

As I raced off the edge of the curb, one pump heel slid down into the storm sewer grate. I stumbled. I caught myself. Instead of plunging to the ground in my usual fashion, I was held fast to the grate by my stuck shoe. I reestablished the grip on my umbrella holding it for maximum coverage while wiggling my foot. The shoe was wedged tight; I couldn't dislodge it. When a malicious green van came screeching around the corner veering towards me, I wiggled my foot

51

harder.

The van didn't make any attempt to slow down. It sped up.

The van missed me by a fraction of a scream. I bounded back up to the curb but not before the tire splashes doused my skirt, legs, and feet. My shoe hadn't come with me. It was filled with water, still stuck in the grate.

I stooped down and gave a vicious tug on the darned thing. The heel snapped off, remaining lodged in the grate. I gave the heel a hard yank. My frustration pulled it free in time for me to get out of the way of the next vehicle driving by, but not in time to avoid another dousing.

Perfect.

I had to find the McClintock office building wet from the waist down. At least my old, bent umbrella had saved my hair, coat and blouse from the rain.

A sudden gust of wind caught the umbrella, which tried to launch me, Mary Poppin's style, into one of the huge concrete planter boxes that protectively lined the street side of the Federal Reserve Bank. The weakened ribs give way, and everything flipped inside out. The umbrella's ribs—mine were fine.

I felt the rain begin to soak my hair and face as I wrestled with the wind controlled umbrella. A rain-coated, wide-brimmed hatted man stepped out of the reserve bank and approached my struggles.

"Allow me," he said. I relinquished the useless thing and watched as his skilled, strong hands forced the umbrella to revert to its original intended shape so it could perform its expected function. He held the umbrella over my head and placed the handle back in my hand. When I didn't secure my grip right away, his warm fingers curled around my cold, wet hand. I gawked foolishly up at the warm smile that showed between his neatly trimmed blond mustache and beard.

Uncomfortable at his touch, his closeness and how attractive I found him, I stepped away and mumbled a 'thank you' to the hatted head and turned to run to my appointment—except I still didn't know which direction.

I turned back to my rescuer and asked, "Excuse me. Do you happen to know where the McClintock office building is?"

"Of course." He pointed to a building catty-corner to where we were standing.

My gaze traversed the street to land on a flashing jewelry store sign. I turned back to him. "That?" I asked, turning and pointing to the Oppenheimer Jewelry sign.

"It's the building next to it." He took a hold of my shoulders and turned me, readjusting my line of sight to the red brick building he had pointed to.

"Thanks," I said, feeling the warmth of his hands through my thin raincoat just before he released me. I looked at the building and then back at him. My mouth had acquired an idiotic grin that had become as unruly as my umbrella. My eyes continued to drink in the pleasure of his smile, and my feet refused to give up their soggy stance to move away from him.

As the rain continued to drip from his hat's brim and the edges of my umbrella, I got another white teethed, heart-melting smile that crinkled the corners of his Mediterranean blue eyes. They were all clear and sparkly fresh, and I wanted to drown in those perfect complements to his tan face.

He returned my gaze for the briefest of time, and then tipped his head against the wind, turned up the collar of his raincoat and dashed through the traffic to cross the street, disappearing into a corner coffee shop, leaving me to fend for myself again.

I looked longingly at the coffee shop wondering if they had any marzipan muffins to go along with that hunk of gorgeous. The tea and toast I had for breakfast had deserted me long before Mr. Blond Beard had.

When my umbrella turned tail again in the next heavy gust, I closed the errant thing, no longer trusting it. Instead, I followed the man's lead, pulled the edges of my raincoat collar together, and held them there against the onslaught of wind and rain to protect my silk blouse underneath.

I ran, or rather hobbled and squished to the building Mr. Blond Beard had pointed out for me.

Once I reached the red-bricked facade, I stopped short, allowing the rain to beat against my clutched jacket and exposed face and hair.

My phobias were dancing around me as I stood rooted to my little spot of concrete in front of an ancient masonry building. I allowed my gaze to travel all the way up its front as I stayed outside of the building long enough to count all twelve stories and read the plaque attached to the building's corner.

Chicago Landmark
206 Jackson St

> This original construction completed in 1898 is the work of world-renowned architect, Richard Williams, and is the first of its kind to feature six tall granite-faced columns anchoring the entranceway to the ten upper floors. The granite and stainless steel elevator cabs complement the multi-colored, patterned stainless steel and terrazzo lobby to combine striking vintage charm with functionality.

I stepped out of the rain to a spot under the building's front overhang and leaned against one of the two-story tall pillars, breathing deeply of the rain-washed air, I counted slowly to fifty before proceeding forward to the closest of six glass entry doors.

I was not usually so calm about tall buildings, but since it was only half as tall as all the other buildings wedged in around it, I figured that would cut my acrophobia in half.

A directory listed a long string of accountants, lawyers, consultants and a host of other commercial type businesses, but I found no *Quarterly Repository Magazine* on the list.

The lobby's dangling "information" sign had a handwritten note on the vacant desk saying, "Be Right Back." I stepped off to the side of the desk, away from the flow of traffic, people rushing hither and fro, to wait for the receptionist to return.

I glanced at my watch, worried, shrinking back farther to the wall when the sign's 'right back' stretched into ten minutes. At eleven minutes, I pulled out the square blue knitted yarn swatch I'd done as a gauge before knitting Frank's Zig Zag scarf. At twelve minutes, I hid the swatch in the palm of my hand and began rubbing the yarn's softness against my cheek.

I was going to be late for my interview unless I could force myself to approach one of the people rushing in and out of the building to ask them where the *Quarterly Repository* offices were.

At the fifteen-minute mark, as I was taught in my Dale Carnage course, I began to do a practice talk in my head. Once I knew exactly what I was going to say and how I was going to say it, I searched the crowd to find the least intimidating person to approach for directions.

The business types, men and women in dark suits with black umbrellas and black attaché cases wouldn't do. Too busy. Too cold.

The customer types, people in business casual, going to meet the business types wouldn't do either. Too nervous looking.

An elderly man sat alone in one of the overstuffed chairs in the lobby area reading a newspaper. No. Not him. I didn't want to talk to anyone who partially obscured their face behind reading material.

A wet, scraggly haired, bearded man in a ratty, dirty, frayed leather coat, black Stetson hat, holey jeans; carrying a scrubby looking backpack, and wearing dark glasses came through the outside doors into the lobby area. Once through the door, he shook himself. Water flung from him like fleas off a drowning dog.

He strode across the lobby and sat on one of the three vacant overstuffed chairs near Mr. Newspaper. The newspaper lowered a bit when the new arrival pulled out a crumpled pack of cigarettes and appeared to ask Mr. Newspaper if he had a match. Mr. Newspaper stopped his reading to pull out a matchbook. The scraggly man tore off one of the matches from the cardboard book and stuck it to the bottom of his cowboy-booted foot. The match flared to life. The flame was brought to the end of the cigarette where it caught, and the glow grew. Mr. Scraggly shook the flame from the match and tried to give the matchbook back to Mr. Newspaper. He refused the tiny book and its unlit contents. *Yeah, I wasn't going to take anything from that man either, not even directions.*

I was fast running out of plausible, approachable options when a girl, long legs showing below her short anime-style skirt, pink pigtails bouncing, came in through the front door. A man in a black hoodie sweatshirt, black jeans, black sneakers, black eye shadow and gold nose piercings entered through the door just behind her. Miss Anime collapsed her see through umbrella and shook the water off before snapping and strapping it shut. She looked unintimidating, and she was already heading in my direction. I stepped out away from the desk to ask her for directions when she got within distance.

She was just beyond Mr. Goth's reach when he quickened his pace, got up behind her and pulled her to him. He swung her around and roughly kissed her while his hand snaked up the inside of her crop top.

My closed umbrella up like a bat, ready to come to Miss Anime's assistance. When she pulled his hand away and resettled it on her shoulder, melded into his embrace and started kissing him back, I put my lucky umbrella down and rubbed the swatch against my heated cheeks to cool them. I scurried to an obscured spot against the wall and turned to examine the polished brass light fixtures hanging there.

That was not my business. I was not there to spy on eccentric lovers. I was just waiting for the information receptionist.

I ached for Frank.

When I got up the nerve to put the swatch away and look around again, Miss Anime and Mr. Goth had finished their public displays of affection and she was already at the desk I was standing near. She flipped the "Be Right Back" sign face down and stepped behind the information desk.

She looked confused when I asked her where the *Quarterly Repository* offices were.

"There aren't any banks in this building," she said, chomping on a big cud of gum.

"It's not a bank. It's a magazine company," I said.

She pulled a laminated building floor plan from the drawer of her desk, frowned, read and chewed for several seconds. She blew a gigantic pink bubble while reading; when it popped, it released a smell of strawberries. My stomach growled. I should have eaten more for breakfast.

"Nope. Nothing here by that name." Another bubble popped. Atomized flavor filled the air.

"Are you sure? This is the building the man on the phone told me to come to for my interview. I'm already late, and I desperately need this job."

She looked me up and down. My humanity must have shown through my dripping wet hair, soppy wet coat, and streaky makeup because she gave me a big bubble gum grin and picked up the phone on her desk. She asked someone on the other end, "Hey, Dad. There's a lady here asking for the *Quarterly Repository*. Do we have one of those?"

She smacked her gum while listening. Her gaze all the while glued to my face. "Unhuh. Unhuh. Okay. I'll tell her." She replaced the receiver. Before she said anything, she pulled a bit of gum out of her mouth with her fingers and pulled it into a long, pink taffy-type string. She used her tongue to twirl the gum up and back into her mouth.

I swallowed a sudden rush of saliva.

"My dad says he just rented out space in the dungeon last week," she told me pointing to a spot on her building floor plans. I leaned over the desk to take a look at the large expanse of rooms she was pointing to.

"Dungeon?" I squeaked, vocal chords and leg muscles tightening, getting ready to leave the building.

"Don't worry." She leaned in close to me over the width of the desk. "We just call it that because the sub, sub-basement is part of the original crazy asylum basement. People say that's where they kept their worst cases locked up. The architect for this building had that old basement dug out some more, included it in the plans and built up right over the top of it. I haven't gone down there lately. That level was used as a storage area for the businesses in the building. A few weeks ago one of Dad's friends asked him if he could lease a set of rooms in the sub-sub out. Since it was mostly wasted space, my dad agreed. I didn't know what the new firm was fixing the place up for. I only know they've been taking a lot of construction equipment down there. I heard they also put in a few more lights so I'm sure it won't seem so dark and abandoned now."

I examined the floor plan, a series of large and small squares with spots for doors and no windows. My brain conjured up visions of women with wild hair, in long nightgowns gliding down dark hallways with sputtering candle flames flickering before them to light their way into madness.

When I turned towards the outer doors, intending to leave, Miss Anime said, "Hey, wait. Didn't you say you really need this job? The sub-sub is not that bad. It's not as if it goes as far down as the underground tunnels. Now there is one place where I'll never go." She shuddered. "Especially after that worker was found with his head so bashed in they had to pick the pieces off the walls of the tunnel."

I began to gag and thought I might vomit right on the spot before I got myself under control. Good thing my stomach was empty.

She quickly said, "I'm so sorry. I didn't realize you had a weak stomach. Forget I even mentioned it. That incident didn't even happen in this area. It's nothing to worry about. There isn't even any connection from the deep tunnel up to this building. The tunnel is just there for rain water removal anyway."

To rid my mind of brain matter scatter, I pictured myself back in a happier time—the last time Frank kissed me the way Mr. Goth had kissed Miss Anime. I rubbed the swatch in my pocket and achieved some level of calm. I had to find a way to get $2,000. I couldn't give up. "I guess I could try to forget it for the sake of my sanity. Where did you say the magazine's offices were?"

"Take one of the elevators behind me down three floors, all the way to the bottom, as far as it will go. Look for the door that says Office Suite 101 B3."

Before I could thank her, she set the "Be Right Back" sign in its upright position and headed down a short hall to enter a door marked "Ladies."

After watching her go, I turned back to the bank of elevators as a small tremor pulsed through me.

CHAPTER 8

I probably should have used the stairs, except I had developed an unhealthy fear of stairwells in addition to my healthy fear of elevators. I tamped down my claustrophobia, stuffed the thoughts of bashed heads and deep, dark tunnels aside. For Gordon, Keiko and my father, I screwed up my courage and hobbled through the first elevator door that opened to lure me in; grateful the building designer used the granite construction for the shaft and not the elevator car itself.

I shriveled against the stainless steel wall when Mr. Newspaper stepped into the elevator behind me, a folded newspaper under one arm and a bulging satchel stretching out the other. We did the awkward "don't look at each other" elevator-positioning dance—while waiting for the elevator doors to close. He moved off to one side. I stepped over as far as possible in that cable-suspended metal box trying not to stare at the small, unusually shaped black birthmark on his left cheek. It resembled a fly—one flattened by a flyswatter.

When the doors took an unusually long time to close, I pushed the 'door close' button several times in an attempt to get the elevator to move faster. Mr. Newspaper eyed me wearily; both arms came up to hug that satchel to his chest as he retreated to the opposite corner of the car. When the elevator stopped, he burned a path out the door before the doors could slide all the way open. He barely got himself and his satchel squeezed out and into the hallway.

The hallway was painted a flat dull green and smelled of damp earth and must. I traversed the airless, dimly lit hall until I found a dirty door with a small sign and entered the reception area of the *Quarterly Repository*. I discovered two ladies there ahead of me. They were already sitting on folding chairs—business types, the ladies—not the chairs. The chairs were standard issue church potluck metal. There were three doors and a huge desk on the far side of the room. The only unoccupied chair was a padded office seat behind the big vacant desk, apparently the reception desk. That would have been too cheeky of me to sit in that chair, so I stood near the front door, soggy from sweat and rainwater, my leg cramping from keeping one foot poised well into the air, so it wasn't obvious the heel of the shoe was in my purse.

I didn't try to speak to the dressed-for-success women, with their dry hair and intact shoes. Talking to strangers is not something I'm comfortable with—having failed my *Dale Carnage* course. The course they must have passed because they were busy talking to each other.

"I've offered to do the job as an unpaid intern. I need the experience to widen my resume. Starting out with a starting firm will be a great start to my starting my professional assistant career." Miss Dyed Shocking-Red Hair said to the perky nosed woman with her dry blue suit and shoes that matched.

"I doubt they'd need an intern," Miss Perky Nose told Miss Dyed Hair. "I graduated at the top of my class at Defried Business Institute. I have ten years experience in this type of work. Seeing that they are a start-up firm, they'll need someone like me, someone with experience, to help them grow their business. I'm sure they'll find me an invaluable asset." Miss Perky Nose told Miss Dyed Hair.

Miss Dyed Hair sniffed.

Miss Perky Nose sniffed back.

They both turned to me. "Are you here to interview for

the office receptionist position, too?" Miss Perky Nose asked me.

I graduated at the top of nothing. I've never even wanted to be at the top of anything—I'm afraid of heights. I pushed myself harder against the wall and wrapped the edges of my coat tighter around me. I was seriously considering leaving before I embarrassed myself any further.

The middle door behind the desk swung open. Mr. Fly from the elevator stepped out into the office reception area accompanied by a balding white haired, black man dressed in a purple and white striped shirt, black pants, rainbow-colored suspenders and black thick-lensed glasses that had a periscope type jeweler's loop attached to the upper rim. The black man was exceptionally small in stature, only about two inches taller than me, and exceedingly old, at least 50.

Mr. Fly tossed his newspaper in the trashcan by the desk and said to the other man, "Pleasure doing business with ya. See ya next time." He and his collapsed bag strode out the door without a glance at any of the hopefuls in the reception area.

The other man watched Mr. Fly go, and then lifted up his thick lenses to survey the room. He squinted at each of us in turn, put the glasses back down and gazed at the stack of papers he was holding in his hands.

The violet scented, lavender-colored paper I'd typed my resume on was on top of the stack. "Which one of you is Imogene Warren?"

"That's me," I said raising my hand and waving it so his thick glasses could see me over by the door. "I'm Sorry I'm late. I stopped to help a lady who was having trouble." That wasn't exactly a lie. I did help a woman—she just happened to be me.

I unevenly stepped forward to shake his hand and follow him through the door he'd come through. We passed into a long, dark hallway that had three doors, one marked on a metal plate as "storage." The second had a similar plate for "mechanical room," and both those had additional handwritten signs that said, "Keep Out." The third door, the one we entered, was unmarked. It was an office. A stark room with a wooden desk and two wooden chairs, a wastebasket, and a computer. Nothing else. It was reminiscent of their sparse reception area.

I sat down wondering what type of questions he would be asking me and how I could make my incompetent, pampered life seem less pampered and more competent.

"So it says here you know how to type and answer the phone."

"Y...y...yes. I...I answer the phone all the time at home." I hadn't put on my resume that I typed my deceased famous billionaire mystery writer aunt's manuscripts. I thought that might make it appear as though I didn't need a job, which I did, so I didn't dare expand on the typing issue. I also was hoping to avoid the whole double-agent-spy father issue. I sat quietly, my shaking hands wedged into my raincoat pockets. My fingers were alternating between running over the bumpy raised letters of my credit card to furiously rubbing the yarn swatch.

"You have a problem keeping your trap shut on what goes on at work?"

I recovered from the shock of this crude question quickly and answered truthfully. "I...I don't leave my house much, and it is difficult for me to strike up a conversation on any sub...subject so you'd never have to worry about my talking about my work to anyone." I didn't think it was necessary to reveal that I had no friends to talk to.

I tried to relax a bit. I pulled one hand out from my pocket when he unfolded his arms and grabbed his suspenders and snapped them.

"My goodness," I added to the echo of the snap. "I hadn't realized the magazine industry was such a secretive business."

"Yeah? Well, we're just getting started." Snap. "This is a new venture for us, my business partners and me." Snap. "We've never done this kind of work before, and we don't want anyone to steal our ideas or...our story lines. You know how it is when you've got a good way to make money. Everyone always wants a piece of the action."

I twirled my silver bracelet around on my wrist. That could have well been true. Everyone was always after me to reveal the ending of my aunt's murder mystery novels. She'd been buried in the ground for months, but her publicist and agent still called me almost daily asking about the status of the two novels she was working on at the time of her death.

The suspender snapping paused; he looked around the room and shuffled the papers on his desk. In the silence that intervened, I tried to think of what I'd read in *Working Woman Weekly* about how to make yourself stand out in a job interview, how to sell yourself to potential employers.

"I know all about what you do," I said.

"You do?" There was an unpleasant edge to his voice. He picked up a letter opener from the desk. To avoid his piercing gaze, I focused on the irregular, dark area of skin on the back of his right hand. That spot resembled a map of Italy or some other foreign country. He didn't appear Italian. I looked up then away when he squinted at me over his thick glasses, and a sneer took over his face.

"Oh." I pulled the second hand out of my pocket and held both up as a caution against this sudden change in the atmosphere of the room. "I don't mean to imply that I know the magazine industry. It's just that I read a lot of magazines."

He dropped the letter opener. His eyes un-squinted. The sneer stopped. "That's nice...that you read a lot of magazines." A pleasant look returned to his face as he picked up the letter opener again and ran his fingers along the length of the blade. I tried not to stare at the dark marking on his hand, so I looked up again and saw his eyes, sharp, intelligent, studying me. I doubted they missed much.

"I don't read magazines now. I canceled all my subscriptions." I told him shoving my hands back into my pockets where my swatch was.

"Say. When you did read, just what kind of magazines did you read?"

"Knitting, crocheting, fashion, clothing: women's magazines mostly." I pulled my hands out to rest them on my lap to appear open and friendly like I'd read in *Working Woman* but when the silence continued I had to clasp them together to keep them still. I didn't want him to see the shaking and know I'd omitted one magazine from my list. I couldn't tell this little man I read *Cosmopolite*. That would have been too scandalous. Women on the cover always show a lot of skin and the stories all revolve around sexually pleasing your man. It was the one subscription I hadn't canceled.

"You don't read any true crime magazines, do you?"

That took me off guard. "No. Is that what you do here?"

"No! We are not into crime. No, sirree. We run a wholesome, upstanding business here. All we need is someone to answer the phone, keep an eye on things while we get the business operation set up and running. We need someone to alert us when we have people out front. You know, so we can do our job and get things moving faster without having to watch the door and all."

"I certainly can watch the door. I've done that at home before."

He smiled at me, and I smiled back. He looked down at my resume briefly, then leaned forward and asked, "You ain't related to that double agent guy named Warren are you?"

I swallowed hard. "Only distantly." He was a distant memory, so I didn't lie—exactly.

The interview lagged uncomfortably again as my interviewer put down the letter opener to fiddle with a pair of long-handled scissors on his desk.

Remembering Mr. Twerk's scissor actions, I fidgeted in my seat again. That old wooden chair gave a loud creak that caused me some embarrassment.

I tugged at my memory of what that magazine article I'd read suggested I do to make me a standout interview candidate. *Show an interest in their business.* "If you don't mind my asking," I began. "Just what does the magazine specialize in? What kind of articles will you run?"

The scissors clinked to the floor. He bent to grab them up and set them on the desk before answering. "We're sort of a generic magazine business. A little of this. A little of that."

"Oh." Another uncomfortable lull. *Show an interest in the interviewer.* "Are you the editor of the magazine?"

"I'm the one with the know how to get the job done, and I'll approve the final run so, I guess you could say that makes me the editor." Double suspender snap. "Yeah, I like the sound of that. I'm the editor."

He looked at the single lavender sheet that was on top of the other stack of papers on his desk. I wished I'd been more of a liar when I typed that resume up.

"You got any family on the police force or in law enforcement?" he asked me after looking over my skimpy resume, which provided no professional references, no college degree, no bi-lingual abilities. It said only my name, address, phone number, high school diploma, on-line courses and typing skills. My typed resume was only a half a page. I should have used a bigger font.

"No. My only family is my half-sister and her brother, who happens to be my cousin. Except I don't see him anymore because he's on a tether release from prison." I purposefully didn't mention that he was in prison because he was trying to kill me, and we don't see each other because I have a restraining order against him. I didn't want to give the wrong impression about myself.

"That so? You know anyone in law enforcement?" he asked.

I thought about this for a long second. Both hands went in my coat pockets again, and I was rubbing the swatch so hard I'm surprised it didn't unravel. I was pretty sure I was in love with an FBI agent, but he worked undercover so I couldn't give this man any information on him.

"No," I lied. I guessed the lying thing was becoming a habit.

"Good."

I brightened considerably when the diminutive black man

with the colorful suspenders smiled at me, crumpled my lavender paper and flung it into the trash along with the other papers on his desk. "You're hired. We're on a tight deadline. My partner, Rocko, and his brother, Randy, and I are in the back almost all the time getting things ready for our first run, so we need someone to man the phones, handle the equipment and supply deliveries and guard the front door while we work in back. There's a special delivery scheduled for later today. Can you start right now?"

"I'm hired? Don't you want me to take a typing test or anything?" My stomach growled, reminding me that I hadn't eaten much for breakfast because I intended to be home for lunch.

"Nah, your first assignment is to tell those dames out in the front area they can go home. The job's been filled."

CHAPTER 9

After those huffy ladies left in a snit, my interviewer provided me with a brief verbal set of duty instructions before he disappeared into the back room area.

While the men worked in the back, I was to keep an eye on the front door. If anyone came in, any person at all, I was to push the red buzzer mounted under the right-hand corner of the desk to alert them in the back that someone had entered. I was also to answer the phone when it rang. I was required to work late some evenings because some of what they had to do could only be done after 5 o'clock when the building closed, and the rest of the building occupants went home. I would also be required to run occasional errands.

I committed these instructions to memory and sat down in the receptionist chair and swiveled around in joyous circles until I was dizzy. I put my hands on the top surface of the desk—my desk—to steady my wooziness. Then I wiped the black dust and grime that covered the desktop off my hands onto my skirt. Good thing I wore a dark skirt. I turned the desktop computer on and smiled at the blue start-up screen, thrilled that I had beat out those reception room ladies.

I didn't need diamonds, expensive cars, new clothes or a high-rise apartment to be happy. I had my first real job—aside from the work I had done for my Aunt Tilly.

I was anxious to greet the first visitor to the office, and I couldn't wait to answer my first phone call.

The phone was one of those old-time things with a barbell receiver that sat on top of a clunky square base. The receiver grip was filthy with ground in dirt. That grunge had no doubt accumulated when the men in the back stopped working to answer the phone; that's why they needed me, their new receptionist.

The disgustingly dirty phone rang while I was still recovering from my chair twirling. I couldn't bring myself to touch the gripping grime part of the phone, even though I knew I had to. It was my job to answer that revolting phone. I couldn't screw this job up. If I got fired, I couldn't pay Keiko. If I couldn't pay Keiko, and she left, I'd be all alone in my 21-room house until Gordon returned from his trip to Nepal.

I never liked being home alone. The house was too big with too many nooks and crannies to ever ensure you were truly alone, and I scared easily.

With the phone continuing to ring loudly, I pulled a hanky from my purse, covered the handset and delicately picked it up. Then I froze. I should have practiced the phone answering thing rather than twirl because I didn't know how I should indentify myself on the phone.

No words came out of my open mouth.

"Hello?" the caller said after I failed to say anything or even provide a greeting.

"This is the receptionist for...this...magazine company," unfrozen, I spoke in my cheeriest voice. I hoped the caller knew the name of the magazine company he was calling because my nervous brain had forgotten it.

What was it called? Gentlemen's Quarters? Reproachful Weekly? Generic Non-Crime?

I wiped my free hand on my skirt and began opening desk drawers for a pencil or a pen to take notes.

"You the chick they hired to answer the phone?" a distant, harsh voice squawked. I moved the receiver a little closer to my ear—without touching it. The ear, of course, I was touching the receiver.

"Yes. I'm the receptionist."

My first official call. I was a real receptionist.

"Good, put the chief on the phone."

"Yes, sir. Right away, sir." I gave up my search for a pen and sat the receiver down to go to the back and get the man who hired me, whom I presumed must be the 'chief.'

Before I could reach the back door, a horrible thought overtook me. I turned back to confirm it.

Yup. I had just hung up on my first caller.

I re-cradled the receiver on its stand and re-cradled my butt in the twirly chair—non-twirling this time.

A red-haired, broad-shouldered man wearing dusty green overhauls and leather work gloves barged out from the back area, slamming the door against the wall so hard I lurched in my chair.

"Why didn't you answer the phone?" he bellowed at me.

I cringed and scooted my chair away from him. He was a bruiser, the unibrow, high frontal ridge, knuckle-dragging kind. His large frame towered over me. My hands trembled violently. I gripped them together to keep them still. I couldn't find my voice; only a tiny mouse squeak came out of me. "I did."

The phone rang again. Forgoing the hanky, I snatched up the receiver. I nearly dropped it, but recovered my fumble and cheeped "Hello" into it, finding my voice as best I could.

Mr. Bruiser turned away and retreated to the back room muttering, "Brother. Boggs sure can pick 'em. I told him it was a bad idea to bring anyone else in on this."

I cleared my throat into the phone and quivered, "Qu...qu...quarterly Re...review, this is Miss Warren speaking," into the mouthpiece.

"Yeah, Toots. We got cut off. You were getting the chief for me. Is he in?" I hoped the man that hired me was the chief. I didn't want Mr. Bruiser to be chief of anything.

"I'll check. Whom shall I say is calling?"

There was a long pregnant pause on the other end of the

line before I heard his echo-ey voice bark out, "Mr. Ruff." A dog whined somewhere in the background or maybe it was Mr. Ruff's attempt at humor.

I carefully set the receiver on the desk, but I couldn't get the backroom door to open. The knob seemed to be stuck. I pulled up a bit of my shirt and used it to grip the handle better. That didn't work.

I brought my one heelless shoe up and braced it against the doorjamb while I tugged and twisted the knob.

Nothing. That door was not stuck. It was locked tight.

I knuckle rapped softly on the door, fearful the bruiser would come barreling out again. When the barreling didn't happen, I knocked a little louder. I didn't want to face Mr. Bruiser again, but I also didn't want him angry with me for messing up this call.

To my relief, the man who hired me opened the door a crack and peeked out at me through his thick lenses.

"Hello, little lady. Is there something you wanted?"

"There's a man on the phone. A Mr. Ruff." I gave the name the same dog barking inflection Mr. Ruff had.

"Okay. Thanks."

He came out and picked up the receiver. I listened to his half of the conversation.

"Yeah. Whatta ya want? You were just here. You're supposed to be returning that 'package' today so we can get another tomorrow. ...What do you mean you couldn't return today's package because some of it was missing? How's that even possible?...Wasn't that on him when you picked him up? Why would anyone remove it....Randy! I'll bet he took it off 'em. That kid has got to watch it. He'll get us all in trouble. ...Nah. Don't do that. Too risky. We can't be getting the..." He looked pointedly at me before continuing. "Customers too upset. Better take the package back without it. Tell her we kept it as insurance to ensure she don't squeal. She makes too big a fuss, I'll make Randy cough it up and will get it back to her. ...Listen. I told ya I'd take care of it."

The man who hired me slammed down the phone, and

then he headed towards the backroom door.

I spoke up quickly before this man could disappear through that locked door. "Sir, what shall I call you?"

He stopped, his small body framed in the dim light of the doorway. "You can call me Mr. Pilfer."

"Thank you, Mr. Pilfer."

Mr. Pilfer's hand was on the doorknob getting ready to close the backroom door when I gathered up my courage again, grabbed the knob on my side of the door, and asked in a rush, "How would you like for me to answer the phone here?"

When he looked back at me confused, I rephrased the question, slower this time. "What type of greeting should I use for callers?" I was hoping he would provide me with the business name of the magazine so I wouldn't have to ask him and appear foolish for not remembering.

He said, "'Hello' would be nice."

CHAPTER 10

My next hour on the job, I sat facing the office entry door, practicing my made-up receptionist greeting.

"Hello, I'm the receptionist here. Welcome to our office. Pardon the dust. We are still under construction," I said, standing up in the vacant reception area to face the door.

"What's that you say? You want to:

"A. pay to advertise in our magazine?

"B. sell us your glossy professional photos for our magazine?

"C. pitch a freelance story idea to our magazine?

"How lovely. Someone will be with you shortly. Would you please take a seat."

I even practiced flourishing my hand, Vanna style, towards the two folding metal seats along the side wall.

No one showed up that first hour. Not even someone who made a wrong turn and ended up in our back area of the sub, sub-basement and needed flourishing hand directions out of that hole.

Being an agoraphobic, you'd think I would have been happy that no one came into the office, but I wasn't. If I remained the only one ever in the outer office, how was I going to get to push that little button Mr. Pilfer showed me under the corner of the reception desk?

73

After a time, I gave up watching the door to straighten my desk—, which was at a crooked angle to the room.

I wished I had brought my crocheting with me. That would have kept my hands and mind occupied. My over-active imagination was turning the scraping, bumping, and scratching noises I heard from the back area into asylum ghosts and dead men with lobotomized brains coming to get me.

It's not good for me to host my fears for too long; they feed off each other. I had to find something to engage my mind or it was going to be as brittle as a box of crackers and just as crumbly by the time 5 o'clock quitting time rolled around.

I wanted to clean the phone, so it would be clean for when it rang the next time, so I hanky-handled and called home for cleaning advice. When Keiko didn't pick up, I worried she was already out job hunting, and I'd be returning to an empty house.

I was disgusted with myself for being so useless. As a newly independent, employed woman of the world, I should have been able to find a way to clean without resorting to asking my maid. The room marked "maintenance" probably had a ton of cleaning supplies. I tugged on the door to the back area and found it opened easily this time.

I tiptoed past the voices coming from Mr. Pilfer's closed office door. I wasn't sneaking exactly, but I wasn't totally above board either. I was trying to avoid Rocko, whom I suspected was the louder voice I heard behind the closed door.

Once I got back to the main backroom work area and saw no one around, I relaxed a bit. Dirt, cardboard, and wooden boxes were scattered about along with wheelbarrows, shovels, picks and various wood and metal tool thingies.

I ignored the 'Keep Out' sign on the maintenance room door because I was sure the sign was put up there to keep non-employees out.

The maintenance room was a wide room with various pieces of equipment lining the walls. The lighting was good enough for me to see the floor here was dirtier than the rest of the place. A piece of plywood lay at the center of the floor, edged in built up dirt. Another piece of plywood leaned up against one wall. I stepped around the makeshift wooden flooring to search the shelves lining the room for cleaning supplies.

I was moving the numerous printer ink boxes aside so I could grab a roll of paper towels when I heard a barely audible melodious childlike voice chanting, "Ring around the rosy, pocket full of posies, ashes, ashes, we all fall down." I paused, recognizing that as the song of death sung during Europe's black plague epidemic.

I was sure Rocko and Mr. Pilfer were in the office, just as I was dead certain I was alone in the back area. I surveyed the shelves, boxes, tools and various items around me. No one was in sight, and there was nothing large enough for anyone to hide behind.

The faint refrain of "Ring around the rosy..." begin again.

I had not forgotten what Miss Anime said about the building being built over an old insane asylum. A line of goose bumps raced up my arms. I backed out of the room, slowly closed the door, and started down the hall limping from my mismatched shoe heights.

As I neared Mr. Pilfer's office door, the voices inside were so loud I couldn't help but hear their conversation.

"I just don't understand why you went and hired her. I don't like it."

"She lends an air of credibility to the business. What magazine company doesn't have a receptionist? Did you want to keep having Randy answer the phone and do look out for the door?"

"No. of course not. Randy can't handle that. He's best at doing the heavy lifting and manual labor. I thought we agreed we'd get one of our previous partners to do look out for us. That woman you hired is too damn goody-goody."

"You got rid of your previous partner. Remember? Let's face it. All our previous partners are too greedy to be trusted.

Even as much as I trust Flynn, he's growing suspicious and wants in on what we're doing."

"What'd you tell him?"

"Nothing, but it's getting harder and harder to stall him. I know that Warren girl is a goody-two-shoes. That's the whole point—credibility for when anyone comes snooping around."

"I'm telling ya. I don't like it. I catch a whiff of her making trouble for us; I'm going to get rid of her, too."

I jumped when I heard a sound like a fist hitting a wall.

"Cool down. She's harmless. If we remember to keep the back door locked at all times, she's so naïve that she won't suspect a thing. More importantly, anybody who shows up and sees her will never suspect a thing. You let me handle this part of the business. I'll deal with Flynn and the girl."

"All right, but I still don't like it. We don't have much time left, and the only sure thing we have is Jones. He'll do his part when the time comes. He'd sell his mother's prize race horse to the glue factory if it would wipe out his gambling debt."

I heard a low chuckle. "Yeah. He'd sell his mother if that's what it took to keep him at the poker table."

I tried to walk quietly back to my desk, but I stumbled over a stack of checkered flooring tiles and landed near an unopened box. I probably didn't let out a peep, but to my ears, my dropping to the floor rang out like a call to mass at the Sistine Chapel.

I didn't stick around to see if the men in the office heard my fall. I got my harmless, goody, but broken two shoes back through the door and at my desk in double time, my cleaning errand forgotten.

I sat down so hard in my chair it almost rolled out from under me. I pulled out my blue swatch and began rubbing it against my chin and cheeks, my heart doing double time.

What was it I was supposed to not suspect? What had I gotten myself into? Apparently not the magazine business.

I was reasonably sure that whatever I had become involved in, it was something a girl like me shouldn't be in.

I took several deep breaths and with the help of my

worry cloth, managed to calm myself, so I was the picture of innocence when Mr. Pilfer opened the backroom door a bit later. He looked around the reception area.

"Anybody come in or out of here in the last few minutes?" he asked me.

"Not that I saw," I told him. That was not a lie. You can't see yourself doing things unless you have a mirror.

"Well, if anyone does come in, be sure and push that button under the desk, so we know about it in the back. Rocko doesn't handle surprises well."

CHAPTER 11

The thought of being involved in something illicit terrified and excited me at the same time. It was the same feeling I got whenever my aunt handed me one of her Penelope Pembrooke mystery novels to type for the first time. Reading the story as I typed it, I had no way of knowing how the story would end. I typed, hanging on every word waiting for the climax, waiting to see if I was right about the identity of the killer. I was seldom right.

I envied Penelope, the heroine of the novels, and her ability to conduct investigations that lead to the apprehension of criminals. Being a knitting agoraphobic, I never thought I was capable of leading an exciting life like my heroine.

However, there I was, in the midst of intrigue and I felt my life was changing. Mr. Pilfer hired me because I was dense and the least likely to arouse suspicion as to the true nature of the business being conducted. If I wanted to, I could discover the true business being done. The fact that my employers thought me a dupe could work to my advantage. I could become the Penelope of the novels.

Based on what I had heard, I knew my employers weren't in the magazine business. If I could figure out what business they were in I might be in line for a crime stopper reward.

I was eager to start my investigation, but until I could find a way to get into that off-limits back room; where the illegal stuff was taking place; I'd have to settle with exploring the places I did have access to.

I went through every drawer in the receptionist desk looking for clues. Aside from a few miniscule pieces of lint and obvious trash, I found only the receipt from the used furniture store showing the purchase of the desks and chairs used in the office and another slip of paper for some commercial grade flooring tiles—special order from Spain.

There were three doors behind my desk. The center door opened into the back work areas. The bulb that lit the closet behind the door on the right was dim, the shelves almost bare with nothing of interest. The closet was too small for my claustrophobic tastes so I shut that door.

When I opened the door to the left of my desk, I was met with a series of boards across the opening. I put my eye up close to the spaces between the nailed boards. I could see nothing but darkened gloom.

I needed to discover any easy way to investigate the guys and their activities in those back rooms.

How foolish I was to think that after years of typing my aunt's novels for her, I could unravel the mystery of my employer's illegal business when I hadn't even been able to get out of the backroom without stumbling.

I needed a way to gather information on the sly. I cursed Mr. Twerk for canceling my home internet service as a cost savings measure. I couldn't use the computer at home to gather information.

I returned to the computer at my desk, fingers itching, brain twitching. I entered Mr. Pilfer's name in the internet search engine and came up with nothing. The names Rocko and Randy were not enough to conduct a search so I entered the names of the all the tools I could remember from the back room; pick, shovel, boards, wheelbarrows, and metal bars. I got a bunch of retail sales sites popping up. Clearing the cookies and the search engine first, I began searching for magazine company start-up information hoping to find something useful to trap my employers with.

How To Start a Business said that to start publishing a magazine you need an office—check. You also need a website, advertisers, article writers, a commercial printer, marketing and selling venues. Uncheck. Uncheck. Uncheck. Uncheck. Uncheck. Uncheck. Not only did we not have the necessary components to start a magazine company, nothing I read indicated dirt accumulations or bulging satchels were part of a magazine production, but what did I know about the magazine business?

I kept typing in everything I knew about the company I was working for and kept coming up empty-handed for everything I typed in. Discouraged with my lack of serious sleuthing skills, I brought up my personal e-mail account and typed a quick e-mail to Gordon's account.

> *Dearest Gordon,*
>
> *I miss you terribly. Things are not the same with you gone. The house makes all kinds of creepy noises. I don't know how to set the house alarms and doorbell is broken and won't ring. I can't pay the household bills. I accepted a job working for strange men in a creepy asylum basement of a building downtown so maybe Keiko won't have to leave me all alone.*
>
> *I've not seen or heard from Frank in weeks.*
>
> *Martin is out on bail and Mandy has chosen him over me.*
>
> *Thanks for checking the car over before you left. I feel more secure knowing you gave it a once over. I still haven't found my garage door opener and house keys, so I've been*

using yours. I figured you wouldn't mind since you are gone on holiday for a spell. You will probably have to get a duplicate set made up when you get home if I haven't found mine by then.

Oh, BTW, I'm all out of sugar cookies.

I swiveled back and forth in my chair as I proofread what I'd typed. I then hit the backspace key until I got to 'I miss you terribly'. I let that sentence stay and typed after it "I hope you are having a great time in Nepal. Take care of yourself and don't fall off Mount Everest." I hit the send key and felt a weight lift from me. Gordon was the best. He deserved this vacation break to help his friend.

I presumed that since I hadn't heard from Frank, he must not be able to send or receive e-mails while on undercover assignments but that didn't stop me from bringing up the Penelope Pembrook e-mail account and e-mailing the account he had used to converse with me on my aunt's website. I wanted to enlist his advice on undercover investigative techniques that would allow me to explore the back room.

Hello Undercover Fan,

Surprise! I have a job. I bet you never thought I'd give up knitting at home, but I have done just that. Mr. Pilfer liked me and hired me on the spot. Except I think that isn't his real name, because I've heard him referred to as Mr. Boggs. I now work at the McClintock Office building. In the basement to the basement. The men I work for claim they are starting a magazine company. I've only worked here a few hours, but my guess is they are up to no good. Instead of staplers, staple pullers, ink pens, paper, ink, glue, and all the things a magazine receptionist needs to stay busy, my desk is stocked with only lint and trash, and they keep what's going on in the back room a secret.

They had a customer who came in today with a heavily stuffed satchel. After he was in the backroom a while, he left with his bag empty. They must be involved in something illegal, but I don't know how to prove it. Yet.

I heard Rocko say the back room door is going to always be locked tight to keep me from snooping. Do you have any tips on how I can sneak undetected into a back room where I think they are doing the illegal business? If you tell me how to get in there, I will also need a tip on what to do if I'm caught snooping because Rocko is a huge guy with a bad disposition.

I wanted to type 'I miss you terribly and things are not the same without you' into the closing of Frank's e-mail, but I didn't want to sound pathetic so I just added '*your Genie*' and hoped he'd read between the lines and know I was his and how much I regretted not making him my 'Undercover Man' when I had the chance.

I opened the door to the back room again, heard no voices, and seeing no one about in the hallway I put my brave investigator facade on and crept down the darkened hall wondering why I heard no sounds at all in the back area. Nothing. Nothing from Mr. Pilfer's office door either so I crept to the maintenance door and opened it just enough to see inside. No one was visible.

There was only one method of egress, past my desk. *No one had left the backroom so why was no one around?* Here was an excellent opportunity to begin my investigation. I opened the door to the other room in the back and found the same emptiness. There had to be a secret access panel hidden somewhere for those men to disappear the way they did. I ran my hand along the edge of a board covering one wall. It was loose, not affixed to the wall, so there was no need to find a latch or spring that hid the secret room I knew had to be behind the board. I tipped the board towards me. It was heavier than it looked. When it started to drift away from my control, I let it settle back against the wall.

When I heard scraping sounds coming from the maintenance room, I scurried back to the reception desk. I decided it was best to leave exploring the back rooms until I got Frank's expert advice. I didn't want to get flattened by wood or caught by Rocko.

My father may have been a double agent spy and my aunt a popular murder mystery writer, but placing myself in imminent danger for the thrill of it was not something I'd inherited from either of them.

CHAPTER 12

I sat silently in my chair with my elbows on the desk, my head in my hands. I was deep into something I knew nothing about. I likely wouldn't receive a response from either Gordon or Frank anytime soon. I was alone and afraid and wondering what I should do about my employment situation.

Should I quit my job and turn over what I knew to the authorities? What exactly did I know? The men who hired me weren't good housekeepers? They leased space that might have ghosts? They didn't want to bring in their previous partners because they were greedy?

All I knew for sure was that Rocko had said something big was up. He hadn't wanted to hire me, and he wanted me to stay out of the back work area. *Was that enough to go to the police with?*

I was lost in dark thoughts when two red bandana sweat-banded men entered the office. Both men had the sleeves torn off their sweat-drenched tee shirts to reveal their bulging biceps.

I stood up. My practiced receptionist words stuck in my throat.

"We got a delivery to bring in. This door the best one to use?" The man with the strongest smell and the biggest underarm tee shirt stains asked me, motioning to the front door of the office.

My fingers were busy searching the corner edge of the desk for the button Mr. Pilfer told me to push. I rushed my fingers up and down the edge in a panic, but I couldn't find that darned button.

"Just a minute," I told the men. "There is something I'm supposed to do." I dropped down to a crouch on the floor to see the underside of the desk clearly. I found and pushed the red button several times.

I got my head above the level of the desk high enough to see the men and said, "Hello, I'm the receptionist here." I popped up to full height and swept my arms out to encompass the vacant reception area.

"Welcome to our offices. Pardon the dust. We are still under construction. What's that you say? You want to, to...to..."

Seeing their blank looks, I said, "Never mind. Someone will be with you shortly. Would you like to take a seat?" I Vanna gestured to the two pathetic folding chairs.

Both men looked at each other, at me, then at the room and then at the two folded up chairs. "Nah. We got a bunch more deliveries to do. We just need to know what's the best way to get this thing in here. The elevators seem big enough to use, but this door seems too narrow for the RO14 to get through." The man speaking untwisted his bandana and used it to wipe his face and underarms.

Mr. Pilfer rushed out and had the two sweat-soaked men bring the boxed gigantic fancy, high-resolution printer in through the only exterior door we had—the door leading in from the main building hallway.

I watched the two men struggle to bring a monster piece of equipment in. They dolly-rolled it in past my desk easily enough, a man holding each side of its bulk. Then they came to the back area door.

I hid a smile as those two men grabbed, pulled and coaxed that machine through the doorway while Mr. Pilfer paced back and forth in the reception area, urging, "Careful now, careful now. That's a very sensitive printer. Don't damage it. Work it through carefully."

He scurried behind the men when they finally squeezed the machine through the doorway. Mr. Pilfer was so genuinely concerned about this important magazine printing equipment that I began to have doubts about thinking that he was anything other than a newly established, inexperienced magazine editor.

I replayed the conversation I'd heard in the back room in my mind, trying to decide if my employer had actually said threatening things about me or if my mind was conjuring up danger.

When the two delivery men came back out to the reception area several minutes later, they requested I sign the delivery slip so they could be on their way.

"Shouldn't Mr. Pilfer be the one to sign this?" I asked.

"He said to get your signature on it." The biggest man pulled a pen from behind his sweat-banded ear and offered it to me.

I opened desk drawers hoping a pen would magically appear inside one of the empty drawers.

The man wiggled the pen he was holding.

"Thank you, but I'm sure there is a pen in here somewhere." I frantically began opening and closing desk drawers, knowing there wasn't a pen or pencil, but still searching for anything I could use to sign my name to that paper, anything but his pen.

I found a bunch of lint and dirt, pencil lead and the sales receipt in the top drawer—just as before. I knew the next two drawers were empty, but I opened them anyway. I didn't have a pen. I didn't even have one of those little paper clippy things that hold the paperclips inside magnetically until you shake them out. *Darn it.*

The bottom drawer unexpectedly jingled when I slammed it shut in frustration.

One of the sweaty headbands hitched up his sagging jeans and flashed his ink pen in front of my face again. I quickly picked up the pencil lead from the top drawer and holding it pinched between thumb and forefinger managed to sign my name on the appropriate line before the lead broke in two.

The sweatier of the two took the signed form, used it to rub his nose to dislodge a drip of something that I hoped wasn't what I thought it was, and then he peeled off the bottom yellow customer copy and held it out to me.

When I didn't readily accept the form from him, he grunted in disgust and slapped it on the desk where I vowed it would remain throughout the eternities.

After the grunge brothers left, I got down on my knees to check out the drawer with the jingle. I reached in and felt around the flat bottom until I got hold of something. I pulled out an odd little strip of leather with a buckle attachment. There were some stones adorning the leather and a couple of metal loops at the center. If I'd had Mr. Pilfer's special glasses, I could have examined the stones closer to see if they were valuable. As it was, the band was too big to be a bracelet and too small to be a decent necklace. I threw the thing back into the drawer and shoved the desk drawer closed again.

Now that I knew my employers were legitimate businessmen, and I had nothing to investigate, I returned to the computer. I hooked back into the building's wifi system and did an internet search on the McClintock building in Chicago.

That building was only interesting for its historical architectural worth. Seems there had been a hospital in the general area of the McClintock building, but it wasn't for the insane, and it didn't operate long before the city bought it up so they could begin construction on the Deep Tunnel, an enormous underground storm sewer drain of some sort that would store and channel the rainwater that had nowhere else to go. The tunnel prevented flooding of the streets and buildings whenever there was extensive rain. The water was stored in areas of the tunnel for a slower release into Lake Michigan.

Once the drain system was in place and the city was done

with the land, a man named Richard McClintock bought the land and what was left of the building to build the current McClintock Office building.

Building research was boring. Being broke made any online window-shopping a bore, too.

I'd always enjoyed typing on a keyboard when I had typed the Penelope Pembrooke manuscripts from my aunt's longhand notes, making sure her manuscript was properly formatted. Manuscript typing was one of the only things, besides knitting, I did well. Now that I knew this was a real magazine company with its own super duper printer, I wanted to do something that would benefit my employers in their business endeavors. *Business Weekly* said in their lead article last month, "Ensuring your employer's success is to ensure your success."

Knowing a magazine needed lots of articles, I figured I'd type a few articles up for them. Write what you know *Writers* magazine had suggested. I had a hard time coming up with something useful, but ended up typing a 699-word article on "How to Pump Your Own Gasoline." I checked my writing over on the screen and was pleased that I'd accomplished something useful.

I wanted to print the article out so I could proof it in print, but, unfortunately, I didn't have a printer at my desk and the super deluxe printer in the back was still being set up and would probably be off limits to me anyway. I unclasped my USB bracelet and saved the document there so I could print it out at home.

Building on my first success, I thought I'd try my hand at writing an article on to "How to Pay Your Household Staff Without Money."

I got writer's block on that one, so I stopped working on it three lines in. Just as well. It was best not to give Mr. Pilfer any ideas about paying me in anything other than money.

Devoid of writing inspiration, I dug the newspaper Mr. Fly threw away out of the trashcan to get fresh story ideas. I purposefully avoided the stories about the stealth missile.

Given the state of my hunger, I also skipped all the restaurant ads and reviews.

I went straight to the stories of politics, crime, and celebrities and began reading an article titled "Rich Get Bagged." It was a silly story about rich people finding plastic grocery shopping bags tied to their front yard trees. If the bags had been designer handbags, then the wealthy people who found them in their tree branches probably wouldn't have complained. But since the bags were common plastic, the rich filed complaints with the police alleging that their yards were being littered with trash. The paper chose to run a story on their plight believing this was a new style of vandalism that targeted only the wealthiest homes in the wealthiest neighborhoods.

I lived in a wealthy suburb. I didn't recall any bags fluttering from trees in my yard that morning so I concluded the vandals must have caught wind of my financial woes and determined I wasn't worthy of plastic mayhem.

When I got to the paper's sports section, I saw where Mr. Fly had circled a bunch of team stats and written a lot of numbers in the margin of the pages. I pulled the scribbled on section out. None of it made sense to me, so I put the sports section back in the trash where it belonged.

CHAPTER 13

One o'clock came and went. I was fighting severe hunger, sitting at my desk twiddling my thumbs when the lights in the room began to flicker and dim. I jumped up in a panic wondering if we were experiencing an earthquake or another natural disaster. If the building lights went totally out, it would be like I was buried underground. I didn't have a survival kit with me. I didn't even have a flashlight to see my way out of the building. Before I could have a full-blown panic attack, I remembered my cell phone was in my purse. I didn't have phone service, but the phone had a flashlight application that I was sure would still work even without the phone service.

After a few minutes of flickering, the lights stopped acting up. Everything became quiet again, except for the growling of my stomach.

The back door opened a wide crack and a man's smooth-shaven face and close-clipped sideburns peered out at me.

Was the man, who had to be Randy, making sure I was working? Was he going to report my lack of activity back to Rocko?

My stomach gurgled. The door opened further. Randy and I made eye contact. We both looked away. He quickly closed the door.

When I heard the door open again, I pretended to be

busy at work typing, but I was just re-typing one of the stories from the newspaper. The one about the plastic bags.

After a few seconds of staring at me sprint typing, Randy closed the door, nothing said.

I could sympathize. I don't much like talking to strangers either.

Randy opened the door again at 1:40 and stuck his hand out through the opening with four crisp, slightly soiled five-dollar bills clutched tight.

"Rocko said you go get us lunch at McDeed's." He remained behind the door jam, shaking his fisted dollars at me.

I had passed a McDeed's restaurant that morning while lost. It was on the block behind the McClintock building, a little farther down the street. I could walk there and back—no problem, provided I didn't drown from the rain. If I took the alley that bordered the McClintock building and its neighbor, the Opalheimer Jewelry Store, that would shorten my trip. I'd only half drown.

I held out my open palm under his fist, and the released bills cascaded down into my hand.

"What does everyone want?" I asked him looking up at his face, speckled with dirt. He looked to be mid-twenties.

"I dunno." He opened the door wide and looked around the room. He resembled his older brother in stature and coloring, except something about him wasn't as threatening or as dull. His eyes were brighter. His face friendlier.

"Burgers I guess. I like the McDeed big kid's burger meal," he said to me, and then this grown man put his head down and looked at me from beneath his thick lashes—all shy like and whispered, "Sometimes they put toys or a little book in the bag. If they do that, can ya make sure it's a book with easy words or a boy toy like a car or gun or sump'in? Rocko gets mad when I play with the little dollies they sometimes put in the bag for me. I like 'em, but he doesn't. He thinks girls and dolls are stupid."

"Girls and dolls aren't stupid. Doesn't he have a mother?

91

Would he call her stupid?" I asked defending my gender, my dislike of Rocko increasing.

"We had a mother, but she's gone now. That's why I gotta stay with Rocko. Momma tol' him he gots to take care of me. She said I need to listen to him and do everythin' he says on accouna I cain't stay on my own ever since the accident where my head got hurt." He hid his face partially behind the door he was holding open.

I was instantly ashamed of my thinking a man like Randy was trying to catch me goofing off at work. This poor man's mother died leaving him saddled with a man like Rocko.

"I'll make sure they give you a toy Rocko would approve of," I reassured him. "But no guns. Guns do not make good toys."

A tiny grin lit his face, and he skipped happily back to his jerk of a brother while I and my empty stomach headed out to get three burger meals.

I was a little light-headed from hunger and vigorous typing, but when I reached the front doors to the building, I turned around, deciding to use the bathroom before I went out into the drizzling outdoors. I found Miss Anime in the public bathroom on the first floor, gazing in the mirror, reapplying her candy apple red lipstick. I'm a little shy about using public bathroom stalls when others are near.

"I'll be glad when this rain finally stops." She looked at me via the mirror reflection.

"Me, too. How long has it been raining like this?" I asked, wondering what difference it would make to me, but feeling inclined to say something.

"Oh, that's right. I forgot. You probably can't hear anything buried away in the sub-sub. It's been raining off and on today. The weatherman says this is the rainiest November in over 50 years. I feel positively soggy every time I step outside."

Miss Anime left the restroom, and I was finally able to do what I'd gone in for. I was going to cut through the side alley as a shortcut, but when I rounded the corner of the building and discovered the lobby man with the holey tan jacket scrounging through the alley dumpster, I stepped back to the building's edge to rethink my plan. I'd read stories about homeless veterans with Post Traumatic Stress Disorder living on the street because they didn't get the mental and physical help they needed.

I didn't know if the man was dangerous or not and I hadn't a clue of how long it would it take me if I went the long way around. I peered around the edge of the building. Maybe he was just taking a smoking break. He was probably harmless.

The man leaned into the dumpster, grabbed a hold of something heavy, and hefted out a bulging, black plastic trash bag. He ripped the top of the bag open and began rummaging inside, pulling paper and debris out, looking at them, then dropping them on the ground to get to the next item. The dirty, worn backpack with the bedroll bungee corded to the bottom sat near the open dumpster confirming that he was homeless.

I remembered that feeling. Homeless. Dumpster diving. Stench. Rats and Moon Pies.

I gave a shake of my head when the man flung the bag and all the trash back inside the dumpster. The lid slammed down with an echoing bang as he sank to sit on the ground, empty handed. His head turned my way. His eyes were shielded behind tinted glasses, but I could feel his shaded eyes watching me as I turned and left my plan of a shortcut behind with him and the trash in the alleyway.

I took the alternate route, to the corner stop light and down the street to the next stop light and over a half a block. The glitter from a ten-karat Hearts-Desire diamond engagement ring in the window of the Opalheimer jewelry store caught my eye. I stopped and stared at the huge rock on display. My mind conjured up a vision of Frank slipping an engagement ring on my finger. A man in a suit stepped out of the store and handed me a sales flyer. He looked at me looking at the ring in the window.

"It's a beauty isn't it? We've got a huge shipment of

diamonds coming in next week if you'd prefer a different diamond, a bigger one perhaps?" His smile was smug.

"No. No. No, thank you." I handed the flyer back to the man. I couldn't afford diamonds and had no intentions of ever marrying again.

I chastised myself for wasting time as I ran the rest of the way to the fast food burger place, mortified that I'd even allowed such a horrible thought as marriage to enter my mind.

A few late-lunch diners were at the McDeeds. There was a line of customers at the counter, but not more than I could handle. More would have given me indigestion—if I'd had anything in my stomach.

I had no idea of what kind of burger to get Mr. Pilfer and Rocko. I only knew Rocko was not someone you wanted to give the wrong burger to so I read the menu billboard in its entirety five times before I approached the end of the line.

"Say, aren't you the lady with the naughty umbrella?"

I turned around. Mr. Blond Beard was directly behind me in line. I didn't recall him being there when I got in line, but hunger can be so distracting.

"Oh, hello." I turned back to the menu board.

I could feel that he'd stepped closer to my back, tailgating. I moved forward a fraction until the smell of the old spice aftershave on the man ahead of me stopped me. If I moved any closer, Mr. Old Spice would be taking me to meet his parents.

I didn't like Mr. Blond Beard crowding me so I turned roundabout and stepped a little off to the side of the line to get some of my personal space back and to clear my nostrils of spice. With a motion of my hand pointing to my spot in line, I said to Mr. Blond Beard, "You must be in a hurry. You can go ahead of me."

"No. I'm not in a hurry." He smiled that dental ad smile and didn't budge a fraction from where he was standing. If anything, he advanced slightly forward making it awkward for me to step back into my spot in line without touching him.

The line advanced, and I rushed into my former spot

before the opening got any smaller.

Mr. Blond Beard edged forward again.

I looked behind me at the four customers that had accumulated. I would be next at the counter after Mr. Spice. If I had gotten out of line then, it would have taken forever to get back up to the counter, so I stood my ground and decided to tough the situation out. My stomach gurgled in affirmation.

The customer at the counter was finishing up his order.

I was almost to the counter.

Mr. Spice stepped up to the counter and began reading the long list of burgers he'd been designated to pick up. I regretted my choice of service lines when the line next to mine advanced while I was standing still—sandwiched in with Mr. Blond Beard at my heels and Mr. Spice at my front.

At long last, I stepped to the counter and ordered Rocko a triple threat, a sandwich with three paddies and three slices of cheese. For Mr. Pilfer, I got a quarter pound beef burger and for Randy, the big kid's meal with a boy toy. I had enough of the $20 left to buy something small for me from the twenty— but I had my junior burger and fries rung up and packaged separately from the other items. No one implied I could use the money Randy gave me to buy myself lunch, so I didn't.

"That's a lot of food for a little girl like you to be eating." Mr. Blond Beard said. His eye laugh lines deepened; he was joking.

"I am hungry enough to eat a gelding, but don't worry, you're safe; most of this is for my bosses."

"Funny and a working girl. Where do you work?"

He was shamelessly holding up the line to talk to me. The girl behind the counter was patiently waiting for him to tell her his order. From the way she was ogling him, I am sure she was willing to wait as long as he needed. He had her full attention even though he ignored her to talk to me.

I took a closer look at him, wondering if he was captivating enough to continue to hold my attention. His sandy hair and tan face were handsomely beguiling. The well-tailored blue suit showed off his lean body to good advantage.

Nope. My opinion hadn't changed since our morning encounter in the street. He was extremely attractive and movie star handsome. Robert Redfordish in appearance—back when Robert Redford was young and made appearances—but that was all.

People in line behind us weren't as equally impressed. They were making impatient noises and shuffling forward a little, like drivers who want to hurry up the car up ahead of them by riding on their bumper.

"A magazine company," I told him. Tightening my grip on the food bags in my hands, I rushed outside.

Once I confirmed that Mr. Blond Beard wasn't following me, I stopped to pull a few fries out of my bag and eat them. I was so hungry; I decided to take my chances with Mr. PTSD, so I ran to the alley to get back to my desk and eat those delicious fries.

I entered the alley's rear entrance. There was no sign of Mr. PTSD.

So far so good.

I was just about level with the dumpster when I noticed two blue-jeaned legs and muddy white high tops angling out into the alleyway.

He was still there, still sitting where he slumped down 40 minutes ago. I didn't know if he was demented or dangerous, but I was not going to stop to find out. I made a decision on the fly. I ran full speed to the dumpster. I stopped in front of it, screeching to a full halt. I flung my white bag with its junior burger and less than full complement of fries down on the ground next to Mr. PTSD. I then sprinted the rest of the way to the front door of the McClintock building.

My stomach was having a fit over my altruistic actions, so I stopped at the reception desk to catch my breath and to ask the girl with the pink hair if she had a stick of gum I could have.

CHAPTER 14

Arriving home from work, I didn't pause to take off my dried on sticky clothes, broken shoes or coat. I didn't wait for Keiko either. I hobbled directly to the kitchen, opened the refrigerator, pulled out a sausage link and started eating it cold.

Keiko came in, grabbed the partially eaten sausage out of my hand and admonished me saying, "This not sushi, Missy Imogreen. Must cook."

"The package said, 'pre-cooked' and I'm too hungry to wait for cooking."

She put that sausage and another unbitten link on a plate. "You do like this." She poked each sausage twice with a knife from the drawer, put the cold sausages in the microwave and set the timer for 2 minutes while she fished two hot dog buns out of a plastic bag.

When she pulled the plate out of the microwave, the wonderful scent of cooked sausages filled the kitchen.

"See. Quick," she said cradling each sausage down into its soft bun and then handing them to me.

The phone rang just as I got the sausage to my mouth.

"Repotters call all day," Keiko said.

I smiled as I answered the phone, prepared to tell the "repotters" to shove off.

"Miss Warren? We were wondering if you'd found those unfinished manuscripts?" I didn't have to see the twitchy mustache to know it was my aunt's literary agent, the one she'd been working with before her death. He and her publisher seemed convinced that if I would turn over her two unfinished manuscripts, they could have someone ghost write the endings and sell them for a tidy profit.

"The manuscripts aren't lost." I twirled my bracelet around on my wrist. "I know exactly where they are, and I'm not going to have my aunt's work be capitalized on by another author. She's the only one who could do the endings justice, because she was the one who knew how the stories were supposed to end."

"But if you'd just listen to reason. I'm sure the endings could be figured out if we had the beginnings of the manuscripts."

"I'm not interested."

"Please understand our interest is strictly for the fans that love her and want to read more of her mysteries."

"The fans who love her will want a story that she wrote and not a phony ending. Good-bye, Mr. Rosenthal." He was still pleading when I hung up.

The phone immediately rang again.

"I told you; I am not interested..." I said.

"You had better be interested," Darth Vader said.

I gasped when the sound of his mechanical breathing caused me to panic. "What do you want?"

"I want those documents. I know you have them."

I shut my eyes tight and said, "I don't know what documents you are referring to."

"I think you do."

"Well, I don't!" I hung up, my appetite lost.

Mr. Twerk must not have been able to get all the utility companies to hold off for a bit. I worked all evening trying to figure out how to pay the overdue electric bill that came with a shut-off notice in that day's mail. I didn't have enough money to pay the utilities and still pay Keiko. I decided Keiko came first. I put check I'd made out to the gas company in the envelope for the electric company. I figured when the electric company opened their envelope, they would decide it was an honest mistake and send the check back to me so I could reissue. That would buy me sufficient time to receive my first paycheck from Mr. Pilfer and pay the bill.

I knew it was cheating to do that. I did intend to pay them; I just couldn't do it right then. I left the unsealed, unstamped payment envelope on the hall stand for Keiko to take care of and headed to the cookie jar in the kitchen. I opened the lid and inhaled their sweet goodness, but when I saw the credit card bill on the kitchen counter, my appetite deserted me. I set the lid back down on the jar.

I needed $2,000 to start Mr. Chilton looking into the allegations against my father. I needed to pay the credit company. I also needed to do something fast to get the utility bills paid or Keiko and I would be frozen popsicles sitting in the dark. Well, maybe just I would be a frozen confection as I was certain Keiko would have left my employ by then.

Next morning, I was brooding and sullen to Keiko's cheerfulness. She fixed my breakfast while I scuttled out to the front porch to retrieve the morning paper. Thankfully, there were no reporters in sight.

"You read paper loudly for me?" Keiko asked while she sliced mushrooms and spinach to add to my omelet.

I perused the stories for something suitable to read aloud. The front page was plastered with news of my father and the stolen plans. I skipped those. I also skipped over the police reports on break-ins. I didn't want the details of how many there were to make Keiko nervous; she'd be too frightened to sleep at night.

"Here's an interesting story continued from yesterday." I began reading, not knowing if Keiko even understood what I was saying.

"Madeline, a Portuguese Poodle, cousin to the president's dog, has been reported missing. Police do not suspect foul play but are asking people to be on the lookout for her. She was last seen outside her home yesterday when the butler let her out for a potty break. She is wearing a diamond studded leather collar with emerald accents. In addition to the dog's connection to the president, Madeline won best in show at the Westminster Kennel Club three years running and is a highly sought-after breeding bitch."

I held the paper up to Keiko's face at the counter where she was chopping veggies. "Here is a picture of her."

"People take dog for owner money," Keiko declared looking up only briefly at the picture while slicing radishes into little flowers.

I looked at her, then back at the picture of a carefully groomed dog sitting on a plush pillow with a sparkly collar around the neck and a big bow on top of the little carefully coiffed head. The owner must dote on the dog, probably would be willing to pay a lot of money to get the dog back. Something about the dog seemed familiar even though I'd never been to a dog show.

I never had a dog, but then I never wanted a dog. I'm afraid of dogs. They all bark and bite, but if I had wanted a dog, I knew Gordon would not allow my dog to be dognapped. That was, if I'd had a dog and if I had still had Gordon.

Feeling maudlin, I went on to read the next article on the page while Keiko arranged sliced sausages, veggie flowers and a molded rice teddy bear into a Benito box for my work lunch.

"Fad vandalism in the Chicago suburbs is on the rise. Ten homes in the upper north side have had vandals tie plastic bags to the trees in their front yard. Initially, it was thought the tree tying was related to a benign gang initiation rite, but since the homes are all in affluent neighborhoods, the police now believe the bags might be some way of marking the houses for robbery. As of yet the houses have been left undisturbed, but authorities are asking homeowners to be vigilant and to keep their doors locked and their house alarms on."

"Gang bull's eye," Keiko said sticking a sprig of parsley in the rice bear's hand, then drying her hands on a kitchen towel.

"You might be right." How astute of her to deduce a plausible explanation. I wondered if the police had been smart enough to return to their original supposition of gang activity in conjunction with the plastic bags.

Keiko handed me the insulated lunch container that was shaped like a smiling white kitty sporting a pink bow over one ear. Before I went to brush my teeth, I hid that container and the newspaper inside my handy oversize purse along with a kid's book for Randy, a few balls of yarn and a crochet hook for me. My cell phone was useless for making calls, but I threw it in with the other things because I wanted the flashlight application—just in case the lights flickered again.

As I drove my car down the long, tree-lined driveway, I took careful note of each tree I passed. Nothing plastic fluttered in the breeze, and I had only a slight feeling of unease upon leaving my house. My phobia was better, but my mood was not.

Keiko was good company, and I knew she knew her way around a mop, but Gordon wasn't going to be coming home soon enough for me. I should have paid closer attention when he showed me how to set the house alarm. Setting the alarm was not something I was good at so most nights I didn't even try.

My morose mood and the gloom of heavy-laden gray skies followed me all the way to the Well's Street self-parking garage. I quickly fobbed the car locks and all but ran the few blocks to my office building to beat the rain. I slowed my pace upon approach to the massive columns that supported the ten stories above them.

A thin reed of smoke was escaping from behind one of the pillars. I could just make out the brim edge of a black Stetson. Then I saw him, soiled jacket, backpack, ratty blue jeans and all, head to toe visible in the reflection of the glassed front doors. On this overcast day, he used those mirrored sunglass lenses as an obvious attempt to conceal his drug crazed eyes.

Just like my observations, I felt him watching my reflection from his concealed spacing behind the pillar. He may have been leaning casually against the granite surface blowing a long curling stream of smoke upwards, but something about him told me nothing about him was casual.

My heart thudded at the unexpected sight of the man. There was a law prohibiting smoking near the entrances so obviously he was not a law-abiding citizen.

"Pay him no mind. He's mostly harmless." Miss Anime stepped up to my right. She easily crossed the expanse to the building's entrance, opened one of the doors and entered. I swooped in behind her. As she made her way to her desk, I glanced behind me. The interior of the building was reflected off the doors now, but Mr. PTSD's cigaretted glow remained as a visible reminder the man was still out there.

"He's been hanging around here for a couple of weeks. I think he's a mule or something." Miss Anime opened a drawer on her desk and flung her pink leather purse covered in kitschy bling inside.

"I can't put my finger on it, but there's something not right about him. He doesn't resemble a mule though, more like a sly fox," I said looking cautiously back at the doors, expecting him to come through them after me.

"I meant mule as in drug runner, not mule as in Hee Haw." Miss Anime laughed. "I've seen him exchanging things with people when he thinks no one is looking, small packages and slips of paper and stuff, but he never seems to bother anyone else; I figure he's harmless." She extended a hand to me. "You're back again today so you must not mind working in the basement dungeon."

"Yeah. They offered me the job, and since I didn't see any ghosts or dead bodies, I took it."

"Good for you and hey, that stuff about the basement

having ghosts from the asylum is just an old tale. Don't let it bother you. Some city inspector was just in last month and declared everything down there in tip-top shape."

"Well, thanks. I'd had better get down there to my work desk. I have to man the phones and reception the people coming in and all."

"Stop by if you get a break. It's boring up here." She extended her hand to me. "My name's Rē."

"Thanks. My name's Imogene. Imogene Warren."

She had a firm handshake for a girl in pink pigtails.

"Ray is an unusual name for a girl."

'Rē. It's short for Remote. My dad, Rolland Chance, owns this and few other buildings in the area. He makes me work at the information desk here to earn my allowance. He has some weird idea it will make me appreciate my wealth more if I have to work for it. Cheeze. How old-fashioned."

I gave her an incredulous look. "Your name is Remote Chance?"

"It's a kicker isn't it? I figure it's better than him naming me Nada."

CHAPTER 15

I found the outer door to the magazine office open a smidge. When I entered, I noticed my computer was already on, the top drawer of the desk pulled out and the items on the top of the desk askew. The closet door was wide open, too, with one of the folding chairs pulled inside. Some of the items on the shelves inside the closet were tipped over. A host of banging and scraping noises were coming from the backroom. I hesitated to open the back room door and check on things because I was concerned that we were in the midst of a burglary and I didn't want to confront any burglars who might be back there burglaring.

When the office lights began flickering, and I heard a whirring, drilling sound from the back, I sighed, pulled the folding chair back to its spot along the wall, closed the closet door, and shoved in the desk drawer. Randy must have been bored and messing around in the reception area after I left the day before. He probably left the doors open and whatever Mr. Pilfer and Rocko were doing in the back was interfering with the lights again.

I put the lunch Keiko packed for me in the desk. The dust was thick over everything again.

Darn. I had remembered to bring a light source but had

forgotten to ask Keiko for a bottle of cleaner.

I found the door to the back room locked tight—just like the day before. Setting up the high quality multicolor digital paper printing machine must have been taking them longer than they expected. I didn't mind the noise. That noise and the printer delivery was sure proof I'd soon be reading the first issue of *Quarterly Repository.*

I didn't waste my time on receptionist practicing or waiting for the phone to ring or someone to walk in the front door. Instead, I got into my bag and took out a single sheet of crochet instructions, two balls of yarn and the crochet hook I'd brought to start crocheting a blanket for the homeless man in the alley.

I held the green and cream yarns doubled and crocheted a chain. When the chain was about three feet long, I worked a pattern of "single crochet in one chain, chain one and skip the next chain" all the way across the chain, being careful to end the row with a single crochet. Then I chained one and turned the piece so I could work a single crochet in each chain space and a chain stitch over each single crochet of the previous row. Being careful always to start and end each row with a single crochet, I worked steadily on the blanket for a while.

It had been an unseasonably warm and wet November, but December snows were expected to be heavy. The afghan blanket needed to extra thick to keep Mr. PTSD warm through the winter. If the magazine business remained slow, I could maybe get the majority of the blanket done before the first issue was released and things got busy.

I was going lickety split at single crochets and chains when one of the balls of yarn escaped me and rolled across the floor. I retrieved the yarn and with great dismay saw how much filth had accumulated on it. If I didn't get some of the dust and dirt removed from my work area, the blanket I was making would end up as filthy as the phone that never rang. From the looks of him, Mr. PTSD probably wouldn't have cared if the blanket I made him was dirty, but I did.

Never gift anything but your best, no matter to whom you

are giving it.

I got a few more rows done before the man with the fly birthmark came in toting his big, heavy satchel—just like the day before. Just like before, he patently ignored my greeting and bypassed me to head for the back door. I fumbled around trying to find the red button under the desk to push it.

Before I could find the button, Mr. Fly's pounding on the back door summoned Randy, who opened the door for him.

"Which one are you picking out for next time?" I heard Randy ask Mr. Fly.

"It hasn't been decided yet. We have several good prospects marked." Mr. Fly grumbled and hefted the bag up higher—almost dropping the bulging load as he moved through the narrow doorway.

"Can I pick the next one? Pretty please. I like the little black ones with beards." Randy followed closely at Mr. Fly's heels.

"We'll see. Anything we pick will have to be worth—" The door slammed shut. Locking automatically, muffling their voices.

Mr. Fly was a rude man, but Randy hadn't paid me any attention either. I shrugged it off. I was not offended at being ignored. I thrived on being ignored. I lived for anonymity. I was thrilled to be rejected by things that creeped me out, and Mr. Fly's fly birthmark was creepy. I know it was an unkind thing to say, but I couldn't help it that bugs scared me.

I brushed the yarn ball off as best I could and slid it back into my bag along with the few inches of the blanket I'd managed to crochet. I crossed the room to the storage closet and opened the door.

That closet was smaller than the building's elevator boxes. Tighter and crampier, but if I were quick, the room was roomy enough to hold me and my claustrophobia for the few seconds it would have taken for me to find something to clean with.

I stepped inside and began searching for cleaning supplies among the rolls of toilet paper and stacks of paper sacks and tipped over cans and boxes. It was all so confusing. I wished I'd gotten a can or box of whatever it was Keiko used to dust and clean with at home. The can on the top shelf was the only thing that even looked vaguely familiar.

I was struggling to reach the spray can at the back of the top shelf when I heard voices coming through the wall from Mr. Pilfer's office.

"I've already given you your share." Mr. Pilfer's feeble reedy voice didn't carry well, but it could still be heard through the thin wall of the closet.

"You ain't fooling me, Boggs." The voice of Mr. Fly came on strong, loud, demanding. It had to be him. He was the only visitor who had gone back there. "I know you got something bigger going than what you're letting me in on. I want in. Stop leaving me with only the penny ante stuff."

I visualized Mr. Pilfer fiddling with his glasses or the scissors on his desk when I heard him say, "There is nothing to get 'in' on. We're only doing this because we need some cash to start up a legitimate business here. Nothing more."

"Heinrich Rockford's never done anything legit in his life. He couches everything in terms of what he can get. He even takes his brother's disability check from him. If this magazine business of yours is so legit then why ain't I heard of it? Why don't you got a website or anything published yet?"

"It takes time to get a business started."

"Yeah, time and money. After doing time for money, I'll bet you're planning on doing it again."

My closet claustrophobia hit me hard just then. I needed to get out of there. I stretched up and grabbed the can from the top shelf. I rushed out of the closet before I could pass out from its confining space.

I got a grip, on my panic and the can and started willy-nilly spraying the dirt-streaked floor by the back door. The liquid pooled up in tiny, reflective puddles. I didn't think it was supposed to be doing that, so I read the back of the can. "Lessons Rusted Parts, Frees Sticky things, Stops squeaks."

The liquid was spreading, leaving a thin oily sheen on the

tiled floor.

I went back to the closet so I could retrieve the mop and swish it around like I'd seen people do on television, but when I opened the closet door, I couldn't bring myself to step back inside. I had an invisible claustrophobic barrier preventing me from going back into the boxy little room with its muffled shouting voices.

I was trying unsuccessfully to get my phobia in check so I could grab the mop when Mr. Fly came running out of the back room with Mr. Pilfer following close behind.

"Don't do anything foolish, Flynn," Mr. Pilfer yelled to Mr. Fly's racing form. They hit the area where I sprayed the floor and went sliding, arms flailing, halfway across the room.

Mr. Fly got his balance first and was out the door and gone. Mr. Pilfer slipped and landed on his butt.

I rushed over to help him up. "I'm so sorry, Mr. Pilfer. I was trying to clean the floor because it was so dirty. I guess I grabbed the wrong can of cleaning stuff." I took a hold of his upper arm to help him up. He and I both slipped a little before we got to a dry area of the floor.

"Don't worry about it, Miss Warren. It's probably just as well I didn't catch him. He and I used to be business partners, but we have been on the outs lately. It's a shame he ran out of here thinking the wrong thing about me. He's under a misimpression about this latest business venture. I'll go after him in a bit to see he doesn't do anything foolish. Please don't mention this to anyone. I wouldn't want Rocko to catch wind of it. Another incident would be bad for business."

Before he left to pursue Mr. Fly, Mr. Pilfer got me a jug of liquid marked "sodium hyperclorate" and some paper towels from the back room, so I could clean up the WD-4D I'd sprayed on the floor.

The sodium hyperclorate burned my eyes, nose, and throat, made my hands stink and turned the hem of my skirt white, but at least the floor was clean enough for my ball of yarn to roll across.

The McClintock building was spooky after the all the daytime business workers went home. At 5:15 half of the building lights shut down, leaving the office, hallways and bathrooms dimly lit. Rē had warned me this would happen. It was all done as part of a huge grant her father had received to do energy conservation in the building. Rather than replace the lighting with energy efficient lights, Mr. Chance had chosen to put in timers to shut half the lights off. I had wondered what Mr. Chance had done with the rest of the grant money but didn't broach the subject with Rē. He was her father, and who was I to criticize anyone else's father for their unscrupulous actions.

It was only my second day on the job, but Mr. Pilfer had asked me to stay in the magazine's reception area until 9 o'clock to keep an eye on things and answer the phone. I was afraid to be out that late and didn't see why my staying was necessary. Rē had told me that the building's outer doors locked at 5:15. People could leave the building after the doors locked, but no one could enter. Mr. Chance hadn't wanted to pay a security guard and so he'd given Rē the job of keeping an eye on things at the information desk during the day and kept the exterior doors locked after hours.

Mr. Pilfer appeared to understand my reluctance to stay when I explained how frightened my maid was to be alone in the house with all the threatening phone calls I'd been getting. At seven o'clock, he sent Randy out to keep an eye on things and answer the phone so I could leave.

Randy came out covered in dirt. I didn't want him sitting at my desk, but didn't see how I could stop him. I doubted anyone remaining in the building would venture down here with the lights only half working. It was too creepy.

I gave Randy one of the *Dreampuff* picture storybooks I'd brought for him.

"Gee, Thanks." Randy turned the book over and over in his big hands.

"You're welcome. It was one of my favorite books when I was a little girl. It's about a tiny white dog named Dreampuff."

"No one hurts the dog in here do they?" He scrunched up his face and began flipping through the book, looking at the pictures.

"No. Of course not. This is a happy book about Dreampuff's adventures in the big city."

"Good. I don't want no one to hurt no dogs. I like dogs a lot. I 'specially like the ones named "Scotty.""

As I left the magazine office, I saw Mr. Fly coming down the basement corridor towards me. With only half of the hallway lights lit there were eerie shadows on the walls. Mr. Fly had a box marked for 'bananas' under one arm, and he was dragging an empty black plastic garbage bag along behind him. Something about the vacuous look on his face scared me.

I said, "Hello," but Mr. Fly just stopped and stared at me. No recognition showed on his face, so I hurried past him.

I ran the full way to the self-parking garage in the dark and was quick to get in my car, lock the doors and head straight home.

I hit the opening on Gordon's garage door remote control several times when I got home, but the garage door refused to go up. The Bentley dealership insisted I had the remote with me when I got in the cab and left their lot. The Chevy dealership claimed they had put the remote on the Malibu's visor before I drove away. They both had lied. Keiko had searched the car and found no remote.

I blared the car horn and continued to blast it until finally, Keiko came outside to see what was going on.

"I can't get this thing to work," I told her, holding up Gordon's remote opener through my car window and continuing to press the button.

"No power," she said.

"I put new batteries in it this week."

She pointed to the three-stall garage. "No power in car house."

She pointed to the house. "No power in people house,

110

too."

I looked at the house for the first time since my arrival home. All the windows were dark. Seems the power company either hadn't gotten the check or they already knew about the switching the envelopes trick.

We ate cold dinner by candlelight, with the phone ringers turned off. I stayed up the entire night, unable to sleep in total darkness.

CHAPTER 16

The next day I headed to work early. I went through the McDeed's drive through and got their breakfast special with a strong hot coffee before parking my car.

Mr. Pilfer looked at the array of breakfast spread out on napkins on my desk and frowned at me over the top of his glasses.

"Let me get this straight. You need an advance on your paycheck to pay your maid?"

"Yes. No! I've already paid my maid, but I had to call up the electric company to get my lights turned back on. They wouldn't do that unless I promised I'd be there today to pay my bill. I didn't have the heart to ask my maid to give me her paycheck back so you see I can't pay my electric or gas bills because I've paid my maid."

He stood stock-still and continued to peer at me over his glasses. The jewelers loop gave him a "cyborg" look, and I began to think my asking for an advance may have been harder than asking Keiko for her paycheck back. My upper lip quivered, and a small twitch had started in the corner of my left eye, but I stood my ground. I'd already asked Keiko to seek alternative employment. Next month, without Keiko's wages to pay, I would be able to pay the electric bill; this advance was just to cover the current month's bill.

Mr. Pilfer shook his head and walked into the back room. My hopes shattered, my tears fell and mingled with dirt on the floor. I dropped like a stone into my chair. There would be no twirling for me. My only hope was to beg Mandy for some of the money I had turned over to her. My head sank down to rest on my desktop, dejected.

The door to the back room opened. I popped up. Mr. Pilfer stepped out towards me with five new one-hundred dollar bills that he thrust at me. "How you spend your money is none of my business, but you can't tell Rocko I gave you these. It doesn't bode well for our business plan to be doling out money we had other uses for."

I did a happy little quiver all over before I thanked Mr. Pilfer over and over again.

"You won't regret this," I told him. "I'll work very hard. You can ask me to do anything, and I'll do it. I can do more than type and answer the phone. I can set up a business website for you. I can type articles for the magazine to run. I've been practicing by typing the articles from the newspaper. I even wrote a few articles all on my own."

"You have?" he said. "Say, I would like to see those articles. I've always wanted to be a writer myself. I've met a lot of interesting people over the years. Might be good reading if I wrote about 'em."

I spent the next few hours happily researching website hosting companies and typing up articles on crocheting blankets for babies and the homeless in hopes that Mr. Pilfer might find my articles good enough to print in his magazine.

On my lunch hour, I ran to a nearby bill paying location and paid the electric bill in cash before I stopped to get burger meals for Rocko, Mr. Pilfer, Randy, and Mr. PTSD. I already had the lunch Keiko had packed for me that I was going to eat, but I wanted to treat everyone with the last 100-dollar bill I had.

Mr. Blond Beard was sitting at a table texting on his phone when I entered the McDeeds. He immediately came along side me in line and said, "Where have you been all my life?"

"Home, knitting."

He laughed, and we chatted about the unseasonably warm and rainy weather as he walked with me up to the counter to place my order. I handed the clerk my last Benjamin Franklin. He pulled a pen from the cash register drawer and made a faint brown line on the bill. Satisfied, he put the bill in the till and gave me back three twenties, a ten, a five and some change.

"Big spender," Mr. Blond Beard said. "Got more where that came from?"

"I wish. By the time I pay my weekly parking bill, I'll be broke again."

"Then you need to let me buy you dinner."

Keiko was going to the Bull's game that night with a friend she met at class. That meant no hot dinner for me. His offer was appealing, but I reluctantly told him 'no.' I didn't want him to think I was interested, because I was not. I was sure Frank would contact me any day so we could resume our romance.

Randy was so happy with the extra toy I got him that he danced around the reception area, hugging the two little plushie puppies. He opened the bottom drawer on my desk and pulled out the leather strap and showed it his inanimate animals.

"I knows this is too big for you guys, but see how pretty it is? I can't get ones that's smaller for you both to wear because Rocko says I can't be around any more dogs after what happened, but you guys probably don't care." He put the leather band and the two dogs into his oversized pocket and grabbed the lunches and took them into the back room before I could question him about the leather band.

I had brought the morning paper to work with me, so I didn't have to read it at home by flickering candle light if I didn't get the money to turn the lights back on.

114

The paper dismayed me as I read the front-page headline. Seems that about the time I was finding my power shut off, a man was struggling for his life in Lake Michigan.

Body Found in Lake Michigan

Chicago, Ill. – Late last night a man's body was pulled from Lake Michigan in the Rouge Street pier area. Authorities say the body was found in 60 feet of water near the Deep Tunnel duct that is used for controlled release of rainwater from the tunnel into Lake Michigan. Police say the death is being ruled as "suspicious." A full autopsy has been scheduled.

I was horrified that someone would go swimming so late at night and in so much water.

The next story headline was no better.

Government Investigates Warren Espionage

Washington D.C. –The Pentagon has denied rumors that the stealth missile plans have fallen into the hands of the Russian government.—

I thought the front-page news stupid and searched for the funnies, always a better read.

Except when I went to turn the thin newsprint pages, I found the edges were sticking, and I had trouble separating them.

I rubbed the tips of my finger pads together. They were slick and smooth. The cleaner I'd used the day before had removed all of my fingerprint ridges, leaving me with little to grip with.

My aunt had once written a story titled *Narrow Escape*,

115

where the killer had soaked his fingertips in bleach before going into a house within full view of the neighbors to kill his victim. None of the suspect's fingerprints were found at the murder scene. When the eyewitnesses testified that the suspect couldn't have killed the victim because he wasn't wearing any gloves, no gloves were found at the scene, and the suspect's fingerprints weren't found at the scene either. The police let the killer go. Penelope, teen detective, knew from the lingering smell of bleach that the killer had soaked his hands in bleach to remove his fingerprint ridges. She solved the crime and got the crime stopper reward.

The world needed more people like Penelope Pembrooke. The paper I was reading was full of awful news.

I did an internet search, and there it was, sodium hyperclorate, a fancy name for bleach.

I didn't know why my employers had so much bleach around there and thought maybe they were planning to perform criminal deeds. We were next door to a jewelry store, one that was expecting a shipment of diamonds.

My instincts kicked in and overrode my fear of the closet. Removing fingerprints meant these guys were into serious no good. Something strange was going on in the back room, and I couldn't wait until I got instructions from Frank. I needed to find out what my employers were up to.

I stepped inside the closet where I could at least hear the voices in Mr. Pilfer's office. Before I could get a full-blown case of claustrophobia, I was distracted by Rocko's firm booming voice through the wall.

"Flynn got us a pretty good haul this last time, but now that he's gone we're gonna have to go out and do a couple more jobs ourselves if we want to be ready to move forward with phase two on time."

"I don't know." I could just barely hear Mr. Pilfer's thin voice. "Randy's become a problem. I'm starting to have second thoughts about this whole thing. Things are starting to go sour. I don't like what happened to Flynn. We've got the equipment and the setup. Miss Warren could start a website for us. We

116

could make a good living at the magazine business if we really tried."

"What happened to Flynn was his own damn fault. Don't get all high flutin' on me and forget why we started this business," Rocko said. "I ain't going to give up on my dream to be filthy rich. The magazine business is for paupers."

I stepped out of the closet fearful they could hear my heavy, gasping breath and know how concerned I was about their using the magazine business as a front for illegal activities.

Worried I was going to find myself back on the street job-hunting soon, I wondered if it would be socially acceptable to use Mr. Pilfer as a reference if he was a dangerous criminal.

I sat and stewed at my desk, wondering what I should do about what I'd heard. I needed my paycheck to pay Keiko her last paycheck, and I now owed Mr. Pilfer five hundred dollars. I needed two thousand dollars to engage Mr. Chilton's services.

I know it wasn't right to play along and act ignorant of their actions just because I desperately needed the money, but I didn't know what else I could do.

Maybe if I found out as much as I could about the business they were doing in the back room—if I got more information—I might find that what they were doing wasn't illegal at all. Of if it was illegal, I could gather proof of that before I went to the police.

I needed at least two paychecks—maybe even three or four paycheck's worth of evidence.

I jumped when Mr. Pilfer came out and told me, "Rocko and I will be going out soon. We need to get this done today; it can't wait. We may be gone for several hours. You'll need to keep an eye on things as we're expecting another delivery." He gave me one of his weak, grandfatherly smiles.

I wrung my hands together and breathed a sigh of relief that he didn't seem aware that my opinion of him had changed. I managed to say, "Okay."

When he looked directly at me, I tried to meet his gaze with a steady gaze of my own and failed. I averted my eyes and rubbed the back of my hand over my brow to smooth my hair out of my face to cover my guilt.

"Randy stays," he said to me, putting on his coat and buttoning it up. Then he added, "Sorry, but he's been a handful lately, and he'll only get in the way if we take him with us."

Rocko came out of the back with a banana box just like the one Mr. Fly had been carrying the night before. Randy followed close at Rocko's heels, almost stepping on them.

"Why cain't I go?" Randy asked.

"You've been nothing but trouble, and I'm tired of cleaning up your messes. You stay here," Rocko said.

Randy hung his head. "I saided I was sorry." A sigh heaved out of his chest.

Mr. Pilfer reached up to put a hand on Randy's broad shoulder and told him, "We need you to stay here and make sure that new delivery of supplies goes where we need it in the back room. You think you can do that?"

Randy's face brightened a little as he looked down at Mr. Pilfer. "Is it important?"

"Very important," Mr. Pilfer told him.

Randy smiled a broad grin. After the door closed behind Rocko and Mr. Pilfer, the smile dissipated and Randy viciously kicked one of the metal chairs. The chair collapsed to the floor.

I seized upon this opportunity. "What's the matter, Randy?"

"They don't let me go with them." Another kick at the floored chair.

"Why? What are they going out to do?" I was hoping he would open up and spill the beans; let the cat out of the bag—so to speak.

"To bag up a prize." Not the bag I was hoping for.

"What kind of prize?"

"A prize I want. If I coulda go with them, maybe I could keep one of them. They cain't need them all." He crossed his arms, kicked the wall and left a scuffmark.

"Keep what? What is it they went to get?"

"Stop askin' me questions I can't answer." The next kick clattered the second chair to the floor.

He stomped into the backroom and slammed the door.

That was a dead end.

I went back to my internet search for clues. I typed in 'Heinrich Rockford.' Rocko's picture popped up on the screen of an arrest record site. The website prompted me to give them my credit card number to see the felonious charge details. I needed that information and didn't want to wait until my credit card was available again, so I typed an e-mail to Frank.

> *Dear Undercover Fan,*
> *Is there any way you can provide me with information on the previous felony convictions of Henrich Rockford? He's the one I told you I believe is involved in something shady again and would like to be able to know what he has done in the past so that I can be on the lookout for evidence of what he might be up to now.*
> *Thanks,*
> *Genie*

I had cleared my computer screen of my search efforts and the e-mail before I took up my hook and yarn again. I pushed the button under the desk a few minutes later when I saw a big-box discount store delivery man come through the front door wheeling in a dolly stacked high with several cartons.

Randy made a big deal of showing him into the back room. The man handed me the invoice before he followed Randy. Since this delivery guy was well dressed in a tan jacket and slacks with no nose drippings or sweat, I took the paper slip when he offered it to me.

Randy held the door open while the boxes were dollied into the back area. Randy's chin was jutted out, and he was striding with his head held high while leading the way into the back room to show the delivery man where the boxes were to go.

I read the invoice after the man left. Twenty rolls of paper towels, 25 LED emergency battery operated lights, six handheld flashlights, 30 packs of batteries, two specialty ink pens, six jugs of bleach, six 10-gallon buckets, a ream of heavy weight paper, masking tape, specialty plastic wrap and miscellaneous bolts and screws.

A strange mixture of items to be sure, but nothing sinister stood out. Everything pointed to a legitimate business with legitimate supply needs though even with my fear of the dark, I thought 25 emergency lights were a bit excessive.

I pressed the button under the desk, and Randy appeared. He seemed in a better mood. "Did everything get delivered into the back room okay?" I asked Randy in what I hoped was a conciliatory tone.

"Yeah, Rocko will be proud of me. I got it all back there and in the right spot."

"What is all the stuff being used for?" I asked twirling around an all-day sucker that I'd pulled from my purse.

Randy eyed the sucker, distracted. "I cain't say."

"That's a shame. I was saving this sucker for a friend. I was hoping you and I were friends. Friends share secrets. Friends share suckers." I let that hang in the air a moment.

"That's all stuff for the Grand Opening," Randy blurted out. "I'm not supposed to say because it has to stay a secret so I cain't tell you anything more."

"That's okay Randy. Friends keep secrets. I won't tell anyone you told me."

I didn't want to give up my sucker, and I was still confused about much of what I had eavesdropped on, but I felt better about the people I was working for after that delivery and Randy telling me about the grand opening. These men may have had shady pasts, but maybe they were working to turn their lives around and clean up their act—or maybe not. I had no way of knowing for sure.

I couldn't decide if Rocko and Mr. Pilfer were working hard to get their first issue completed and off the presses or if they were planning on using bleach to obliterate their fingerprints when they did something awful—like rob the jewelry store next door.

I'd seen their work area in the back. It was filthy, so it was just as plausible that they were going to use the bleach to clean and sterilize for when they had their grand opening. The floor tiles stacked in the hall were probably going to be installed just prior to the grand opening.

My area, the front reception room, was just as filthy and could have used a good cleaning, also. Too bad they were keeping everything in the back where I was not allowed. Had some of that stuff been up front, I could have cleaned my work area, too,—if I'd known how to clean.

I was jittery with excitement when I got a response to the e-mail I'd sent to Frank. When I opened it up, I found it was not the response I'd hoped it would be.

Imogene,

The FBI has an interest in Henrich Rockford. What is your association with him? Why do you believe he is doing something illegal? What type of evidence do you have access to? Can you access his computer files?

The e-mail lacked a signature line. My heart was hoping for warmth and familiarity, something that showed he was thinking of me as much as I was thinking of him. I didn't get what I wanted. I guess men don't think like women, or his interest in me had started to wane. Sorrowfully, I placed my fingers on the keyboard and typed back.

Frank,

A man named Pilfer hired me to work for him. I don't know his first name, but I've heard him called Boggs, and his partner's name is Henrich Rockford. They are supposed to be starting a magazine company called Quarterly Review, but initially, some things here didn't add up. I contacted you because I believed what they are doing may have been illegal, but I misinterpreted some things and no longer believe that now. Sorry to have bothered you.

Imogene

I had wanted to type, "do you love me or not?" like we were first graders but I refrained from making a fool out of myself in print. To my surprise, Frank typed immediately back.

Can you send pictures of the set up they have for starting the magazine company? Please provide as much information as you can about what you know about their business. Then erase these e-mails.

Your assistance is appreciated.

I flipped the screen off, disgusted with his 'appreciation.'

As much as I didn't want to believe it, my sister had a point about Frank. He wasn't exactly extolling his love for me.

CHAPTER 17

It was a long, difficult weekend. I couldn't get the impersonal way Frank had addressed me out of my mind. I thought a few sugar cookies might help, but when I went to the cookie jar, it was empty.

After I had received another call from my Darth Vader caller, I had to have a cookie.

I searched the pantry for a remnant of a cookie. They only thing that came close was a lonely graham cracker at the bottom of the cracker tin. I settled, but after that first stale bite, I threw it out. I expanded my search to the kitchen cupboards. Reaching on the top shelf of the cabinet nearest the stove, I pulled out a small box labeled "recipes." Inside I found recipe cards, some were typed, and some were handwritten. I flipped through the cards in the "sweets" section. I flipped past Topsy Turvey Cupcakes written in Aunt Tilly's hand, and skipped the typed up Pumpkin Gnash recipe.

My breath gave a hitch when I found the card "daughters' cookies" in my father's neat, precise handwriting.

My father had hand written that card.

I cradled the card next to my heart, now understanding the significance of the apostrophe placement. My father always made sugar cookies. He decorated them with white frosting and green sugar crystals whenever Mandy came to

123

visit. I liked pink frosting with rainbow candy sprinkles, so he made those for me.

I collected the ingredients I needed to make the cookies and began following the recipe. I was to whisk the dry ingredients together in a bowl. The whisking resulted in flour flying out of the bowl and onto the counter and floor, but since most of it stayed in the bowl, I forged ahead with my baking. When the instructions called for "creaming the butter and sugar together" in a separate bowl, that's what I did— guessing at the amount of cream needed since it wasn't mentioned on the card.

With the oven set to 350°, I started pouring out the cookie dough onto a cookie sheet. Feeling proud of my accomplishment, I set the timer for eight minutes and sat down at the table to wait.

The smoke alarm went off before the timer. The kitchen filled with smoke while I scrambled to find oven mitts. I pulled the burnt cookie puddles out of the oven and threw that smoking mess in the sink. Setting the oven to "broil" didn't turn out to be a good idea for getting the cookies done quicker.

No cookies for me.

The only bright spots in the day were that Vader had given up calling, and I received a neatly hand-written letter from Gordon in the mail.

My Dear Imogene,

Travel is difficult given the recent earthquake in this area, but after many trials, I arrived at my destination safely. I'm using the mail services as many of the utility services are down, and internet access is spotty or non-existent. My friend's trouble is more serious than I initially thought. I don't know when I'll be able to come home, but I would like for you to keep my apartment secured until then. I've transferred money to your account to assist with any expenses associated with my request.

As ever, yours,
Gordon

I was relieved to know that all was well with him. And that he was able to send me some money, but without my home internet access, I had to wait until I got to work to check my account to verify the amount of his deposit. I put the letter in my purse as a reminder to check my account on Monday. It didn't matter what the amount was. I was grateful for any amount. I just wanted to make sure I had enough to buy cookies.

Monday rolled around, and I had to pack my own lunch as Keiko had returned to her job hunting. I made two peanut butter and jelly sandwiches, the only kind of sandwich I knew how to make. I got the newspaper from the front porch and shoved that into my bag along with the sandwiches. I also scrounged up a few more of the books I'd had as a child. I put one in my purse, intending to dole them out to Randy one at a time so as to keep on his good side. I didn't want any more chair kicking episodes.

Randy and the others were already in the back when I arrived at work, so I set about trying to find ways to keep myself busy. I was on a downer over Frank's not even lukewarm response to my e-mails. I wasn't keen on crocheting, so I pulled out the newspaper. The front-page news had a picture of the man who was hit on the head and downed in Lake Michigan. I knew him as Mr. Fly but the police had identified him as Flynn, ex-prison con. I wasn't crazy about all the bad stuff that was going on in the world so I typed the newspaper stories backward so I wouldn't have to read them.

I was startled by a door slam when Randy came out from the back with the stick of the sucker I'd given him dangling from his mouth like a cigarette.

125

"Got any more of those suckers?" He asked.

"No."

"Then can I have more of those little books about dogs?"

"Huh, oh yeah, sure. I brought you *Dreampuff's Adventures at Disney*." I put the newspaper down and reached into my bag to get the book I'd packed that morning. The newspaper's front-page story and the picture of Mr. Flynn were face up on the desk.

Randy pulled the empty sucker stick out of his mouth, picked up the paper and put it up close to his eyes, squinting. "This has got a lot of tiny big words. Does it say anything about a merman?" Randy shoved the newspaper in my face and pointed to the story of Mr. Flynn's death. My sensibilities jumped up a notch.

"No. That's a story about that man who came in here a couple of times. You remember him don't you?"

"Yeah, I thought he was a nice man, but he wasn't a nice man. He wasn't nice at all."

"That man was found in the water. The police think he was drowned on purpose." I shuddered as a line of goose bumps trailed up my spine and down my arms.

"What's wrong? Why you shake like that?"

"I just don't like the thought of anyone drowning in water. I'm afraid of water." I hugged my arms around my chest to stave off the next round of shivers.

"Water ain't nothing to be afraid of. I love to swim. Mamma taught me how."

"I'm glad you can swim. I don't know how to swim because I've never been in anything bigger than a bathtub, and even then I prefer a shower."

"Oh. That's too bad. You can never be a mermaid then." Randy placed the paper back on the desk.

"Randy!" Rocko's voiced boomed from the back. "You better not be out there blabbing your mouth."

I shoved the second book of the "Adventures of Dreampuff" into Randy's hands and told him, "You can keep it. If there are any words you don't know, remember you can just

126

come back and ask me."

"Randy!"

Randy flinched, jumped and hastily hid the book under his shirt. "I gotta go."

I jumped up before he got away and held the door open for him as a gesture of kindness. That allowed me to flip the self-locking tab to the unlock position after he disappeared into the darkness of the back room.

As the three men I associated with worked steadily in the back, I gave up on typing to work on my crocheting, biding my time until I could get into the back room undetected.

I didn't like that I was always being excluded—unless I was the one choosing to exclude myself, or there was a mutually agreed upon exclusion. The people I was working for may not have been swell guys, but Rocko scared me. I wished Frank had given me some hint of what Rocko's past crimes were so I knew just how scared I should be.

I detested being at the lowest spot underground. I was terrified that the defunct lighting would go out entirely. The men I worked for hadn't bothered to even provide me with one of the flashlights that had been delivered for when the lights flickered.

I had been employed there only a few days and I didn't see how I could go on working under those nerve-jangling conditions for much longer. I had to find an above-board, above-ground job, but I had to make sure I had a new job lined up before I left the magazine company; I couldn't afford the disruption in income.

I took out the newspaper I'd brought and folded it so the murder and espionage headlines weren't staring up at me. I searched the help wanted ads—without luck.

I threw the paper in the trashcan and returned to the dinosaur-age computer to start on-line searching for my next job, one where they weren't so secretive. One where the lights always worked properly. One that wasn't in a dugout basement of a former asylum.

My on-line job hunting left me just as disappointed as the newspaper want ads. Employment agencies all required a degree for nursing, teaching, hairdressing and all the other interesting jobs. Even being a city sewer system inspector required a science degree. I didn't have a degree in anything and no time to acquire one.

Focusing on the computer for so long caused my eyes to cross when a pop-up sprang up on my monitor advertising "faithful women wanted."

Could finding another job be as easy as an on-line pop-up?

I was faithful, and I wanted a job, so I clicked on the advertisement.

A long row of men's pictures populated my computer screen. Below each picture was a sign on name and a come-on tag line advertising each man's dating availability.

Oops.

I'd gone from help wanted to help-mate wanted.

It could have been a blessing in disguise if I wasn't already in love with 'ole what's his face who never called and only sent me impersonal e-mails. That memento swatch of yarn I'd been carrying around with me was getting frayed. Frank had refused to ever let me take his picture—something to do with his job requirements. I wanted to ask Janey for a keepsake picture of Frank when I was there, but I didn't because I was afraid she'd guess my feelings for him.

I decided to search the dating website to find a picture of a man who resembled Frank. If the resemblance was close enough, I could pretend it was Frank, carry that picture around with me—and get rid of the frayed yarn square.

I typed in Frank's physical characteristics. Male. Tall. Handsome. Dark Brown Hair. Brown eyes flecked with blue. 140-155 pounds. Above average intelligence. Athletic build. Mid-twenties to early thirties. High moral integrity.

"No match found" popped up on my screen. I already

knew that; there was only one Frank. I just wanted a picture facsimile to tide me over until the real thing came back.

The 'Make A Wish' dating company began to populate the screen with a line of male pictures—their suggested Frank alternatives. A sneaky 'bait and switch' operation. *We don't have what you want, but can we interest you in one of these guys?*

Disgusted, I searched for a way to end the testosterone parade. Before I could hit the escape key, I found one of faces in the line-up looked familiar.

I clicked to enlarge the picture. I was certain it was Mr. Blond Beard without his beard and mustache. Maybe he had a brother or cousin that looked like him—like Mandy and I closely resembled each other. Either that or someone used an old picture of Robert Redford for their on-line dating picture. His handle was "Mr. Right" and the caption below the picture read, "Gentleman seeks company of lovely lady for serious dating with marriage intentions."

"You are a fine looking man," I told the picture on the screen, "but you're not what I'm looking for." I shut the computer down, disappointed.

"Time for you to go get our lunch now," Randy said, skipping out into the reception area. It was a little early to be getting lunch. I was suspicious he wanted me to hurry up and leave so he could sit at my desk and twirl in my chair.

I logged off from the singles site and grabbed the lunch list from his outstretched hand. The lunch list was written in faint brown ink, block style print on a rectangle piece of paper a few inches wide and about 6 inches long. The ink was so faint and the handwriting so poor, I had trouble reading the list.

"Did you write this, Randy?"

"Yes."

"What does it say?"

He looked at the paper and turned it around and around, this way then that. He scratched his head and said, "I don't write so well. I think this one here says 'burger and pickles.'" His finger pointed to a line of marks at the small edge of the paper.

"Mr. Boggs...sorry, I'm not supposed to call him that, he likes burgers and pickles so I know that's what I wrote."

"What do the other words say?"

He pointed to one of the light, scratchy scribbles with a lot of 'O's. "That there says Olive Burger. Rocko likes olives. I like the toys." He pointed to where he drew a stick figure with a gun.

I took the paper and rubbed it between my fingers. It felt like fine linen. "This is strange paper. It seems expensive. Are you sure they wanted you to write on this paper?"

"It was the only paper and pen I could find. You won't tell, will you? We gots lots of that paper now, but I'm not supposed to play with it."

"Don't worry. I won't tell." I shoved the list in my pocket. "I'll bring some of my aunt's yellow writing pads and purple ink pens in tomorrow, and you can use them. She used them to write stories, but now she's gone so you might as well use them."

"Really? Your aunt write-ed stories? My mom used to read stories to me. Now I try to read them to myself 'cause Rocko won't. I like the doggie stories you gave me. I can read those just fine, except when I'm working down where the lighting isn't so good."

"I used to have a little light that clipped onto a book so you could read in the dark. I'll see if I can find it at home and bring it in for you."

I didn't mind sharing my childhood toys with Randy. As a young girl, my favorite stories were about Dreampuff, the little white dog that got into mischief all the time, and Bobby the Puppet Boy, who did silly things.

I grabbed my purse and at the doorway turned back to see Randy opening my bottom desk drawer and shoving in that same little leather band that he'd taken out before. When he saw me looking, he put the band back, closed the drawer, sat down in my chair and smiled a broad grin.

"Randy, do you sometimes put things in my desk

drawers?"

"I didn't put nothin' in there."

"That's not what I asked." I went to the drawer and pulled out that strap of leather. "Do you know what this is?"

"Sure. It's a dog collar. I'm keeping it for a little dog I'm going to get as soon as I finish up helping Rocko and Mr. Boggs get the grand opening done." He beamed with delight. Then his face fell.

"Darn. I'm not supposed to talk to you anymore about the grand opening."

"Why not?" I asked. "Is there something going on that I'm not supposed to know about?"

"I don't know what you mean." He didn't look me in the eye. He swiveled the chair away and looked up at the ceiling. He tapped his foot against the leg of the desk and began to whistle.

I used an old Gordon trick from my childhood and said, "That's okay. I already know all about it."

He swung back to face me, eyes wide. "You know all about Tea Biscuit, Lady Jane, and Misty?"

"Of course," I said, hoping he'd say more.

"Well, good. 'Cause I cain't tell no one about them. Rocko promised me I could have a dog if I keep my mouth shut." He then made like he was locking his lips with a key that he threw away.

That was all right. Those names he gave me sounded like racehorses. He'd given me a few clues, and that was all I needed to resume my stalled investigation.

CHAPTER 18

To my dismay, Mr. Beard was at the McDeeds again. Thanks to the classifieds, I wasn't surprised when he approached me.

"Well, this is getting to be a habit," he said to me, laugh lines crinkling. "Are you coming here every day just to see me?"

I pulled the piece of paper Randy gave me out of my pocket and holding it up so he could see it and know I was there on business said, "Not unless you are an olive burger, a burger with extra pickles or a kid's meal."

The eye laugh lines around his eyes straightened then disappeared. I guess he would have preferred I was there to see him. He recovered quickly, however. No smile but he bowed deep from the waist, straightened and placed his hand over the area of his heart said, "Madame, I am crushed."

Satisfied I'd gotten through to him I folded the paper and slid it back into my pocket. I rubbed the little piece of knit yarn I had in there before I pulled my hand back out.

I wished Frank would call so I could hear his voice.

The patrons coming in through the door began to weave their way up to the counter; I followed suit. I was surprised after my rebuff to find Mr. Beard remaining so close at my heels. Like before, he was standing too close behind me. He was so close that when he bumped into me, I stepped off to the side of the line to get away from him—keeping one foot stretched into the line so no one could accuse me of cutting.

Randy wanted a drink to go with his kid's meal, so I had to juggle to keep the cup upright while I grabbed the food bags.

"Here, let me help you with that." Mr. Beard made as if to take the drink from my hand.

I moved the cup and bags away from his reach almost tipping over the cup. "No. I can manage. I don't have far to go, just over on Jackson Street."

"Very well then, good day." He tipped his hat and returned to the counter where I heard grumbles about no save-ies.

I was in a hurry to deliver the food to the guys in the back and get back to my desk so I could eat my lunch, but I took the time to set the bag of burger and fries I'd purchased for Mr. Mr. PTSD down near him.

He grumbled something.

I said, "you're welcome", but I didn't wait to hear a response. I wanted to eat and get started again on my sleuthing.

I rearranged my desk and placed my computer monitor so the screen couldn't be seen from the back room doorway, a trick I learned from Jorgji. They were keeping the back room off limits, but I had a few tricks up my sleeve to outsmart them.

That afternoon I kept returning to the closet hoping to hear a conversation about something useful for my investigation. As near as I could figure, those papers with the linen feel were used for people to write down their bets on the horses. That light brown ink Randy had used for the lunch list must be ink that disappears after a certain amount of time passes so no evidence of the bet would be left behind.

Mr. Flynn had to be the one who figured up the betting odds using the sports section of the newspaper. He then went out, collected the bets, wrote them on that fancy paper and brought them in for Mr. Pilfer and Rocko to process. They must have been doing a rousing business if that bulge of the satchel Mr. Flynn had carried was any indication of the number of bets he had brought with him.

I spent a little time researching how bookies make money, but none of the sites gave a clue as to the types of papers used for placing bets. Reading about odds, predictions, statistics and vig, the percentage deduced from a gambler's winnings by the bookie, made my brain feel like it was going to explode so I carefully wiped my browser history and started crocheting on the homeless man's blanket so I'd have something more than computer surfing to show for my day's work.

"Hello, Gorgeous."

I looked up from my crocheting to see Mr. Beard from McDeeds standing in front of my desk with his hat in one hand, his blond hair curling at the temples where it touched his beard, his mustache twitching a little.

I hadn't heard him enter.

"Hello. Are you here to see Mr. Pilfer?"

My fingers searched the underside of the desk trying to find the little button I was to push whenever someone came into the reception area.

"No. I'm here to see you." He twirled his hat around on his index finger.

I stopped my fingers from searching under the desk for the button. I didn't think Mr. Blond Beard counted as a business customer if he was there to see me.

"Why do you want to see me? How did you find me?"

"I wanted to give you this." He held up a white rectangle of plastic.

My hand went immediately to the pocket where I kept my credit card. That pocket was empty. The Visa Select card was maxed out and probably would stay that way for a long time, but I wasn't about to give that card up.

"How did you get that?" I asked as I took the useless piece of plastic and stared at it. My name, Imogene C. Warren, was on there in raised lettering. It was my credit card all right.

"You dropped it today at McDeeds," he told me.

"I don't know how it got out of my pocket." I took it and quickly shoved it into one of the empty desk drawers. I wasn't sure, but I thought maybe his bumping into me at the McDeeds line was not accidental.

"Thank you, Mr....." I couldn't very well have called him Mr. Blond Beard, now could I?

"Garrett Edmond." He extended his right hand towards me. It was large, warm and firm—just like I remembered from our first encounter.

He held my hand a little longer than was polite before I pulled it away.

"Thank you, Mr. Edmond."

"Please, call me Garrett."

"All right. Thank you, Garrett."

"And you might be...?" He smiled. Lots of straight, white teeth showed.

"The receptionist."

He laughed. It was a deep laugh. I didn't detect any malice or depreciation in it. "Is that what I should call you? Miss Receptionist?"

"Oh, forgive me. I'm Imogene Warren—the receptionist."

He took hold of my hand again and shook it. "Nice to meet you Miss Imogene Candless Warren, receptionist." He still had a hold of my hand, but he had stopped shaking it. "Now that I know you better, I'd like to get to know you better."

I gently pulled my hand out of his grasp, fearful he was the hand kissing type, and I was out of Sani-wipes. I glanced nervously at the back room door. I had been instructed to let the men in the back know when someone was in the reception area. I hadn't done that. It wouldn't do for them to come out and find Mr. Blond Beard there.

I fiddled around with some papers on my desk, trying to come up with something to do or say to get him to leave when he looked around the reception room and said to me, "Oh, I'm sorry. You're working." He glanced down at my crochet project, and a slight smile tugged at the corners of his mouth. "Perhaps you'd allow me to take you to lunch sometime?"

"I don't think so. I bring my lunch. I only pick up the workers' lunches, so they don't have to stop what they are doing."

"Dinner perhaps?"

"Perhaps." I thought if I gave him hope, he'd leave.

"How about tonight? You get out at five? I could pick you up after work, so you don't have to drive back to Winnetka first."

I looked at my watch. 4:10. I put my hand in my pocket. The Frank yarn swatch frayed a little when I rubbed it. I would have to repair it before putting it in the laundry to be washed.

"I don't think that'd be a good idea. I think it best if you leave. I need to get back to work." I started typing something at random, thankful I'd turned the monitor screen, so my gibberish wasn't visible to him. He got the hint and left.

At quitting time, I was happy to see Randy coming in from the back room. I quickly popped up to greet him, making sure the latch that automatically locked the door was still in the unlocked position so if I could get to work early, before Rocko, Pilfer, and Randy, I could take a peek into the back room and get pictures to please Frank. I wasn't any good at hacking into computer networks, but I was willing to try that, too, if that was what Frank wanted.

I found Garrett waiting for me when I left the building. I had said I wouldn't go to dinner with him, but he was persistent. As I continued walking, he linked his arm through mine and asked, "What does it take for a guy to get a date with you?"

I heard a low growl coming from down the sidewalk. It was the homeless man looking even more scraggly than ever. He was drinking something concealed in a paper bag and unsteadily weaving as he walked.

I was grateful that Garrett walked me safely to my car; Mr. PTSD staggered somewhere behind us the whole way, creeping me out.

Mandy's Bentley was in the driveway when I got home, so I drove the Malibu into the garage and headed in through the kitchen straight to the cookie jar before my sister could assault me with her latest acquisition. She seemed to be falling into her newfound wealth headfirst.

"Yip, Yip, Yip," was coming from the front area of the house. I had managed to get the doorbell working again, but in the process, I must have changed the sound from a scream to a bark. Gordon would have to reprogram the bell again as soon as he got back from his trip. I preferred the blood-curdling scream of the old doorbell over that of a yipping dog.

"Ain't he cute?" Mandy said coming into the kitchen. She was holding up for my approval a stark white puff with two black beads centered for eyes, a black button sized nose, and a mouth full of sharp little teeth. The dog stopped barking to growl at me.

"You bought a dog?"

"Not just any dog. He's a high-pedigreed Pomeranian. His name is Mr. Mister. I'm going to call him Mr. M for short." She hugged Mr. M to her chest, and he stopped growling long enough to lick her chin. "See. He loves me already."

No small feat there. Maybe his name should have been Mr. Miracle.

"How nice for you and Mr. M," I said. My insincerity was lost on her and her chin licking dog as I opened the frig to poke around for a snack.

"He's a special dog. There's not another one like him."

"Un huhh", I said absently moving the stuff to the front of the shelf out of the way to get to the pudding I'd hope Keiko had saved for me.

"Listen to me going on and on about my dog," Mandy said in her I-want-something-from-you voice. "I should be asking you how your interview with that magazine company went."

"I got hired. I've been working there for a few days."

"That's wonderful!" she said with faked enthusiasm. "Tell me all about it. Are there any cute men at work?"

She would ask that. Not, 'what type of employee benefits do you have, what wage are you being paid, is it union or non-union?' Nope. My sister only wanted to know if there are any cute men.

"I'm not there to meet men."

"They're all dogs, huh?"

"No. The man who hired me, Mr. Pilfer, happens to be very nice. He's small, old, with thick glasses, and a little bookish looking."

"He sounds like a man Martin used to place gambling bets with."

I twirled this thought around in my head. Mr. Pilfer did look to be the bookie type. That fit in with my assumption they were conducting an illegal gambling business.

"Anybody else?" she asked.

"There are two guys who work in the back room. Rocko is big, tall with a bulbous nose and close-set eyes in a meaty head. Then there's Randy, Rocko's brother. He's a big man who chronologically is probably in his mid-twenties, but his brain is stuck on the more joyous aspects of youth."

"None of them sound like good romance prospects. You meet anyone else? Anyone interesting come into the magazine office?" Mandy gave me a wide-eyed innocent look. She and the little dog in her arms did a little sashay back and forth when she asked this. Usually, this put me on alert that she was up to something, but I didn't see any possible connection between her and Garrett.

"Just a man I met on the way to my interview." I opened the pudding lid. "He wanted to take me to dinner, but I said no. I think he works downtown in the business district because he gets lunch at the McDeed's in that area."

"Well, is he cute?" She leaned forward to study my answer, so I thought about the question before answering.

"Yeah, he is very nice looking in a movie star sort of way.

If you like the blond, tan, buff kind of look." I opened the pudding lid and pulled a spoon out of the drawer.

"Like that kind of look? Are you crazy?" Mandy waved her free hand in the air. "Never mind. I forgot who I was talking to. You thought that FBI creep who pounded Martin unconscious was good looking."

"He is good looking. And he saved me from being strangled to death by Martin."

"That was just a misunderstanding between you and Martin. He wasn't going to kill you."

I slammed down the pudding dish, and chocolate pudding sprang out onto the table.

Mandy handed me a towel from the counter and gave an exasperated huff. "Well, it was. Anyways, if your FBI crush is so good looking why isn't he looking at you?"

I laid the towel over the chocolate mess on the table and got a Japanese cookie Keiko had made from the jar. I shoved the whole cookie in my mouth, so I wouldn't have to answer. The cookie didn't taste very sweet, but it was better than nothing.

"What size are Mr. Movie star's hands?" Mandy asked. Her dog growled when she reached down to mop up the mess I'd left on the table. I flushed at the memory of Garrett's warm, strong hands on mine as he handed me back my umbrella.

"I don't know and why do you want to know?"

"You know what they say, 'big hands is a sign of big something else."

"Amanda!"

I headed out of the kitchen with another cookie in hand. She followed me, the breathing white mop in tow.

"Garrett is a very nice man, but since I turned down his offer of dinner, I doubt I'll be seeing him again."

"You turned down a date with a handsome man who could be Mr. Right? Why? Are you still waiting around for that FBI guy to show up?"

I refused to answer her. She had Mr. M's growl as

confirmation enough.

Mr. M had not stopped growling a low toned growl at me since their arrival. We were now in the parlor eyeing each other warily, he in Mandy's arms, me defenseless. I didn't know if he was after me or my cookie, but the threatening noises were unnerving me. I wished my sister-cousin would get to the point about what she came here to get and take her dog away.

"Mr. M stop that growling," said Mandy to her dog giving him a minuscule pat on the head that I think was supposed to show him she meant business. He growled louder and threw in a few yaps for good measure. He obviously wasn't in cahoots with her plan. She shook him a little when he didn't stop growling. I believed he was grin-growling at me, mocking my fear of him.

Mandy set Mr. M down, but then picked him back up from the floor when he sniffed one leg of the sofa.

"Maybe you could have your butler-guy come and take him for a walk so we can have a little talk?" she asked me.

"I already know about the birds and the bees, besides Gordon is not my butler anymore. He has retired from servitude to travel. He's already packed his bags and is somewhere distant even as we speak. If you want to talk, I can hear you just fine—even with that dog making threatening gestures at me. Just make sure you keep him away from me."

"Well, that's what I wanted to talk to you about." She did one of her I'm-your-sister-and-I-never-got-to-live-with-my-dad-because-he-lived-with-you sad-eyed looks.

I sighed. This was going to be good.

"I was out shopping for a new sofa to go with my newly purchased apartment when I passed the pet store and saw Mr. M in the window. He was so darn cute. The sales lady at *Dog Gone Good Dogs* said he'd go fast, so if I wanted him, I had to get him right then. I just had to have him, but I'm not quite sure my apartment building allows pets. I was hopin' you'd keep him here until I got that all worked out?" Her lower lip came out so far a bird could have perched on it.

I gave a glare to the offending creature before I gave Mandy my response. "Keep him here? Are you insane? He's acting like he wants to rip my throat out."

Mr. M growled in affirmation.

"I think he's just being overly protective of me. I have this carrying purse." She held up a square bag with a shoulder strap that looked like a cross between a Vera Bradley backpack and a Louis Viton suitcase. "He can stay in here while I'm gone. I shouldn't be away too long. I have a few cans of Little Prince Dog food to give him if he gets hungry and some bottles of Evian Aramis pure water if he gets thirsty." She held up a plastic grocery bag that had the plastic stretched into the shape of several cans and bottles.

"He drinks Evian Armais water?"

"Only if it's chilled first."

"You have got to be out of your gourd! I am not taking care of a dog that thinks I'm a chew toy, and that thinks he's royalty who has to have chilled boutique water. What do I do if he needs to get rid of what he eats and drinks? I didn't relish having to deal with either end of this dog."

"Here's his leash." Mandy pulled a six-foot long cord out of a side pocket of the dog carrier. "Just walk him outside and he'll do the rest. Please? Pretty Please?" She hugged him to her.

Mr. M was suddenly silent, his black beads in his white face trained on me. His little doggie brows went up in an expressive plea as he cocked his head to one side. He looked so blasted sweet he could have been a Facebook post. I felt myself weaken.

"Pretty please with a sugar cookie on top? I'll make you the kind you like, pink with rainbow sprinkles. All warm and soft—just like you like 'em."

I hadn't had a good cookie since Gordon left. That is the problem with family. They know all your weak points.

"Okay," I relented, against my better judgment. "I'll dog sit for you for a short spell so you can go to your apartment and make arrangements to keep him. But you better come back with cookies."

Mandy threw her free arm around me and hugged me tight. Mr. M bit one of the buttons off my blouse.

CHAPTER 19

I awoke to the sound of whimpering. I groggily fumbled for the alarm clock and slammed my hand down on the shut-off button. The whimpering continued. I opened one eye to check the time. The whimpering wasn't from the alarm clock. It was a full two hours before my alarm was set to go off.

Mandy never came back for her dog and refused to answer my frantic voicemail messages. Mr. M was in his carrier beside the bed, where I had to zip him in for the night and cover the suitcase thing up with a towel to stop his constant barking and growling.

He whined again.

Grabbing my robe and his leash I slid my feet into my now open-toed slippers. I grabbed the bath towel and threw it over Mr. M the minute his little growling form came charging out of his carrier.

With his head covered, I managed to attach the leash to the metal rings on his faux diamond studded halter before his teeth could get a purchase on my arm. I held the leash with arm extended so he and his teeth were as far away from my body as I could get them, and we headed out into the predawn hours so he could get rid of the princely supper, slipper parts, blouse button and partial sock that he'd consumed the evening before. I pulled the morning paper off the front step as we headed back in.

I'd heard the way to a male's heart is through his stomach, and I'll admit that Mr. M was more docile after he ate most of my microwaved frozen breakfast eggs, but I was not taking any chances. I encircled the front door knob with the loop end of his leash to keep him in check until Mandy could get there to pick him up, or Keiko got up to go job hunting again, whichever came first.

Mandy and the dog had such a love fest before she dropped him off, I was sure the fixed doorbell would ring any minute to herald that she was there to pick the little chin licker up.

I settled down with a cup of hot tea and left Mandy another voice message that she had to come and get her dog now because I wanted to get into work early. I didn't expect an immediate response. Mandy was never an early riser.

I straightened the paper out. Skipping the front page entirely I went directly to the Lifestyles page to read my horoscope. Madame Zarina, queen of the planet alignments, assured me that I would soon run into the man of my dreams, but that our happiness could only be found through great personal sacrifice. *Hah, fat chance of that being accurate.*

The weather prediction on page one showed rain drops with more of the same for the rest of the week. Now that was a prediction that was sure to come true. Chicago continued to be deluged with an unseasonably high amount of rain and warm weather for November.

My second cup of tea found me reading about the recent rash of dog thefts. Unlike times when people rounded up dogs running wild in the streets to take them to a dog refuge, these dogs weren't feral, and they were not just any breed of dogs. These were high society dogs, bought with a price tag as hefty as their pedigrees. The dognappers were taking the dogs and ransoming them for as much as $20,000 each; the money had to be paid in new, uncirculated five-dollar bills. The police were baffled by the strange payment demands but figured it was because the dognappers knew that lower denomination bills would be difficult to track.

Hmm. Maybe I could ransom Mr. M for the money I needed? Nah. I didn't think a ransom demand would work if the dog owner knew who had their dog.

I called Mandy. She still wasn't answering her phone, but I left a voice message that threatened her with her dog sitting fees and lost wages if she didn't hurry up and get there before I had to leave for work. She didn't answer, and when I tried to call her again, her voice mailbox was full.

After breakfast, I dressed in sturdy dark pants and a blue cotton shirt that I got from Keiko; skirts and silk blouses no longer seemed proper attire for working in a dustbin. Keiko had also provided me with a bottle of cleaning stuff, so I could give the office a cleaning in my spare time—which based on the past few days was bound to be plentiful.

The doorbell didn't ring before I had to leave, but I knew Keiko would soon be getting up, so I left her a note to turn the dog over to Mandy before she went out job-hunting and I left Mr. M with water and food and a full run of the house.

In retrospect, that was not a good idea.

CHAPTER 20

I hadn't gotten an early start to the day as I had wanted, but judging by the eerie quiet of the basement, I had at least beat the boss trio into the office. I wasted no time getting my camera out of my purse. I also pulled out the can of cleaner to use as a decoy in case my employers caught me in the back room. I could always use the excuse that I'd gone back to clean. No one who knew me would ever believe I had gone anywhere to do cleaning, but no one here at the office knew me.

I couldn't find the light switch in the back room so had to work by the light of the flashlight app on my phone. The pictures were grainy and dark, but they showed the collection of boxes, mud, boards, tools, wheelbarrow, and an assortment of items stored in the central area. I was just about to click a picture of the printer and move on to the items in the maintenance room when I heard a crash coming from the maintenance room area.

I turned to run back to the reception area, heart thudding. In my haste, I stumbled over one of the many cardboard boxes stacked around the place. One box fell and broke open, scattering the contents across the floor.

I scrambled back to my feet; my phone light dimly illuminated the green colors of the scattered papers. I didn't take the time to stop and pick the papers up, but I did scoop as many of them back into the open box as I could manage in the few seconds I dared. I tipped the box back upright before sprinting to my desk.

When Mr. Pilfer arrived in the office a few minutes later, I was sitting at my desk trying to control my breathing and the flush to my face.

"Good Morning, Miss Warren. You're the early bird today." He smiled a broad smile at me.

I looked down at the floor so he wouldn't see the guilt in my eyes. When I saw a small piece of paper attached to the bottom of my shoe, I quickly tucked my foot under the desk. I looked back up at him to see if he had noticed it. His smile never faltered, so I gave a timid smile back.

"Good Morning," I said, hoping to engage him in a distracting conversation. "I wanted to get an early start today so I could...show my appreciation for the advance on my wages." I slid my foot farther under my desk.

"Think nothing of it. It was nothing. I'm glad our efforts are helping someone kind and good, like yourself."

His kindness made me feel like the early bird who deserved to be eating worms. *How could I betray Mr. Pilfer by sending pictures of his operation to the FBI just to get back in good with Frank? What kind of person had I become?*

Rocko and Randy showed up just then.

Mr. Pilfer lost his smile.

Once they were all in the back room, I reached down and pulled off my tennis shoe. There attached to the sole was a small strip of white paper, a long strip with a pre-glued edge that had stuck to my shoe. I'd seen papers like this wrapped around silverware at parties, only this paper was bigger and of heavier construction. I doubted the paper was for bundling magazines; the strips were too short and yet they were too long for silverware sets.

One thing I knew for sure. Those strips of paper were nothing ominous. I didn't think anything in the back was ominous or illegal. I wasn't certain those pictures were even

147

worth sending to Frank.

I worried that I was causing undeserved trouble for Mr. Pilfer and Randy by sending pictures to Frank. To poke my conscience even further, I heard nothing but the sound of paper swishing out of the printer the entire morning.

I logged on to my bank account and was overjoyed to see that Gordon had deposited two thousand dollars there. The money was to maintain his residence with me, but it was also just the amount I needed to engage that detective fellow. I called Melton Chilton's secretary and tried to set up a late evening appointment for after I got out of work.

"Mr. Chilton doesn't work evenings," she told me.

"But he has to. I have the money, the retainer he asked for, and I can't leave work and drive there during the day." I caught the sound of my pleading voice echoing off the reception room walls and remembered what Mandy said about my always being whiny. I cleared my throat and began again. "I have to work and cannot meet with Mr. Chilton during the day. If he is unable to assist me with my investigation, I would like a referral to a different agency that can."

There was a short pause. "You say you got all the retainer. The full two thousand?"

"Yes," I told her. "All of it."

"He'll kill me for saying this, so don't let on I told ya, but after work, Mel stops over at the tequila bar for a short one. You might be able to catch him there any time before bar closing time."

I thanked her. Before I could hang up, she said in a rush to so fast it caught me by surprise, "he won't be there tonight, however. He's heading out of town on business."

"Darn it all. I was counting on him to start my case right away. The newspapers are doing a smear job on my father's reputation, and he's unable to defend himself."

"If you're in that big of a hurry for Mel to take your case, he's planning on seeing his kids tomorrow night at seven. He'll be over at that big indoor play area, Whacky Fun, on 5th street at six o'clock waiting for them to show up. He could probably use some company until his kids get there, but don't tell him I told ya that either."

I thanked her again and promised I wouldn't let on what she'd told me when I found Mr. Chilton the next evening.

When Randy came out with the lunch order, I noticed he was unusually quiet.

"Is everything okay, Randy? You're very quiet."

"I gots in trouble this morning for something I didn't do. Rocko's real made at me," Randy said.

Remembering the spilled box, I swallowed hard as a knot started forming in the pit of my stomach. "What was it you got into trouble for?"

"A shelf tipped over in the night and broke some of the flooring tiles Mr. Boggs arranged special for the Grand Opening. Now they gotta do it all over again. Rocko says that shelf wasn't put together right, and that's why it felled and broke the tiles, but I wasn't the one that putted it together. Rocko was. He just don't want to say he did it. Rocko wants me to be the goat he scrapes. I'm always the scrape goat."

My stomach knot loosened. Maybe they hadn't even noticed the box I'd tipped over. I took out of my purse the yellow legal pad and purple pen I'd brought from home. "Will this help make things better?"

Randy's face light up and a smile broadened his mouth. "Wowie, wow, wow. Are these for me?"

"Yup. They used to be my aunt's and now they are all yours."

After I'd brought back lunch for all three men, plus the bag I threw to Mr. PTSD, the men worked steadily in the back long enough for me to upload the pictures I'd taken for Frank. I didn't know what good they would do him. The pictures weren't particularly interesting. It wasn't like they had stored ammo or dead bodies hidden in the back rooms or anything close to it. Well, the wheelbarrow caked in mud was interesting, but the rest of the stuff was just common building materials, shovels, and boards.

I was dismayed to get a terse response back from Frank asking for better pictures and to make sure they showed the labeling on the boxes. This email was even more impersonal than the last. I wasn't about to risk my neck getting professional quality pictures for someone who seemed to have so quickly forgotten our relationship and his talk of love. *That was the last set of pictures he was going to get out of me.*

Rain was pouring down in sheets at quitting time. I didn't protest when Garrett met me in the lobby of the McClintock building with a large umbrella and an invitation to walk to a place close by for an early dinner. His persistence, the rain, and my hunger won me over, but I made it clear I had agreed to go with him for dinner only. Rē waved and winked at me as we strolled past her at the information desk. Mr. Goth was walking in the doors as Garrett and I walked out. I hoped Rē was going to dinner, too.

When Garrett and I exited the building, Mr. PTSD was sitting slouched on the concrete of the front overhang, feet outstretched, his back against one of the buildings supporting pillars. A bottle in a brown paper sack rested at his side. With those dark glasses, it was hard to tell if Mr. PTSD was asleep or passed out.

"That's disgusting. Why don't they call the police and have him hauled away?" Garrett handed me the umbrella handle and put his hand on my elbow to steer me away the homeless man's area near the doors.

"He's harmless." I stubbornly continued to walk towards Mr. PTSD, refusing to allow myself to be herded in a different direction—like cattle. That man by the pillar was probably a war hero fallen on tough times. I didn't like the implications Garrett was making by steering clear of him as if he was trash.

"It's all right; I'm alright," I told Garrett when he tightened his grip on my arm and pulled on me to steer us in the direction he wanted to go. I pulled my arm away, resolute in my desire to show respect to another human being. "He's usually in the alleyway. I think he's only up here by the doors to stay out of the rain."

Garrett re-gripped my arm, loosely this time; there was no insistent tug as he stepped up closer to my side as if to protect me from harm as we strolled to the edge of the front platform of the building. Our path would take us directly by Mr. PTSD. I stiffened when I felt Garrett release his grip on my arm in favor of putting his arm around my waist. Uncomfortable, I let it go in favor of getting past Mr. PTSD without a scene.

Mr. PTSD made as if to stand up as we approached. When we reached the area adjacent to his spot, Garrett stumbled and pitched forward, almost dragging me over with him. Garrett managed to right himself and me in time before we hit the sidewalk below the entry platform.

Garrett swung around and shouted at Mr. PTSD, "You did that on purpose!"

The man saluted us by raising his paper sack then swilled down whatever horrible drink was in hidden by the stained brown paper. I judged it to be liquor.

Garrett stood unmoving staring at the man, his anger palpable in the cool rain washing over the umbrella I held over us. I knew that brown sack contained a liquor bottle when the man defiantly tipped the sack up and swilled more. When he lowered the bottle, a clear liquid ran from the corner of his mouth. He let the dribble remain there. His gaze met Garrett's head on, or at least it appeared that way behind his glasses.

I felt Garrett tense at my side. When he removed his arm from my waist to step closer to the man, I began to worry. Rē and Mr. Goth swept by us, eyes on each other, oblivious to the pugilistic flash about to occur.

I didn't want a scene. "Come on, Garrett. It was an accident."

I took hold of Garrett's arm, but when he shook me off, I moved farther away from the building, farther into the light rain, away from the bum, hoping Garrett would follow me.

151

"No, it wasn't an accident." Garrett stepped closer to the man and gave him a swift kick that connected full force with the man's kidney.

The man grunted and quick as a flash he reached out to snatch a hold of Garrett's retreating foot in an effort to bring him down. Mr. PTSD missed his mark by only a fraction.

Garrett smiled at the near miss and moved swiftly to my side. His arm lightly encircled my waist again. We began to walk down the sidewalk together.

I let out the breath I'd been holding in. Glad that scene was over.

A stream of the foulest profanity I'd ever heard issued forth from the homeless man.

I spun around, glaring in disbelief and anger at the man who had been outside that building every day since I had started my job. Tinted glasses had always covered his eyes—just like they were then, but he couldn't hide his identity from me anymore.

I knew him.

From the way he turned his head away from my stare, I knew he knew that I knew. I didn't have to see those hidden eyes; I recognized that foul mouth.

***

Frank ignored the pain in his back and mentally kicked himself harder than Garrett ever could have. He should have exercised greater control and kept his cool when he saw Imogene and Garrett leave the building together. It wasn't the first time Garrett had been around at quitting time, so it wasn't unexpected.

Genie was a beautiful woman. The kind who didn't recognize her beauty, but men did. Frank had noticed not only Garrett, but another man showing an interest in Genie. That man had been loitering outside the building at the start and end to the last few days. To the casual observer, any man dressed in a dark suit and coat would appear as though he

152

were just one of the hundreds of downtown office workers, but Frank knew better. The man was taking a keen interest in Imogene, his eyes and actions following her every move. It didn't help that she was totally unaware of her innate sexuality when she walked. She wasn't aware that her doe eyes, fresh face, quick smile and guileless demeanor made her compellingly attractive. Unlike Garrett, who didn't seem to be able to stay away, the other man had kept his distance.

Frank just couldn't stand the thought of that pretty-boy getting close to Genie while he had to keep his distance so he could remain incognito to work this latest case in a partnership with Homeland Security.

When Frank slandered Garrett's paternity and his manhood, Frank saw the look Imogene had given him, saw her look of recognition. He knew he'd gone too far. He'd risked the whole operation because he couldn't keep his temper. He pulled the darkened glasses off that he'd been wearing. He couldn't stay incognito with Genie anymore, but even though she was angry, he hoped the look he was sending would keep her from revealing his identity.

He needed to stay holed up outside this building a few days more, going through the dumpster garbage bag for papers, clues and what bits and pieces of information he could find or purchase from his informant.

Frank's express assignment was figuring out what Rockford and Boggs had hooked up for this time, and if it represented a risk to the public, he was authorized to stop them at all cost. Rockford and Boggs went way back to when they were kids tying tin can's on dogs' tails.

Boggs was the brains, Rockford the brawn as they worked every moneymaking scheme known to exist. Then five years ago, Boggs had been sentenced to seven years in the Muddy Spring prison facility for check forgery, gambling, and racketeering charges.

Being incarcerated hadn't stopped Boggs's illegal gambling; he just took it underground in the prison system. He selected a few handpicked prisoners and prison guards to assist him with illegal betting on the inside and business was lucrative.

Rockford got a job working for the city, but the two had kept in constant touch. Then two months ago, a man who worked with Rockford in Chicago's deep tunnel maintenance system had contacted the FBI asking for a meeting. The man said he had information that Rockford was varying from set work routines to meet up with men who were explosives experts. The informant said Rockford had stolen the blueprints for the deep tunnel maintenance shafts and access areas, something the city kept carefully guarded.

Just before the meeting with the FBI was to take place, the informant was found dead in the tunnel, his head bashed in and the information gone.

Rockford was the obvious suspect, but it couldn't be proven that he was in the area where the body was found. The wrench believed to be the murder weapon was found 50 yards away from the body in several feet of water. That, coupled with mishandling of the evidence by a rookie cop caused the prosecutor to shy away from filing murder charges against Rockford.

The city took disciplinary action against Rockford and dismissed him from his job for being absent from his work area without cause, but other than that, Rockford walked free— until additional evidence could be found to levy charges of murder against him.

Frank was brought in, not to assist with the murder investigation; everyone in the FBI knew Rockford was responsible for the murder. The local law enforcement agency compromised the evidence and got it thrown out, so they were going to have to work the case to redeem themselves.

The FBI had assigned Frank and a few other agents to work the case with Homeland Security because Chicago's deep tunnel runs through some densely populated areas of the city as well as parallel to some of the major train lines. The maintenance areas were closer to the surface than the tunnel itself making Homeland Security nervous that Rockford might be working with another organization, which just might have terrorist activities planned.

When Hershel Boggs's time came up for parole, the FBI case manager thought it would be expedient to let the parole request go through knowing Boggs would find and hook up with his old friend, Reinhold Rockford.

When Rockford and Boggs began digging in the bottom of the McClintock building, Homeland Security wanted an experienced agent to work the street outside the building. Someone who's face was unknown in the Chicago area, but who knew how to survive on the streets and take care of himself if the going got rough; Frank accepted the assignment. Chicago wasn't far from Winnetka, and he'd had visions of making a side trip to see Genie while working the case. She'd wanted time to sort out her feelings about him, and he wanted to allow her that time, but he couldn't override this overwhelming desire he had to see her again.

Only his visions had turned into a nightmare when the case took a turn for the worse and Frank saw Imogene approach the building he was watching and go inside, to work somewhere within the building.

Geraldo Flynn, Bogg's last roommate in Muddy Springs correctional facility, had been left without his usual income when Boggs made parole and the bookie business shut down. The roommate was amenable to being a paid informant when Frank approached him with the proposition. They got the man released from prison; he rehooked up with Boggs and things seemed to be moving along in the investigation until Flynn ended up dead in Lake Michigan.

Frank's gut twisted as he watched Imogene enter the building every morning and exit every evening at 5:00, last night much later. When she'd left late with that blond fellow, Garrett, and with the other man following them both, Frank had followed all three of them from a distance to make sure Genie made it to her car okay.

He was so close to her every day and yet so far. He had hoped Imogene wasn't unknowingly mixed up with Rockford or Boggs, but his instincts told him she was.

Unwilling to draw attention to Imogene's involvement or his role in the investigation of Rockford and Boggs, Frank delayed contacting his case officer, or handler in Homeland Security, to tell him about Genie until he got some sense of where the investigation was heading and could figure out what to do to get Genie out of the situation without blowing his cover or placing her in danger.

Now that Genie knew he was here he would contact his handler and see about removing her from the building. With her protected, he would be free to investigate what Bogg's and Rockford were planning without worrying about her safety or her involvement with Garrett and the other man.

Frank knew he had a job to do and, he was not about to be run off by that jackass, Garrett, or anyone else who got in his way.

***

Once I knew Mr. PTSD was Frank, I was not going to give him the satisfaction of knowing that I knew that he'd been there right under my nose, spying on me, so I said loudly to Garrett, "come on, Garrett, leave that BUM alone. We don't want to be late for our dinner DATE."

And then to twist the point home I added, "or any of the activities we might want to do afterward."

Garrett smiled.

Frank scowled.

There weren't going to be any activities afterward, but Frank and Garrett didn't need to know that just then.

***

Frank shrugged off Genie's deliberately taunting him about dating Garrett. He knew her and knew she wasn't planning on doing anything serious with Garrett so soon in a relationship she'd just started. It wasn't in her character.

156

What Frank couldn't shrug off was the pain in Imogene's voice as she linked her arm with Garrett's. Frank couldn't directly follow them this time. Couldn't explain to her. Couldn't stop her from going with Garrett.

She had looked anguished when she discovered his identity. If she didn't care about him, she wouldn't have been hurt. He hated that he'd hurt her—again.

He sighed when he saw the man with the dark suit and coat step out of the shadows of the building and follow behind Genie and Garrett.

Frank stood up and prepared to follow at a safe distance. At least he knew Garrett would be with Genie and able to protect her from harm tonight. Something Frank wasn't in a position to freely do.

CHAPTER 21

Why did handsome men always think their dates would find it romantic to go to the top of a tall building to eat? I stepped quickly into the elevator Garrett was holding open for me, before I changed my mind. I'd have rather eaten a Mark's Gourmet hot dog in the ally with Frank than to have gotten in the Willis Tower's elevator, but I was too hungry, Garrett was too handsome and charismatic, and I was too mad at Frank to forfeit the evening entirely.

The food was delicious; Garrett's laugh was genuine and infectious when I told him all of the things that struck fear in me.

"You are joking, right?" he asked me after ordering the tiramisu.

"I wish I were." I picked at the few crumbs remaining on my plate while we waited for our dessert to be served.

"Then I don't think we'll be heading out to the glassed ledge after we eat."

"Not unless they have a lot of glass cleaner for afterward."

He chuckled. "I've never known anyone to profess to so many fears. It's almost unbelievable."

"Well, believe it. Everyday things that other people love can send me into a tailspin, like Randy who refused to believe I had a fear of swimming and dogs because he loves both."

"Randy?"

"He's one of the men I work for at the *Quarterly Review*. Well, he's the brother of one of the men I work for at the magazine. Randy can barely read so he's not a part of the magazine business. He's just there because his brother keeps an eye on him and gives him odd jobs, mostly manual labor type things."

"Do you like it there?" Garrett waived off our waitress who was trying to refill his already full water glass. My glass remained half-empty.

"I don't like the basement; I hate it, but I like typing, and it's a job."

"What did you do before the magazine business?"

"I typed up my Aunt Tilly's murder mystery manuscripts. Maybe you've heard of them? The Penelope Pembrooke Mysteries."

"Matilda Warren is your aunt?"

"Was my aunt. She died." I twirled my finger around the edge of my almost empty water glass.

"Oh, right." He took a big gulp from his beer. "Are you the niece she raised? The one who inherited her billions?

"I'm her niece, but I don't have the billions anymore. Maybe you've read in the papers how I was swindled out of my money and almost killed. Now I have to work just to make ends meet."

"I do seem to recall something about all that. So you've actually lost everything and are back to square one?"

The waitress set a plate of tiramisu in front of Garrett first, and then set a plate at my spot. I noticed his piece was considerably larger than mine was. Her smile for him was larger, also.

"Square zero." I laughed lightly, not wanting to think about my financial status at that moment. I picked up my fork and focused on my dessert dish.

"So you're there working with these men just because you need money?"

"Pretty much." I looked around the room then back at my drink when I saw the night sky was dark.

"If you're familiar with your aunt's writing style maybe you could finish her unfinished manuscripts and get some money that way."

I looked at him. "I never said she had unfinished manuscripts."

He glanced around, avoiding my gaze. "I must have read it somewhere."

"Just what is that you do for a living?" I asked, covering my interest with a casual sip of my diet coke.

"I'm sort of in the finance business."

I tried to breathe, talk and swallow all at the same time, leaving me with carbonation bubbles up my nose and an embarrassing strangling cough that took my breath away for several seconds.

Garrett pounded my back until my windpipe cleared and people around us retook the seats they'd vacated to see if I was okay.

My face red, my appetite for desert dampened, I began to study Garrett when he wasn't looking at me.

Was he just a man on the internet seeking companionship? Or was that beard hiding more than dimples? Little thoughts niggled at the back of my mind.

How had he known my middle name? Where I lived? Or that my aunt had unfinished manuscripts?

Once I realized Garrett wasn't just a simple bachelor wanting to wine and dine me, I let go of the guilt I felt over leading him on for the sake of a hot meal. I was certain he was after something else—something other than what most men are after when they ply you with dinner, tiramisu, and diet coke.

Jorgji had started out as my financial advisor. He advised me out of my money and almost my life. His deception had begun with a seemingly innocent elegant dinner like this and look where that got me.

Frank wasn't a winer and diner. He preferred spaghetti.

He never took me to high class, high tower places to eat and his dinners never were billed as innocent. He wasn't afraid to speak his mind about what he wanted and how he planned to go about getting it.

I lost myself in the thought of Frank's wants and how he let me know them.

"Earth to Imogene," Garrett said, waving a hand in front of my eyes.

I snapped out of my reverie. "I'm sorry. What were you saying?"

"I was saying I've always wanted to be a writer. Maybe I could do a story for the magazine you work for. What kind of stories do they print?"

That was hard for me to answer since I'd never been directly told. "What kind of story are you interested in writing?"

"I've always wanted to write a story about pigeons."

"Pigeons?"

"Yeah. There are lots of different kinds. Carrier Pigeons, Homing pigeons, stool pigeons."

We both laughed at that. I relaxed enough to take a few more bites of my tiramisu. There was even enough left to pack into a doggy bag so the piece the waitress gave me must have been bigger than I thought.

I waited in the lobby while Garrett went to get his car. I wondered what Frank was eating and if he'd been injured by the kick Garrett gave him.

I wondered if he was allowed to seek medical care. *Did he ever take a break while on assignment? Where did he use the bathroom? What if he caught pneumonia from being out in that damp weather?*

I fretted in silence as we drove the few minutes it took for Garrett to get me to my car in the parking garage—without my having to give him directions—another thing I found disturbing. The garage was cold, dark and almost empty so I was glad Garrett had been gentleman enough to see me to my car door, even if he wasn't gentleman enough to physically open my door for me.

"I had fun tonight," Garrett told me as I unlocked my car and got inside before he got any ideas about kissing me.

I closed my door gently and rolled down the window to talk. I surprised myself by responding, "I had fun tonight, too."

And I had. Garrett wasn't Frank, but Frank hadn't seen fit to call me in months. All I'd gotten from him were impersonal e-mails asking for me to take pictures. He hadn't been willing to assist me. He hadn't even bothered to say hi, even when he was right outside my workplace.

Garrett was the total opposite of Frank. Frank was dark and moody, and street-toughened. Garrett was light and fun. Charming.

CHAPTER 22

I drove home a mess of conflicting emotions. On one hand I was pretty sure I loved Frank. When I was with him, every fiber of my being sang. On the other hand, Mandy was right. Frank wasn't exactly beating down my door to get to me. He'd been literally right outside my door at work and never made an effort to connect with me. In fact, he was cold and hard— patently avoiding any personal connection with me.

I wondered if his feelings towards me had changed now that we'd had some time apart. I hated to think I was mistaken about his feelings for me, but when he removed his darkened glasses, there was a haunted, pleading, apologetic look to his eyes. *Was that an apology for avoiding me or an apology for having lied when he said he loved me?*

I turned into my driveway lost in my clouded thoughts of what was and what might have been. A white form tumbled ghostly across my path. Another white puff billowed out from behind a tree to my right. I slammed on the brakes and felt my seatbelt lock me in place as the car came to a jolting halt.

I cursed Mr. Twerk and his austerity measures that had left me without a means to call for help. I moved fully into the driveway to get off the street and honked the horn several times. Why I didn't know. I was too far from the house for anyone inside to hear the blare. Gordon wasn't there, and

Keiko wasn't home. She was at her evening class learning to speak English.

I watched the loose white form float around the yard. I kept it in my peripheral vision until I decided to stop fruitlessly honking the horn and get out to see if that "ghost" was what I feared it would be.

I crept up towards the thing. Getting closer, I could see what it was that was puffing up and drifting in the breeze.

I chased that plastic shopping bag down until I had it firmly in my grasp and then yanked its partner down from its spot on a tree branch by the road.

The bag vandals had found me worthy after all and had marked by house for some as yet unknown reason.

I hoped my home hadn't been marked for burglary and was even more frightened Keiko was right about the dog ransom thing.

Mandy would kill me if her dog were dognapped.

I might have been in time to thwart the dog snatchers if they were still in the house. I returned to my car, switched the lights off and coasted quietly behind the house to the grove of shrubs, where, like Mandy, I was able to park almost completely out of sight of the house.

In the shed at the back of the property line, I found a rake with hard tines and a long, sturdy wooden handle.

I approached the house with caution not knowing if the burglar-nappers were still in there or not.

The house key remained hidden in its spot under the loose back door step. Looking into the kitchen from the outside window, everything in the kitchen appeared intact and undisturbed, so I entered and advanced through the kitchen, rake at the ready, to confront anyone who might be awaiting me somewhere in the house.

I had trouble controlling my breathing. It seemed either too fast or not at all, no in-betweens.

The dining room buffet drawers were open, but the china display cabinets closed, china settings undisturbed, still on display.

The downstairs rooms were all in shambles. The front living room sofa pillows were torn apart. The tables askew. Books were scattered beneath the bookshelf.

I was about to ascend the back staircase off the kitchen when I thought I heard a faint scratching. A feeling of deja vu rippled through me and my scalp prickled as my hair attempted to stand on end.

I stood stock still, gripping the rake so hard I was losing feeling in my fingers. My ears carefully tuned to the sounds around me. I heard nothing. Nothing at all.

All was dead silent.

Not entirely trusting my hearing, I tippy-toed back to the kitchen phone to call the police and have them check the house over. If my house had been vandalized by thugs and my sister's expensive dog taken, I'd have to file a report with them anyway so why not do that sooner rather than later?

I hadn't even started to punch in 911 when I heard more scratching, louder this time. I did not imagine it. The sound was almost next to me, coming from behind the laundry room door.

I came to the awful realization that I was not alone in the house. Someone was in the laundry room—still vandalizing.

I set down the phone to re-grip the rake handle. I flung the laundry room door open with one hand. I swung the rake at face level with the other hand.

Something hit my left knee. A fluff of white shook itself and zoomed past me to the kitchen door where it whined and scratched to go outside.

Keiko came in as Mr. M and I were going out.

When Mandy hadn't showed to get her dog, Keiko explained that she had left Mr. M in the laundry room so she could leave for class. Since Keiko was unable to tell me that the house had not been like this when she left, I was perplexed at how one small dog could cause so much havoc and mayhem in my life and my house and concluded Mandy's dog was even more sneaky than she was.

After we had picked up the items littering the downstairs,

Keiko and I settled our nerves with hot Chamomile tea and biscuits. Then I called Mr. Twerk at his home and left him a scathing message on his answering machine advising him that he'd better find a way to get my cell phone service turned back on or I was contacting the credit card company and disputing the payment he'd taken.

On a roll, I called Mandy. Martin answered.

"Put Amanda on the phone. Now."

"I can't. She's not here." I could picture his smirk at the other end of the phone.

Her not being there had deflated my bravado, but Martin was miles away and just as handy. "She promised me she would come right back and get this dog of hers. She didn't. Now he's torn my house apart, and I insist she come and get him. I don't want him to stay here even one more night."

"Of course, your highness. She'll be so sad your precious living and dining room are in shambles, but I'm sure she'll be thrilled to hear you've lowered yourself to call us commoners. When she gets in, I'll tell her she has to come get that dog." Then in a Vader voice he intoned, "By your command," followed by a mechanical laugh.

I resisted the urge to slam down the phone. I tightened my grip and said through gritted teeth, "You better stop your little phone games and see that she gets over here to collect this dog, or I'll place a call to the parole board. I'm sure they'd love to know how well the fan is operating in her penthouse."

He hung up on me.

Mandy called me three minutes later. I didn't like the edge to her voice. "What's this about your threatening Martin?"

"It's not Martin I'm threatening. It's you. Your dog has been here long enough. I'm going to not only charge you for dog sitting but for the damages he's caused, too."

"Gosh. You're such a spoilsport. You'd think you'd be in a better mood after being out on a date. Just hold your horses. I have to do a few things before I can come over and pick the dog up."

"Just make sure you get here soon or the little dog gets warm tap water and day old table scraps."

I heard Mandy gasp on the other end of the line. "You wouldn't dare."

"Try me." This time I did slam the phone down. The edge of a cookie recipe card on the counter fluttered in the ensuing whoosh of air. I got down the recipe box to put the card away, but I couldn't do it. My father wrote the recipe on that card. The fact that he had more than one daughter didn't lessen the fact that the man cared deeply for me. I took the card upstairs intending to put it in my keepsake box along with the letter from Gordon.

The keepsake box was nothing more than a thick book that I'd hollowed out as a kid so I could hide some of my possessions from my cousins when they came to visit. *War and Peace.* How fitting.

I pulled the box down from the top shelf of my bookcase and opened it. Inside was the ribbon my mother always wore in her hair, the tin heart that had once sat atop the wand my parents gave me on my sixth birthday, a silver charm bracelet my aunt Tilly gave me when I first came to stay with her, a few old coins, marbles and the lipstick tube I'd taken from my mother's purse before she and my father left on their last business trip, the one that resulted in their deaths from a car crash.

I set the recipe card inside alongside Gordon's hastily written note and then stopped. I pulled both back out and laid the two documents side by side on the dresser. I compared the two. With the writing on both documents next to each other, the truth of my father's demise hit me.

My head swirled, and I saw spots before my eyes. I had to sit down on the bed and lower my head to keep from falling.

All this time. All these years. *Could it be?*

In a rage of betrayal, tears streaming down my face, I tore both documents up into smaller and smaller pieces before I threw them in the trash.

Mandy never showed up to get her dog like she promised me she would. I knew then that lying runs on my father's side of the family.

In bed that night, Mr. M kept barking at my bedroom door—wanting in. The only way I could keep him quiet was to put him in his little carrier next to my bed again, where he went willingly inside and immediately began to snore.

He and I were peacefully sleeping when I was startled awake, not knowing what had awoken me. Confused and disoriented, I lay in the dark for a few moments trying to determine what exactly had caused me to wake up so suddenly.

A noise? A smell? A feeling?

Then I heard it. A creak. I thought it came from overhead, where the hall to Gordon's apartment would have been. Gordon always kept that apartment locked, and he was the only one with a key. I presumed he had taken it with him. No one, and I mean no one, was ever allowed to go into Gordon's area without permission. I now had my suspicions as to why permission was never granted.

Hearing those sounds, I knew I had blundered when I didn't check the whole house for intruders upon arriving home.

I heard that soft creak again.

Mr. M came out of his little carrier bed and stretched up to put his front paws on the edge of my bed. The bed jiggled when he began to shake. A muffled clang sounded somewhere above us. Mr. M cleared the edge of the bed, landed on top where he promptly scratched and burrowed under the covers.

"Fine help you are," I whispered to him. I flung back the covers, got out of bed and picked up the rake I'd brought up to my room to stave off my earlier jitters from finding plastic bags marking my house.

Breathing heavily, I tapped on Keiko's door. She opened it, groggy from sleep, but she followed me downstairs, where I

168

checked all the downstairs entrances. Finding nothing amiss, I screwed up my courage to check the rest of the house. Keiko and I ascended the stairs to where I thought I'd heard the noise. Gordon's apartment door was locked tight with its special security lock. The door leading to the attic peak was also shut tight, but a breeze blew in from an open window in one of the unused bedrooms on the second floor. Figuring Keiko must have left it open to air the room, I closed the window, shrugged my fears off and went back to bed when we found nothing else amiss.

Keiko had already left to go job-hunting the next morning, so I read the paper to myself or tried to. Mr. M kept putting his little paws up in the air and standing on his hind legs and whining.

I called Mandy. When she didn't answer, I left a voice message of Mr. M's whine hoping that would encourage her to get her dog before I had to leave for work. When he kept begging, I put half of my breakfast in a bowl near the front door to keep him out of the kitchen, so I could finish reading the paper in peace.

There was another missing dog article in the morning paper. This time, rather than keep the ransom activity to himself, the dog owner's husband had gone directly to the police and showed them the letter that warned his wife to pay and keep silent or she'd never see her dog again.

Never see him again? I peeked out at Mr. M who was still eating my breakfast.

I resumed my paper reading. The second page had an update on Mr. Flynn's drowning. The coroner said he suffered a blow to the head just prior to the drowning; his death had been ruled a homicide. Anyone with information was being asked to contact the police. I looked at the small picture of Mr. Flynn's face. In this picture, his skin was less saggy. I dug a magnifying glass out of the desk drawer to study the mark on his face. The mark didn't look like a squashed fly. It resembled a galloping horse, like the shape on the back of Mr. Pilfer's hand.

Thinking they both belonged to the same gang as kids, I probably should have gone to the police and told them that Mr. Flynn was in the magazine's office arguing with Mr. Pilfer, but I wasn't overly fond of police officers, and I didn't believe Mr. Pilfer would have harmed anyone, much less a man he called his friend.

I got up to make another piece of toast and peek at the front door. The bowl was empty, and Mr. M was nowhere in sight. *Great.* I couldn't leave for work with him loose in the house. The dog fed on anything he can get in his mouth, including me.

I pulled a chicken sausage from the refrigerator, poked it with a knife and nuked it like Keiko showed me. The aroma filled the kitchen and wafted through the house as I carried it openly on a plate and fanned the smell into every room saying, "here, boy. Come and get it."

He wasn't anywhere in the downstairs. I climbed the back stairs of the kitchen. On the second floor, I came across the room that had the open window the previous night.

I double-checked to make sure the window lock was still locked and then noticed there was dirt on the window sill. I unlocked the window and opened it to look out. The screen had fallen and was in the flowerbed below. Some of the flowers around the screen were smashed, presumably from an intruder's shoes. Someone had been in the house the previous night. They'd pushed out the screen to drop down to the ground below.

I contacted the police, only to be put on hold because, with the intruder no longer in the house, I was a non-emergency call. I gave half a thought to calling back and saying the intruder was still in the house so I could get faster service, but I didn't because I still had to find that dog and get to work.

After waiting for what seemed like hours, I hung up and contacted Chilton Detective Agency.

"Chilton Detective Agency. Twilla speaking." I wondered which hand she was soaking this time.

"Is Mr. Chilton in?"

"Just a minute and I'll check." What was there to check? They had only one large office area and a restroom.

After several minutes, she came back on the line. "Can I take a message?"

I saw Mr. M's little nose wiggle out from under the bedspread on the bed. "Never mind. I've got to go. I'll just ask him about dusting for fingerprints when I see him."

"Suit yourself."

"Come on, you," I said to the lump on the bed. "Don't think you're going to get your own room and bed. You're not even a temporary guest in this house. You're going home today. I'm going to make sure of that."

Mr. M yipped at me as I waved the plate and kept it just out of his reach. He followed me, or rather the sausage, to his carrier, where I flung the sausage in. He ran inside after it, and I zipped the door shut.

I sat his carrier on the floor while I figured out what to do with him and what I should take for my lunch.

Keiko would only be staying with me until she found other employment; I couldn't expect her to cook, clean or dog sit for free.

With Mr. M in his carrier, I pulled from the fridge the only item, other than PBJs, I knew how to prepare. Sausages. One for Mr. M; two for Frank, one for Randy, and two for me.

Frank wasn't sitting on the sheet of cardboard, his usual spot by the dumpster, but the rolled sleeping mat was spread out there. I pulled two of foil wrapped sausages out and sat them down where he would easily find them. I may have been irritated with him, but I didn't want him to starve.

I juggled my diaper bag purse and the doggy carrier down the stairs, afraid if I used the elevator someone might notice I had a dog in the dog carrier. I cautiously opened the office door and peeked in. The reception room was dark and desolate.

Normally I didn't like dark and desolate, but since I was sneaking a dog carrier and its contents into work, dark and desolate worked to my advantage.

I shoved the carrier under the desk, checked for phone and e-mail messages. Finding none, I pulled out my crochet. I wanted to get the blanket I was making for Frank done before snow fell—just in case he was still out there. I didn't want him to freeze to death before I'd had a chance to tell him just what I thought of him.

I held my breath as the three men I worked with came through the front door, walked past my desk and into the backroom. Mr. Pilfer nodded in greeting. Rocko gave a grunt. Randy did a little finger wave. I nodded, grunted and finger waved back.

So far, so good.

At 9:30 I got a phone call from Keiko.

"You sister call. She say she get dog tonight."

Mr. M! I'd forgotten all about him. He'd been pretty quiet for a yipper. I grabbed the handle on the carrier and hefted it up to look inside.

He was asleep, but when the carrier moved, his beady little eyes popped open. He started yipping when he saw me staring in at him.

"Shhh...I don't want anyone to hear you. I don't think they allow dogs in this building."

He yipped again and pawed at the carrier door's zipper.

He must have had to go to the bathroom. I sure did. His carrier was unwieldy, but I managed to lug it up the stairs and out the front doors without anyone noticing us.

Once out in the fog-dampened air I realized bringing that dog with me to work in downtown Chicago was a dreadful mistake. Downtown Chicago is all glass, steel, and concrete. No potty spots exist for dogs.

A whine came out of Mr. M's carrier.

"All right. All right. Hold your horses. I'm trying to find a doggy bathroom." I juggled the carrier from hand to hand and crossed my legs. Both of us were in need. I glanced around, searching for even a minuscule patch of grass or dirt.

Seeing none, I ran across the street to those enormous concrete planter boxes at the Federal Reserve Bank. I sat the carrier down inside one of the planters and unzipped the little door. Mr. M ran out into the concrete enclosure, circling the small ornamental shrubberies planted inside. I waited while he sniffed each evergreen. He sniffed and sniffed.

"Hurry up. Someone might see us."

He gave me a miffed look that I swear resembled the looks I got from Mandy when she thought I was being a 'fraidy cat. He lifted his leg to water a small evergreen bush and after a bit of coaxing I got him back into the carrier, and we headed into the building. My turn next.

"Hey!" I heard Rē shout to me as I passed by the reception desk. "Cute purse. I like the teddy bear one I saw you with, too."

I moved the little carrier door opening away from her line of vision so she couldn't catch sight of Mr. M. "Thanks."

Thirty minutes later at my desk, Mr. M began to whine and scratch at the zipper again. *Another potty break? Had I rushed him too much the first time?* It was too risky to be seen bringing a carrier in and out of the building, so I cut the yarn string on the blanket I was crocheting and used that partial blanket to cover Mr. M from sight. He was quiet under the blanket, so I decided it was safe to use the elevator.

There was only one little old lady in pink tennis shoes and black coat and hat who got on at the basement level. Mr. M stayed quiet under the blanket until the elevator jerked when it started moving again. He wriggled, and I had a hard time holding on to him.

"Do you have a dog under that blanket?" the Pink Tennis Shoe Lady asked me.

Upon hearing her voice, Mr. M poked his head out from under my crocheting.

She saw him and laughed. "He's a cutie."

"Thanks. I'm just watching him for my sister."

Mr. M squirmed and growled at me.

"He doesn't seem to like you too much, does he?"

"The feeling is mutual," I responded. To which Mr. M began snapping, twisting and squirming around so much I couldn't hold on to him; I had to let him down.

The second his feet touched the elevator floor, the door slid open, and he made a mad dash out into the first-floor lobby area; with me in close pursuit.

I heard the pink tennis shoe lady say, "Oh, dearie me," as I stumbled on the hallway rug and the dog got away.

The building's outside doors opened as a visitor walked in. Mr. M ran out. The visitor and I sidestepped each other several times trying to get out of each other's way.

Finally outside, I scanned the area. The dog was lost to the jungle of buildings, or else he'd been run over.

What was I going to tell Mandy? A flattened dog couldn't even be properly stuffed and made to look real.

Then I saw him. He was eating one of the sausages I'd left on the cardboard. I'm referring to Frank. The dog was at Frank's side, front paws up, sitting, begging. Frank tore off a piece to fed it to Mr. M, who snatched it up and began chewing.

I rushed over and grabbed Mr. M's collar, so I could drag his little chewing teeth and struggling form towards the planters.

I didn't dare look at Frank or even talk to him. It wasn't because I was still mad at him—which I was, but I kept silent more out of fear for his safety. Fear that if I talked to him, the pent up longing and love/hate I was feeling would come bubbling out and have me saying things and doing things that would surely have given our relationship and his undercover status away.

So I avoided looking at him and kept my unpuckered lips zipped as I half dragged Mr. M out of the alley.

"Lady. You ought to keep your dog on a leash if you don't want him to get away," Frank called to me.

"He's not my dog," I shouted back over my shoulder. "He's my sister's." Then I said to mostly to myself, but loud enough for Frank to hear, "It appears I've let more than one dog get away."

When Frank e-mailed me that afternoon that he wanted me to do a "report" on the goings on at work. I complied by e-mailing him my crochet blanket pattern. Then when I thought better of it and tried to send an apology e-mail, I found myself blocked by spam filters.

So much for undying love.

CHAPTER 23

Melton Chilton wasn't hard to spot at the Whacky Fun Center. He was just inside the door, sitting on a bench at the entrance to the gated play area watching hordes of screaming, giggling kids wriggle through plastic tubes and bounce in inflated rubber houses.

He looked up when I stepped through the door. He seemed surprised to see me.

"Where's your kid?" he asked me pointing to the "No adults unless accompanied by a child" sign by the gated area. "You even got one?"

"No. I don't have one."

"Oh, then I guess that makes it a dead giveaway that you're here to see me?"

"Sorta." I didn't bother to sit down. It was already 6:30 and I had to get home. Mandy promised she be there at 7:00 to pick up her dog and I wanted to make sure that happened.

"So why'd you sorta come here? What do you want with me?"

"I have the money you requested to start the investigation into my father's spy activities."

"You do? All two thousand of it?" His expression changed slightly, more hopeful.

I pulled out the check I'd written him and handed it over.

He folded it and slipped it into his shirt pocket. I offered him the folder of information I had gathered from the files at home regarding my father. His birth and death certificates, military discharge papers, paycheck stubs from Black and Becker, any and everything I could scrounge up. I wanted to find out the truth.

He waved the file away.

"I don't need anything from you but the money and his name."

"You've got the money, and his name is plastered all over the papers."

"Right. He ever use any aliases?"

"Not that I know of, but I was only six the last time I saw him so my memory might be faulty." I looked at Melton closely. He'd shaved and cleaned up and looked halfway presentable. He had taken the time to comb his hair, and he didn't smell of alcohol, but I wasn't certain this new look was any better than the last. He still seemed dejected.

"You sure you can clear my father's name and find out what really happened to him?"

He shifted on the bench. "Do bears do it in the woods?"

"Depends on what "it" you are referring to," I said. "I also want to know if you can dust a room in my house for fingerprints."

"I can do that. Wanna tell me why?"

"I just need to know who has been in my house. That's all."

"You afraid you've had unwanted company?"

"I'm always afraid." I wished I hadn't torn up the recipe card and letter from Gordon. I could have given him those for a document examiner to compare to see if they had been written by the same person. Since I didn't have them, I kept my suspicions about my father's identity to myself.

The outer door swung open, and two blond haired children rushed in, a boy about eight and a girl about five. They ran straight into Melton Chilton's open arms. He hugged them to him, one in each arm.

He looked up at the petite blond who followed in after the kids. "You're early."

She took off the kids' coats and hung them up on two of the animal tail pegs lining the walls: a monkey and a dog.

"Jennifer insisted we hurry."

"Thank you," Melton told the woman. I looked away when I saw that his gaze held hers for an uncomfortably long time.

"Sure." I turned in time to see her give a little nod of her head.

"Daddy. Daddy. I got a part in the school play," the girl said tugging on his shirtsleeve.

He pulled his eyes away from the woman to look down at his daughter. "That's great, pumpkin."

"Big Deal," the boy said. "You say two words dressed like a peach. Come on, Jennifer. Let's go play. We don't have much time to be with dad, and I want to show him how high I can bounce."

There was an awkward silence between the former Mrs. Chilton and myself after Mr. Chilton and his kids disappeared through the gate and into the bouncy house.

"You the new girlfriend?"

I blinked at her. "Girlfriend? Me? No. No. I'm a client. He's agreed to take my case regarding my dead father."

She visibly relaxed and smoothed back her hair with a shaky hand. "That's nice." Then her hand flew to cover her mouth. "I didn't mean it like that. I mean, it's not nice your dad is dead, I'm just glad that Mel took your case. He's a good detective. The best there is."

"Good to know. That's he's a good detective, I mean and I'm not so sure my dad is dead."

"If he's not Mel will find him. Mel's a good man." She malingered there watching that good man with his kids as they played. Curious about a father who didn't choose to be with his children, except in a play area, I stayed a few minutes to watch her. She had a big smile on her face when all three of them came down the tube slide together—like a train—with

Daddy Chilton the caboose. I remembered what the boy had said about not having much time to be with his father. They seemed to be cramming as much fun as they could into that little space of time. Melton Chilton was definitely enjoying time with his children. He must have said something hilariously funny because they all started laughing as they wandered over to the pizza stand.

After a few minutes of contemplating the changed demeanor in Mr. Chilton, I asked Mrs. Chilton, "If you don't mind my asking, why doesn't Mr. Chilton visit with his children at his home?"

"Same reason we aren't married anymore. I won't let him keep the kids. He made a lot of enemies when he was a detective for the Chicago Police Department. One of them came after me once when I was pregnant for Jennifer. Scared the living Jesus out of me. It started me thinking about the danger he faced every day. I tried to get over it, but I lived in terror day and night after that. Every time he walked out the door," she paused and wiped away a tear that had started to track down her perfectly made up face. "I wondered if he was coming back—wondered if someone was going to come for the kids or me while he was gone.

"I became a wreck, thinking someone would hurt him or God forbid, one of the kids in retribution for someone he put away or killed in the line of duty. Eventually, I just couldn't take it anymore, and I took the kids and went to live with my parents in Naperville. The kids miss their father and beg to see him, so I bring them back twice a month to visit. As long as we stick to public places with a lot of people around I'm able to deal with it."

One look at her pinched, sallow face that told me she wasn't dealing with it. It was still dealing with her.

CHAPTER 24

Mandy snuggled Mr. M up to her face and rubbed her cheek on his furry head. He responded by licking her face. I was so grateful she had finally shown up that evening to get her dog, I would have considered licking her face too if it would have gotten him and her out the door any quicker. I picked up Mr. M's carrier and leash, went out the door and began making my way to her Bentley that she'd parked at the far edge of the drive.

"Wait," I heard her say behind me.

I ignored her and kept walking. She ran after me and grabbed my arm.

I stopped. "Is that Martin in your car?" I turned and asked her at the sight of his blond head behind the steering wheel.

"Yes. He needed to get out of the apartment and get some fresh air, so I had him drive me here. You don't know how hard it is on him being cooped up all day." She was standing next to me in my driveway with her dog, continuing to rub his fur against her face. Mr. M doggy smirked at me.

"You promised me you'd keep Martin away from here. I have a restraining order against him. Which, by the way, prohibits him from making prank calls as well."

"I know. He only did that because he was so bored that he started playing around with his childhood toys. He needed to get out of the apartment. I parked at the far end of the drive so you wouldn't have to deal with him."

I thrust the dog's carrier at her. "Mandy, you'll have to take your dog's things with him to your car. I don't want to have anything to do with Martin."

Mandy folded her arms across Mr. M and hugged him to her. "I can't take Mr. M with me. If he's found in my apartment, my lease says they can kick me to the curb and if I get kicked out where will Martin go? No one will take in a man accused of attempted murder. He won't have a place to stay. I can't risk getting kicked out of my apartment for Martin's sake. My building manager cain't be finding Mr. M in my place."

"He's not staying here."

"It's your fault that Martin is in this predicament. Seems like a small favor to ask for you to keep my dog for a little bit longer."

It wasn't my fault, but I wasn't going to go down that road as I didn't like where the conversation was going. "Well, I'm not keeping your dog. I'm dealing with problems of my own. I can't afford to pay Keiko. If she doesn't have a job, she loses her work visa. If she loses her work visa, she'll have to go back to Japan."

"Why cain't you afford to pay her? What did you do with all your money?" Mandy asked me. Without waiting for an answer—that I would have loved to have given her—she uncrossed her arms, snapped her fingers and continued, "I can pay Keiko. How 'bout we work a deal. I'll take Keiko on as a maid in exchange for you keeping Mr. Mister until I can get the apartment manager worked over to my side."

Keiko was not fond of Mandy and was even less fond of Martin, but I was fond of Keiko and willing to risk her ire if it meant I'd have more time to resolve my financial woes so I could rehire my friend.

"You've got a deal." I went to shake hands and take Mr. M back, but he snapped at me. I said to Mandy, "Just set him on the floor in the laundry room and close the door before you leave."

I didn't want to take Mr. M to work with me again the next day, but with Keiko gone with Mandy, there was no one home to let him out. If I didn't want a mess when I got home, I felt I had no choice but to smuggle him and his carrier in with me again.

Thankfully, Mr. M enjoyed sleeping. He slept through most of the banging and printer noises going on in the back room. He didn't even stir when Randy came out and let the back door slam. Since they'd already given me the lunch order that morning, I was surprised to see Randy.

"You got any more of those purple pens? I dropped the one you gave me in the water, and now it don't work."

"In the water?" I asked, confused about what he was talking about. There wasn't even a restroom in the back.

"Yeah. There's been a lot of rain lately." He flushed a deep red. "I didn't mean to wreck your pen. I'm sorry."

"That's okay. I can bring in another one, but not until tomorrow."

"Okay." He returned to the back room, shoulders slumped.

I felt sorry for Randy, but I didn't engage him in further conversation as I didn't want him to learn I had a dog hidden under my desk.

Curious as to why Mr. M hadn't yipped or made a sound, I crouched down and peered in the carrier.

The zipper was down just wide enough for Mr. M to have escaped. He must have pawed it down. Panicked, I looked around the office trying to find him. There were very few spots where a dog could hide in that meagerly furnished office.

I opened the closet door and peeked inside. No dog. I opened the door with the boarded up insides. A trickle of dirt seeped through the slats of the bottom boards, but with the boards nailed tightly together, there were no spots for even a small dog to get through.

I stood in the center of the room and made a slow circle to see if I'd missed anything or if he had gotten outside of the office. I opened the outer door and peered into the hallway. As I peered, a bundle of white scooted out from wherever he was hiding and whizzed past me out into the hall.

He ran, and I ran after him. He got to the slowly closing elevator doors before me.

If I had been lucky, the doors and dog would have waited until I got close enough to scoop him up. Most days I'm not lucky. That day was no exception. Mr. M dashed inside the elevator, and I was a fraction too late to stop the doors from sliding closed, shutting me out.

I pushed the up elevator button frantically. When the doors didn't reopen, I dashed up the stairs hoping to catch the elevator before it passed by the basement level. I jammed and jabbed at the buttons on the basement level, but the elevator didn't stop there.

I ran up the next flight of stairs and looked around the lobby. I was sure I'd made it here before Mr. M's elevator, but he was nowhere to be seen.

Rē was coming into the building, Mr. Goth's arm draped over her shoulders. They were walking and chewing in unison like a gum commercial.

"If you're looking for your little dog, I saw him run into the alleyway," Rē said to me.

"How did you know I have a...? How did you know he was...? Never mind. Thank you."

I hurried into the alleyway and found Frank feeding Mr. M a piece of apple. "What are you doing? Dogs don't eat apple."

"This one does."

Mr. M looked up at me. Our eyes met, and he took off at a full run down the alley, me in close pursuit. I managed to grab a handful of fur just before he darted into the traffic at the back street. He yipped and barked, but I got a firm hold on his collar and dragged him back through the alley scolding him the whole way.

183

As I dragged, I kept my gaze partially on Frank. Even scruffy, and undercover dirty Frank was saturated in sex appeal, so it was hard to walk past and ignore him, even while fighting to keep a grip on Mandy's dog.

I was glad I'd worn a gardenia-scented perfume and paid particular attention to my hair and makeup that morning.

Once I got near to Frank, I looked at Mr. M. "Don't you dare put yourself at risk like that. If something happens to you, my life will be miserable. More miserable than it already is and my sister will kill me."

Mr. M obviously wasn't too concerned about my familiar problems. He snapped, struggled and fought me all the way down the alley. I could hear Frank's chuckles in the background as I did all I could to keep my hands and ankles out of the way of Mr. M's sharp little teeth.

Mr. Pilfer, Rocko, and Randy stayed busy in the back room with the door locked tight for hours at a time. As much as I was relieved that Randy no longer had time to come out and spy on me, I also missed his company and his cheery disposition.

All the next day I kept going to the supply closet to listen for investigative clues, but since I heard nothing but the printer working, eventually I gave up my quest for clues and just crocheted. I had nothing to report, and I said as much in an e-mail to Frank—which was promptly returned to me as "undeliverable."

Mr. M was contented to sleep in his carrier until I rousted him to eat his princely lunch and go outside for a break. I stopped at Rē's desk so she could quietly coo over Mr. M and pat his little head hidden under the afghan.

"He's adorable," she remarked. He licked her hand.

"He is if you don't have to feed, water, clean up and chase after him. Speaking of cleaning, can I see that floor plan of the sub-sub basement?"

"Sure." She reached into the drawer and pulled out the laminated sheet.

I studied it carefully. I could see the outlines of the office reception area where I worked, the closet and the backroom areas behind that, but the boarded up door area showed a big room with two doors. The door I'd opened off the reception room was boarded up. The other entrance was off the maintenance room. That explained the singing I'd heard when no one was around. It had to be from the room that had the access from the reception room blocked.

When I next took Mr. M outside, I didn't try to stop him from running straight to Frank where I had to go collect him.

"Hello, little fella," Frank said to the dog, but he was looking at me.

I looked into his eyes and found I couldn't look away. It was hard for me to speak, emotion choked me. I finally found my voice and said a soft, "Hello."

He looked down at Mr. M and said low enough that only I could hear. "You'd better take your dog in a different direction when you come out now and stay clear of here. I don't want you to be seen talking with me anymore. It's not safe."

"Yeah, sure." It was hard for me to drag us away. It was even harder to keep my silence. I wanted to ask Frank why I couldn't be seen talking to him, why he refused my request for information on my investigation and why he was so angry at me for not finding some way to rat out my employers.

I tried to do as Frank asked, but that afternoon I walked through the alley anyway. I couldn't help myself. I wasn't close enough to talk to him, but I did buy him a burger and fries, which I flung in his general direction when I passed through the alley. He ignored me. Flinging was not talking so technically Frank shouldn't have been mad at me.

Mandy met me after work that evening so she could see Mr. M.

"So where's this handsome man you've been turning down dates with?" She glanced around the street in front of the McClintock building.

"Garrett Edmond?" I asked as I glanced around to see if he was waiting outside for me. Frank was hidden to the side of the building. There were a few business types loitering at the front of the building, smoking or just taking advantage of the fresh air. I recognized the one man in a black suit. He must work the same hours as me because I saw him a lot when I entered and exited the building.

None of the people I saw were Garrett. "Garrett's walked me to my car a few times, but I haven't seen him since we had dinner together."

"Dinner? You didn't mention this to me." Mandy continued to nuzzle Mr. M the entire way to my car.

"There wasn't much to mention." I unlocked my car door and noticed the man in the black suit was a few rows over.

"Too bad. You need some mentionables." My sister reluctantly placed Mr. M in his carrier in the back seat.

As I closed the door, I noticed that the black suit was looking in our direction with hard, cold eyes. I felt a chill run up my spine. Then his gaze focused on Mandy before he directed his attention elsewhere. My nerves kept making me jumpy.

CHAPTER 25

The next day I opened the magazine's office door to make my daily lunch trip to McDeeds and physically bumped into a hard male chest. I stepped back a pace and fumbled over my own feet. "Excuse me," I said, blushing at my clumsiness. When hands reached out to steady me to keep me from falling backward, I looked up and found Garrett's smiling blue eyes surveying my face.

Garrett acted like he didn't hear the low growl coming from under my desk.

I didn't comment except to look away and say, "Garrett, you scared me. I didn't expect to see you again."

"Well, nice to see you, too," he said. "I came by to see if we could do dinner tonight."

"I don't think that's a good idea. I have to work late, and I'll be too tired to be good company."

"What about tomorrow night? I was really hoping I could see you again before I leave town to visit my mom for the holiday."

"Well...I..." I was trying to find a polite way to turn him down.

"Okay. Okay." He threw his hands up in the air. "I can take a hint. You don't have to make up some phony excuse, like you're washing your hair or something."

I fluffed my shortened hair with my hand wondering how he knew the excuse I'd been thinking of.

"At least let me walk with you to the McDeeds. I promise I'll behave."

Mr. M barked loudly from his carrier spot under the desk. I shushed him and stepped out into the hall and closed the door. I listened for a bit at the door for Mr. M to settle down and stop barking. My employers didn't seem to hear the noise in the reception area, but I didn't want Mr. M to announce to them that I was bringing a dog to work.

"I guess we can walk together—if you're going that way."

Garrett looked back at the closed office door and made no mention of the now silent dog. He linked his arm with mine and said, "Whatever way you're going, I'm going."

I self-consciously removed my arm from Garrett's. I also tried to ignore the glares we got from Frank when he saw Garrett and me walking together, but Frank's reaction gave me a secret pleasure; he still cared enough about me to glare.

That evening Garrett met me outside the building. As I carried Mr. M in his carrier to the parking garage, Garrett came along, asking me how my day was. He asked me a lot of questions about the magazine business, most of which I couldn't answer.

"So when is the first issue due out?" He asked me, opening the back door of my car for me to slide the dog carrier in.

"I don't know. I think it must be pretty soon because I hear the printer going almost non-stop now, and they've asked me to start working later so they can get ready for the big event."

"The big event?"

"That's what Randy has been calling it. I'm sure he's referring to the Magazine's Grand Opening."

"Grand Opening? I didn't know you were having a Grand Opening. Shouldn't there be some sort of announcement or something, so people know about this Grand Opening?" Garrett asked me.

"I'm not sure what they've got planned, but I'm willing to help them with whatever they need for the Grand Opening."

"I see that you're the loyal employee willing to go the extra mile and all that."

"That's right. Mr. Pilfer gave me a job when I needed one badly. I intend to help him all I can and do whatever he asks of me." I saw Garrett give me a puzzled look.

"Thanks for walking me to my car," I said as I slid smoothly into the front seat leaving him holding the door open until I closed it.

He seemed reluctant to let me leave, but once I started the car, he stepped back and I drove away, leaving him standing by my parking spot staring after me.

Garrett was right. If the magazine company was going to succeed, it needed advertising. I knew a little about promotional activities from my time with my aunt.

Filled with excitement, I opened up the digital files my aunt's publicist had developed for her book signings. I modified the documents and loaded my USB bracelet with ideas for the magazine grand opening. I couldn't wait to get to work the next day and show Mr. Pilfer my ideas.

The files were uploading when I got a call from Melton.

"Miss Warren. I've got the results of the fingerprints from the room. Are you on a land line?"

"Yes. Why?"

"Are you sitting down?"

Fear wiped out my advertisement excitement. "Yes. Why?"

"In addition to you, your maid, and your cousin Martin's fingerprints, the lab reports a match for Edward Timothy Warren's prints on file with the CIA."

"What?" I couldn't have heard him right. There must have been more than one Edward Timothy Warren associated

189

with the CIA.

"You heard me correctly. Your dead father was in that room. My guess is he was there recently since cleaning would have erased any older prints."

I stopped breathing. I stopped thinking. I stopped wanting to think.

"Are you there?"

I drew in a shaky breath, still not engaging my brain. "Yes."

"You want me to pursue this further?"

"No, please don't," I whispered. Twenty years of lies pressed me down and swallowed me whole.

CHAPTER 26

The next morning I zombie dressed, zombie fed and watered Mr. M and left him home. I was a hollowed out shell as I drove to work and got into the building, ignoring everyone and everything. Rē saw me walking past her desk and stopped me.

"Genie, what's wrong? You look terrible. Where's your little dog?"

"I left him home. I don't care if he makes a mess of the house. My whole life is a mess. What's one more?"

She pulled me behind her desk and sat me down in her chair.

"What's going on? You look like you've lost your best friend."

I gave a feeble laugh. "In a way I have."

"Tell me about it."

"I found out my father was not whom he claimed to be."

"Oh, honey. None of our fathers are who we want them to be."

"Mine is a despicable man who has done despicable, unforgivable things."

"I don't know what your father has done, but you aren't responsible for anything he did. Don't let his actions taint your life. You have your own life to live." She reached into her pocket and pulled out a wrapped piece of bubble gum. "Here. Take it. There's nothing like a blowing and popping bubbles to make your troubles seem lighter."

Rē was right. Bubble gum is better than Prozac. It's hard to stay down when sticking out your tongue and blowing air creates a big beautiful strawberry bubble. My father may have left me for the second time, but this time, I was not six years old. I was a grown adult, with a grown up job. I had even put together a marvelous marketing and promotion plan for my employers.

Feeling a bit better, I worked up the nerve to push the button under my desk and summon someone from the back room, so I could go back and meet with them about advertising the grand opening.

To my disappointment, Rocko was the first to answer the buzzer.

"What do you want?" he asked me, wiping his hands on a paper towel. He threw the green smeared towel in the waste basket near my desk.

"I just wanted to have a meeting with you and Mr. Pilfer about advertising the Grand Opening for the magazine. I've done up a few sample flyers, and I can post a Grand Opening page on the website I've created if I know the opening date."

His pupils constricted. The muscles in his jaw flexed. "Who said we're having a Grand Opening?"

"I just thought..." I swallowed a lump forming in my throat and continued, "What with all the printing going on it must be about time to notify potential customers of our existence so we can expect great sales. Then be successful—"

"We're in a race to get things wrapped up and ready to go for a Grand Opening all right." He clenched and unclenched his fists. "Only you'll keep your mouth shut about what goes on here if you know what's good for you."

I swallowed the jumping frog that lodged in my throat

along with the previous lump and croaked, "Of course, Mr. Rocko. I was only trying to help the business."

"You can help by staying out of the way and making sure we know when someone comes through that door." He unclenched his fist to point to the outer door. My heart sank to my shoes at his very un- business like attitude.

I was sure then that I was mixed up in an illegal gambling operation, as I'd originally suspected. I should never have given up on my investigation. I should have tried harder to help Frank. It was time to pull my sleuthing skills back out, such as they were and try to gather some concrete evidence. I only hoped it wasn't too late to make amends with Frank.

That afternoon, I printed a message for Frank on the inside of his burger wrapper, "My employers are doing something illegal. Rocko is angry with me, but I think I can get that evidence you asked for. If you still want it."

Just as before, I flung the bag at him on my way through the alley. With my e-mail address tagged as spam, I didn't know how he was going to get a return message to me, but I knew he would.

No message from Frank materialized. By the end of the day, I'd given up on hearing from him. Frank was not by the dumpster when I left for the parking garage either. My heart fluttered erratically when I saw that man in the dark suit from before come towards me as I walked to my car. Fortunately, I was able to mingle in with a group of convention-goers as they all went to the open parking to leave. By the time I got to my car, the man was nowhere to be seen.

Melton was outside my door waiting for me to get home. He joked about stopping by to ease his conscience about not doing more for his two thousand dollars.

"I'm surprised that your father could have gotten past this state-of-the-art alarm system," he said checking over the set up in the central control area. "He must be an excellent spy."

Not wanting to get into the issue of my father lived here for 20 years, I said, "I don't know how to set the alarm thing.

My...butler used to be the one to set it every night. I don't remember how."

"You got the security code?"

"No. I misplaced it."

"That's not good," Melton told me. "You need to show the security company your identification as proof of who you are and have them reset it for you."

I wished I'd taken his advice when I got a throaty call at four in the morning again. The minute I heard the wheeze I said, "It's not funny anymore, Martin" and hung up. I called the phone company and reported it, but that didn't stop my cold sweats from starting.

Frank was not by the dumpster when I entered the building for work the next day. I tried to go about my day as usual. I was brooding about Martin's prank calls and Frank's not responding to my message—both with equal brooding. I wondered where Frank was and if he was okay.

At lunchtime, I still bought him a burger, just like usual. When I walked back from lunch through the alley, it was a relief to see him going through a black garbage bag, which he dropped like hot lava when he saw me.

Between the phone call the night before, the racket in the backroom and being followed by the dark suit when I left work, my nerves were on edge. I decided I had to approach Frank directly and ask him what was up. If I kept my voice low, I felt no one would overhear us.

I walked directly up to him, set the burger bag down next to where he was crouched. When he looked up at me, I wanted to touch his bruised cheek and smooth his unkept hair back from his face, but held myself in check. I began drowning in a pool of liquid desire, and couldn't find the words to speak to him. We were out in the open in a busy alley. I didn't have any idea of why he was there, what assignment he was on or how much danger he would be in if I let on that I knew him.

Before I could turn away, Frank reached out, quick as a bee sting and grabbed my wrist, dragging me down to him. He locked his arms around me, and his hand pushed my head towards his. He laid a huge smooch on my lips. I tasted cinnamon, and my head felt woozy as every electron in my body reversed its spin.

He then shoved a hand down the front of my blouse and hissed in a low voice only I could hear, "act outraged."

He gruffly released me and gave me a little shove away from him before he plunked back down to sit on the ground.

The charged air around me split with his maniacal laugh.

Confused, it took me a second before I came to and realized I had to react as though he was what he appeared to be, a street person who had just accosted me. If I didn't, his cover would be blown.

"You filthy bum," I shouted just before I hauled off and smacked him hard across the face with my open hand. I fumed and stomped off towards the building, so happy I could have jumped for joy.

Once I was inside a stall in the ladies restroom, I leaned against the door, shaken to my core at what I'd just experienced. My body almost betrayed me. Betrayed Frank. I reached into my blouse and pulled out the piece of paper he had thrust there. Inside the fold was a little cinnamon candy heart and a hand-written note.

"Leave now and don't come back. He is a killer," was written in charcoal type pencil. That was all it said.

I didn't know which "he" Frank was referring to. *Rocko? Or Mr. Pilfer? Or someone else? Maybe even Garrett?*

I jumped when the door I was leaning against was rattled from the other side.

"You okay in there?" Rē asked me through the stall door.

"I think so," I responded in a genuinely shaky voice.

"I saw what he did. You want me to call the cops?"

"No. I gave him a good wallop. No harm done." I stared at the paper again with its cryptic note written in Frank's handwriting.

195

"You should take up Karate and roundhouse kick that creep if he ever grabs you like that again."

I ripped the paper into little pieces and flushed them down the toilet before I opened the stall door. "Thanks. I may do just that."

***

Frank didn't know what he would do if Genie didn't take his advice and leave immediately with her little dog. Her note to him the day before had confused him. His Homeland Security handler had told him Genie was working for an investment firm on the third floor of the McClintock building and was nowhere near Heinrich Rockford, the man suspected to be planning a bombing of the deep tunnel. Homeland Security had agents working inside the building, so Frank had no reason to suspect the handler was lying to him.

It had taken Frank the remainder of yesterday to get the story straight. Then he'd spent the night in jail for punching his Homeland Security handler in the face for putting Genie in danger and then lying to him about it.

It took two calls to Merle Hartford, his FBI boss, to get him released from lock up. Frank eagerly took to the streets again; he'd let the bosses haggle over which agency was in charge and who would call the shots. He had informed Merle he wasn't going to work with that handler again so they'd better work something different out.

As far as Frank was concerned, his job hadn't changed; he now had extra incentive for stopping Rockford from completing his plans. Frank didn't care about undercover protocol; he was going to openly approach Genie on her way out and convince her to never come back. While he waited for Genie, he kept trying to calm his nerves by drinking the tea he'd put a whiskey bottle and wrapped in a paper bag. His internal senses were telling him something wasn't right, but he wasn't sure what to do about it.

When Genie didn't come out at quitting time, he began

to pace in front of the building entrance, wondering how long he should wait for her. He needed to get her out of harm's way without putting her in danger or blowing the investigation.

***

I wished Frank had named the killer outright. Rocko was the obvious choice, but I knew how dangerous it was for me to jump to conclusions and miss a vital clue.

I didn't understand why Frank had asked me to get pictures and tell him what was going on if he knew one of the men I was dealing with was a killer. He must have told me to leave because he figured I couldn't get the requested evidence. I felt that I'd failed him.

I had an intense urge to find out what was going on, to get questions answered, if not to help Frank, then to help me. Those answers lay in the backroom—a place Frank didn't have access to, but I did. At least, I did if I could find a way to get back there undetected.

I was surprised at how calm I was at my desk, how easily I resumed my Penelope Pembrooke, detective persona after flushing Frank's note.

When Mr. Pilfer came to ask me if I'd work late the next evening, my voice was steady and sure when I said, "Of course. Since you're working late tomorrow, what time will you be in tomorrow morning?"

"Probably the usual time. We have a deadline, a very short window of opportunity that we can't miss, or our plans will all be for naught."

I intended to be back long before their "usual" time, so I could investigate and not get caught. My only snag was finding a way to avoid Frank; I knew he'd probably have me arrested to stop me from coming back in the building, so I stopped to consult with Rē on my way out.

"That cowboy guy has been hanging around the front entrance again. I'd like to avoid him. Is there another way out of here that will allow me to get the Wells Parking Garage?"

"Sure," Rē told me. "Use the side exit and walk all the way around the back of the building. That street in the back comes out on the other side of the parking garage."

"Thanks. I appreciate your helping me and keeping quiet about my dog."

"No prob. You and your dog are the only excitement I get around here."

***

When five ten o'clock rolled past, Frank couldn't wait any longer for Genie to come out. He decided to go in and get her. Except the handler hadn't actually divulged where Genie was working in the building and now with a broken jaw he doubted his old handler would be inclined to tell him anything.

Frank ambled up to the information desk, trying not to show his concern. The pink haired girl was pulling her bag out of a drawer and getting ready to leave for the night.

"I'm looking for a woman who works in this building. She's about this tall." Frank held his hand up to just below his nose. "Slender, soft brown hair about this length." Frank held his hand up to just below his ears. "Doe eyes. Carries a huge teddy bear purse. Very pretty."

Rē wrinkled her nose and slung her purse over her shoulder. This scruffy dirtball was the man Imogene was trying to avoid. Ré wanted to get home to get ready for a date; she didn't have time to call the police. Since her father had dismissed the building security company, Rē knew no help would be forthcoming from that area.

"Forget it. She's already left for the night. Now scram before I call the cops."

Frank reluctantly went back to his station beside the dumpster, trying to figure out what his best options were. Unable to stand not knowing, he tried calling her cell only to hear it was no longer in service. He then called Imogene's home phone. It rang several times. He was just about to hang up when she finally answered.

"Hello," she'd answered in a tentative voice.

"Hello," she said again louder when he didn't speak.

"Who is this?" She sounded annoyed, but at least he knew she was safely home. He didn't want to worry her so he disconnected without saying a word and was finally able to refocus on his investigation.

CHAPTER 27

I snapped my USB drive bracelet on and made sure the battery in my camera was charged before I left for work early that next morning. A twelve-hour day was too long a time for a little dog to be caged up in a carrier, even a dog who snoozes a lot, so I put Mr. M in my laundry room again, to keep him out of mischief. I set down two of my Wedgewood china bowls on the laundry room floor for him. One I filled with dry kibble, the other with cold water. I added a few ice cubes to the water, folded up the comforter from my bed into a square and sat it near the dryer. Then I took some old newspapers from the recycling bin to spread out on the floor for him—just in case he couldn't wait until I got home.

As I opened the paper up for maximum floor coverage, I saw I had picked up the newspaper that had run the first article on Mr. Flynn's death. I read every word of the article again wondering if Rocko had been the cause Mr. Flynn's death. I didn't suspect Mr. Pilfer who seemed shook up over his fight with his old friend and was anxious to find him and set matters to right.

Try as I might I couldn't help but read some of the story titles as I laid the other papers out flat on the floor. My father's name flashed out at me like a neon sign from one of the many sheets of newsprint covering a corner of the floor. It went against my better judgment, but I read the article anyway.

> **Washington, D.C.** the Pentagon will neither deny nor confirm rumors that Edward Warren, double agent accused of stealing Pentagon designs for the development of a stealth missile, is alive and in hiding.
>
> News broke last week that Warren had provided Russian agents with the missile's plans just before his car crash 20 years ago. Warren's wife died at the scene of the crash, and it was believed that Edward Warren expired later in a hospital in Nepal. Warren left behind one child, Imogene, a daughter, who was not with him at the time of the crash, and a sister, the famous mystery writer, the late Matilda Warren. Jarrod Johnson, investigative reporter for NCC News, has been unable to locate records in Nepal to confirm that the double agent died in the car crash. Undisclosed sources now believe Agent Warren may have survived the crash and took the plans with him when he left Katmandu. The recent earthquake in that area of Asia is hampering investigations.
>
> If the daughter knows the whereabouts of her father, she is not saying. When this story broke last week, Imogene Warren refused to comment. Phone calls to the family residence in Winnetka have gone unanswered.

Wonderful.

I had stopped reading the newspapers, turned the radio and television and phone ringers off to avoid having to deal with the emotional turmoil of my father's story, those threatening from calls from the dark side, the nosy literary agent wanting manuscripts, and to keep my name out of the news. Only while I was in hiding, the story of my father continued on and my name had been plastered in the paper nevertheless.

I slogged through the rain to get to work, thankful that the wet weather made it easy to avoid everyone on my way in, including Frank, who I had hoped was somewhere dry. I entered the McClintock building from the side entrance and got down to the magazine office without incident.

I gave a mental start when I saw Mr. Pilfer was sitting at my desk. My computer was on, and he was studying the screen. I couldn't remember if I had erased my browser history, so I was worried that he had figured out that I was investigating him.

I fumbled in my pocket for my yarn patch and held my breath.

He looked up and smiled at me. "You've done a great job on building the website."

"Thanks." I clutched at the hand-knit fabric in my pocket and wondered if he had been at my computer to check up on my website work or me.

"Rocko is bringing the car around. Most of what we need to do today has to be canceled due to the heavy rain, so I thought maybe we'd close the office for a few hours and take a much-needed break. That'll give Rocko and me some time to go take care of some other things we need to do, so if there is something you'd rather be doing until this afternoon, why don't you put a closed sign on the door and take a few hours off as well. Once the rain stops this afternoon, we'll need to take advantage of the break and work late into the evening. Maybe even all night."

I didn't understand how rain impacted on printing, but I put the closed sign up on the door—no questions asked. I didn't bother to take a few hours off. I got busy trying to get into the locked back room. After numerous failed attempts with a nail file, bobby pin, and my crochet hook, I recalled a technique my aunt had written about using a credit card to trip the latch, but I wasn't desperate enough to sacrifice my only credit card, so I got on-line to see if there was a website with tips for burglars.

My computer sign-in screen was pre-populated with the name Hershal Boggs. A row of asterisks populated the space where Mr. Pilfer had entered his password to access the internet on my computer. All I had to do was hit the return key and the screen displayed the information Mr. Pilfer had brought up to view. In addition to the website I'd created, there were sites on security systems, vault companies, homemade explosives and special welding and cutting equipment.

Now I was getting somewhere. I unsnapped my bracelet and downloaded the information. I knew just visiting a site where these things are sold is not the same as doing something illegal, but it was all starting to make sense. The jewelry store next door was receiving a shipment of diamonds. Even without the shipment, that ring in the window had to be worth a quarter of a mill.

By the time my few hours were up, I felt confident I'd gotten all the information I could without having access to the backroom.

Working late for Mr. Pilfer was the easiest money I ever made. Randy and the others were kept busy in the back. No one came by the office, not even Garrett, who had left town to visit his mother for the holidays. I had enough time on my hands to crochet on the afghan I had started for Frank.

I also had time to cry.

The holidays were rapidly approaching.

The whole country hated my father. I hated him, too.

My sister hated me. I wished she didn't.

Her brother, my cousin, hated me. The feeling was mutual.

It would have been better if I'd never discovered that my father was alive and hiding somewhere in Asia, running and lying. The coward's way, leaving me here to deal with the mess he'd left behind.

There wasn't going to be a Happy Thanksgiving for me.

My mood was full dark, and so was the sky when I left the McKlintock building by the side exit to avoid Frank. I wished I'd had Mr. M with me for company. I had to admit I felt braver when I had him to protect.

I gazed longingly towards the alleyway entrance. *Was Frank out there in the damp dark?*

At least the rain had let up for a while. I imagined Frank was stretched out, staring at the stars or sleeping on the mat he always had corded to his backpack.

As I walked along, I noticed most of the buildings downtown had closed up for the night already—not even the cleaning crew lights were on. Even the Federal Reserve Bank seemed dark and foreboding when I rushed past. I saw a flicker of light flash in one of the windows and then it was gone. Must be their guards used flashlights to do their rounds.

Without Garrett walking beside me, I felt vulnerable. I headed as fast as I could go towards the Well's Street parking garage, now glad Mr. M's bulky carrier wasn't with me to slow me down.

I kept looking behind me. I had a feeling I was being followed. I saw only shadows from the streetlights and an occasional flicker of movement. I told myself it was the tree branches blowing in the wind, but I was lying to myself again. There were no trees.

Once I entered the parking structure, I hesitated to head towards the elevator. I'd parked on the second level, where the open parking for the nearby Marriot hotel was. If I got in the elevator, I might well be trapped.

I could have woven my way around the structure and gone up the inclines the vehicles traversed to get from floor to floor, or I could have entered the stairwell and gone up that way.

When I saw a tall, thin figure in a black suit approach the stairwell door, I crouched down behind one of the first-floor valet parked cars until he disappeared into the stairwell. I decided to use the inclines.

I made it to the second level but coming in from a different angle turned me around. Not seeing my car right away, I got confused.

I didn't know if I was facing north or south.

I spotted my Malibu about the same time the man coming out of the stairwell spotted me. He was between me and my car. When he reached into his coat for something, I ran. I knew I'd made a wise choice to run when I could hear him running as well, his feet heavily hitting the concrete.

Leaving no doubt as to my impending doom, I crouched low and ran in crazy directions around the cars, becoming even more confused and disoriented. The pounding of his feet had stopped and was no longer a drum beat to my ears.

I didn't know if I had gotten away from my stalker or if he was nearby.

When something clanged close by and echoed off the parking garage walls a million times, I ran to a nearby support pillar hoping to hide behind it.

In the dark, I ran straight into someone's arms.

A hand clamped over my mouth, keeping the scream inside me. My arms were pinned to my sides in a death grip by my attacker's other muscular arm. He had no problem dragging me behind the support structure he'd been hiding behind.

He whispered, "Shh. Don't make a sound."

He had to be kidding. I couldn't make a sound with his hand over my mouth. His voice sounded familiar, but I couldn't make out his face in the shadows surrounding us. When I smelled cinnamon and liquorish, I relaxed against him. Fear drained from my body—like air leaking out of a punctured tire.

When he spoke quietly into my ear, "It's all right. It's me." My fear subsided some more.

"I saw that guy follow you in here. I think he's been casing the place where you work hoping to catch you alone."

"How do you know that?" I whispered to Frank.

"It's what I do."

"Oh."

"He'll give up when he doesn't find you right away. When he does give up, you need to get in your vehicle, lock the doors and head straight home. Run every red light if you have to. Have Gordon set the house alarms and keep watch tonight."

"Gordon is in Nepal."

"Shit. Then you need to go stay at your sister's place."

"Martin is out on bail staying with her."

"Double shit."

I winced and tensed.

"Sorry," he said understanding my aversion to swearing. "Is Keiko still employed by you?"

"No. She lives with Mandy now."

Frank had a gun in one hand. His other hand pressed an earbud into his ear. I didn't like the situation at all. We were whispering, but I felt we were being extremely talkative for two people who were supposed to be hiding.

"I'll be okay. What are the odds this guy knows where I live?" I tried to sound brave, but there was a little hitch in my voice that I hoped was too quiet for Frank to notice.

"If you've been getting threatening phone calls at night, he probably knows where you live."

"How do you know about the phone calls?" I said a little too loudly.

"Shhh…" He whispered into my ear. "It's…"

"What I do." I finished for him, making sure only he could hear that. "Yeah, right. Speaking of what you do, isn't being here with me going to blow your cover?"

"No. No one saw me." He pushed the ear bud back against his ear again.

"How can you be sure no one saw you?"

"It's what I do."

His eyes never stopped scanning the area around us, but he kept me hugged tightly to his side behind the pillar while he ducked his head out occasionally, waiting for signs my stalker had left.

That close Frank not only smelled of liquorish and

cinnamon, but of man sweat and dirt, too. His hair was reverting to dreadlocks. His beard was thick and long. I longed to be able to kiss him, but not with those teeth. I couldn't tell for sure in the dark but I though one of his front teeth was missing. There was a dark spot where a tooth should have been, or maybe it was just stuck liquorish.

Instead of my attacker-to-be leaving, Frank said that with his ear amplifier he could hear the faint echo of muted steps as the guy continued to walk around the opposite end of the parking structure floor. Then my stalker turned and even unaided I could hear he was closer to our spot with each step.

Frank's body became a tightly coiled spring, ready to pounce. I remained jello and shook so much I feared the stalker would be able to hear my fear echoing off the walls.

After what seemed like forever, we heard heavy footsteps grow distant, a stairwell door opened and slammed closed.

All was quiet.

Frank whispered into my ear. "He's not gone away. He's still out there on this level, baiting you. Making you think he's left so you'll come out in the open. He doesn't know I'm here. I'm going to take him on, distract him so you can get to your car. Once you're inside, get out of here and do everything I told you earlier."

I didn't ask how he knew my hunter was still out there looking for me. I had a feeling it was one of the things Frank did and did well. Hunting. Luring his prey. As for me, I guess there's always room for Jello.

CHAPTER 28

Frank ran to a spot behind an SUV, stretched out his arms in front of him, braced and leveled his gun at a spot across the floor yelling out to me, "Go, now!"

I ran as fast as I could to my vehicle. I managed to get the door opened and the key in the ignition, despite the sound of gunfire all around me.

My car roared to life.

I floored the gas pedal. Tires squealed and rubber burned. I flew out of the parking structure, hitting the street at 40 mph and bounding around the corner on two wheels.

Gunshots continued to punctuate the night air behind me.

I did as instructed, and drove straight home, cursing Mr. Twerk for my lack of a working cell phone. I prayed the whole way to my house that Frank would be safe.

Once home inside my garage, I stayed locked tight in my car until the garage door boomed down securely. I slumped in my car seat, drained.

Pressing my forehead against the steering wheel, I pleaded with God for Frank's life. I even promised I'd stop having naughty dreams about Frank if only God would keep him alive.

Then I ran into the kitchen. Doubled over at the sink and

puked.

I wiped my mouth on a cold, wet, soapy dishcloth, sank down to the floor and began to cry. Sobbing wracked my body for several minutes. I'd never felt so frightened and alone. Well, except for the time in the laundromat with two hired killers after me.

I didn't know if Frank was dead or alive. I prayed he hadn't taken a bullet meant for me, but I had no way to find out. I was physically sick with dread. All but paralyzed.

I picked up my house phone and listened for the dial tone. I began to push in the 9-1-1 but then remembered what the operator had told me the last time I'd called 9-1-1. If the event was over, it was no longer urgent. I wasn't sure calling the police would help Frank when someone must have already heard those shots and reported them.

The police were probably already at the parking garage, and I doubted they would tell me if they had found Frank dead. They would probably call Frank's next of kin if they had found his body.

Being undercover, did he even have identification on him that could lead to a next of kin?

I couldn't stand the horrible thoughts that pierced my heart every few seconds. I had to find out what was going on, but couldn't figure out how.

How could I help Frank? Who could help me to help Frank?

Janey's phone went directly to voicemail, as did the Chilton Detective Agency's. Agent Steven's phone message advised me he was out for the holidays and to call back during business hours.

The tension of not knowing what to do was driving me crazy. It was worse than hearing nails scrape on a chalkboard.

No. It wasn't worse. Another ripple of fear ripped through me as I listened to the sound of wood splintering.

Then I remembered that Mr. M had been in the laundry room all day. I opened the laundry room door. He yipped and snapped at me as he ran past me to the back door of the kitchen where he yipped in running circles, impatient to be let out.

I was too frightened of his being dog napped and me being killed to go out with him, so I pulled out a big bath towel from the clean linen Keiko had stacked, and spread it out the kitchen floor in front of the back door.

"Sorry, little man. This is the best I can do tonight."

He obediently used the makeshift toilet, then went back to sit in front of his already full water dish in the kitchen.

He looked up at me expectantly, head cocked to one side. He looked so darn cute that even with my worry over Frank, I relented. I dumped the warm water and melted ice cubes out of his dish and pulled a cold mineral water from the frig. I took a few long swallows from the bottle for myself before I filled his water bowl.

The rhythm of him lapping up the water drew my mind back to Mr. Flynn's death by drowning. His threats for more money had made him a business liability.

I wondered if my bosses had learned that I was on to them and their illegal betting scheme. If I was a business liability, they could be the ones who sent the man to the garage to take care of me.

If not that, then I was drawing a blank as to who could be stalking me now. Martin was being monitored by an electronic tether that should have ensured he stayed in the apartment with Mandy, but that wasn't always effective as his fingerprints in the guest room attested. It couldn't be anyone from my past. Jorgji's murdering wife was in prison along with the men involved in the drug dealing and money laundering business.

Who did that leave?

Rocko. Unless Garrett was not all he claimed to be.

If Garrett was a closet writer, he was a dismal failure. I'd yet to see even one solid article from him. My aunt's Tweedle Dumb and Tweedle Dee agent and publisher, who had hounded me mercilessly for her unfinished manuscripts, had been silent and unheard from as of late. They could have switched tactics and decided to eliminate me in hopes of getting the manuscripts after my death.

I couldn't stand not knowing what was happening with Frank back at the parking garage. I kept wondering how I could be of help. I picked up the phone to dial 911 but then set it back down. Whatever had played out in that parking garage had to have been over before I even hit my remote opener to enter my garage. I redialed Janey and Agent Stevens and left messages for them to call right away.

Mr. M finished off the water then sauntered over to check the contents of his food bowl. There were a few kibbles left over from this morning. He could eat those while I mulled things over in my mind.

I kept ignoring his yipping, so he nudged the bowl with his nose—hard. It skittered a ways across the floor and hit me in the foot. Kibble flying.

"That's enough out of you, Mr. Fussy," I told him, picking up the kibble. The floor was still covered in spilled cookie flour I'd never cleaned up after my cookie baking fiasco. Something about cleaning dirty floors with bleach tickled at my mind; then it flew away again.

I opened a can of gourmet dog food and watched Mr. M take delicate little nibbles while I relived the harrowing events of the evening over and over.

Was the man in the parking garage the one who phoned me last night and not Martin? Frank said the man had been watching me. Waiting to get me alone.

I bit my nails down to nubs, unable to eat a bite of anything else. When exhaustion overtook me, I double checked all the house locks and sat back down on the kitchen floor cradling my phone in case Janey or Agent Stevens called me back.

Mr. M, sated on designer food and water, went back to the folded comforter in the laundry room, and a short while later I heard him snore louder than a little dog should be able to accomplish.

It was then I heard the sound of the lock turning on the

kitchen door. I immediately thought my stalker had killed Frank and was coming in to get me.

I was pumped up on fear and adrenalin. Rather than try to fight it, I gave in to my anger. I knew whoever was entering my house most probably had just taken Frank's life in place of mine, and I wasn't going to let them get away with it.

I reached in the cupboard behind me scrambling for a purchase, anything to use as a weapon on the killer. I gripped the first item in the cupboard that seemed solid enough to use to bludgeon someone with.

I stood, ready to face my attacker.

I swung my makeshift weapon as the grime ball came through the door.

He easily ducked away from my swing, swirled me around, and flung my weapon away from me.

Time froze. Then restarted.

"You were going to WOK me?" he asked, picking up the metal pan from where it had clattered to the floor.

I gave my heart a few beats to calm down before I let it race again as I ran into Frank's embrace.

He hugged me to him and then stepped back. He picked up my hand, turned it over, and dropped my door key into my palm. "Don't ever hide your spare key outside. Thieves look under the doormat the first thing."

"It wasn't under the mat. It was under the loose step at the bottom of the stairs," I said, burying my face into his filthy shirt while he hugged me back to him.

"That's the second place they'd look." He was squeezing me so tightly I felt one of my ribs might crack under the pressure, but it was a good feeling.

Frank checked all the doors and windows. Finding them all secure, he sat down at the kitchen table while I made him some hot coffee or attempted to. I scooped coffee grounds into the basket filter, poured water in the back, flipped the red toggle on, and set the carafe under the resulting stream—just like I'd seen Keiko do.

"Why is it so damn cold in here?" Frank asked wrapping

his hands around the steaming mug of blackish-brown sludge—so thick it could be eaten like pudding. He added a lot of cream and sugar.

Not wanting him to know I hadn't been able to pay the gas bill, I racked my brain for a plausible explanation for my heat being turned off and came up with a partial fabrication. "The furnace isn't working. I'll have the heat back on before the snow falls."

"God, I was so worried about you," he told me, standing to hug me to him again.

"I was so worried about you, too. I heard all that gunfire." I said stroking his face or the parts of it I could get to that weren't covered with beard. "I'm so glad you weren't hurt."

I felt him loosen his grip, and his hands came up to take hold my shoulders as he looked steadily into my eyes. "Never worry about me. I can take care of myself. I'm trained to take care of myself. When he got me pinned down so I couldn't move from where I was; I used a classic shooting maneuver and sprayed the area where he was with bullets. I think one of my bullets tore up his left shoulder. There was a lot of blood sprayed on the one wall, but he got away. When a dark SUV came tearing out of the ramp heading in the same direction as you, I figured if he wasn't hurt too badly, he was headed here to finish the job."

"To kill me?" I whispered.

"No. No. He could have done that any time over the last few days. From the way he was shooting, he was a good enough shot to pick you off at 50 yards even in the dark, but instead he just waited and watched. I don't think killing you was his plan. He was biding his time, waiting for you to be alone."

Frank sneered. "The only positive thing about your blondie boyfriend dogging your heels like a love sick puppy was he stuck close to you like gum on a shoe, so you were never alone—until tonight."

"He's not my boyfriend," I said.

Frank smiled, sat down, pulled me down into his lap,

kissed me lightly, and began nuzzling my neck.

"That's a good thing for him," Frank said.

I stood up, not wanting to be distracted. "If the shooter wasn't planning on killing me than you think he was out to..." My mind conjured up all sorts of evil images.

"Yeah. You either have something he wants or he wants you."

Fear punched my gut and my legs buckled. Frank swept me up into his arms and carried me to the sofa where he took the Amish marriage quilt from the back and wrapped me in it. He pulled me to him again, stroking my hair. I felt him lightly kiss the top of my head.

"It's all right. I'm staying here tonight. I've gotten a hold of my new handler and asked to have all the hospitals, and urgent care locations monitored. Anyone around here coming in with gunshot wounds to the left shoulder will be arrested and questioned."

"Handler?" I was uncertain just what a handler did.

"He's my new contact with the Homeland Security main office. He passes along what I learn as a result of my investigation to the rest of the team assigned to this case, and he works to keep me safe. The last handler they gave me caused me some grief. I made the mistake of giving him access to monitor my e-mails for me so I wouldn't miss any correspondence from my moles. He didn't see fit to keep me updated on my private correspondence."

"He was handling your e-mail?" That explained a lot.

"Yeah. I would have had you pulled out of there the minute I realized you were working for Boggs and Rockford, but I wasn't getting your e-mails and unfortunately, my work colleague felt the threat to the public overrode concerns for your safety. Since he was working my correspondence, I didn't know he'd misrepresented himself as me to get you to give insider information on Boggs and Rockford. I only just found out that you were working there when I got your note on the burger wrapper and was able to put it all together.

"My handler and I had a disagreement, but I convinced

him your safety was a priority. Whatever Boggs and Rockford are planning is too close to fruition for you to continue to work there. The new handler is working on a way to get you pulled out of there tomorrow without Boggs and Rockford catching on that we're on to them."

I sank against Frank's chest; he hadn't sent those impersonal e-mails. My relief was so sweet I forgot to shiver with the cold. Then when he began questioning me about my employers and their habits, I got the shakes again at the thought of them killing Mr. Flynn.

I told Frank everything I had learned about Mr. Flynn, Rocko, Randy, Mr. Pilfer, the fight, the dirt, the plywood, the deliveries of equipment and supplies that indicated they were on the up and up, but then I had to admit, "I knew they were up to no good. I just wasn't able to figure out what it was. I thought it was gambling, but not all of it added up. Then when I got that e-mail I thought was from you asking me to tell you/them what I knew about the back room and the deliveries…"

When I finished the story I yawned, put my head down on Frank's shoulder, and stretched my legs out on the sofa. Frank stretched out beside me and held me close. "I need to get you to bed," he said brushing my hair out of my half-closed eyes.

"I thought you'd never say that." I gave him a kiss that turned into a yawn—from lack of sleep.

He didn't kiss me back. Puzzled, I tried to kiss him again. His lips were closed tight and unyielding. I lost some of my sleepiness.

"What's the matter? Don't you want me?" I snuggled in a little closer to him, rubbing my body against his in what I had hoped was a seductive manner, but it was a weak, tired effort. The warmth coming from his body was making me sleepy again. I couldn't hold my eyes open.

"I want you, but not like this. I want our first time to be glorious, not rushed or distracted by the threat of death. I also want you awake and for us both to be naked, which I can tell

you, would put a damper on things if our shooter shows up."
Then he added, "I also want a shower first."

I snuggled in a little closer to Frank and found it was
obvious he wanted me. In a perverse way, I was pleased.
Pleased, tired, and safe.

My eyes completely closed and I relaxed in his arms
enough to fall into a deep sleep for the first time in several
nights.

***

Frank had his handler checking his e-mails while he
worked to learn what he could about the duo he feared were
up to something on a big scale. Frank had watched Genie exit
the McClintock office building later, and later every night, not
realizing she was working for the men he was investigating.
Now, seeing her close up, the dark circles under her eyes and
feeling how thin she'd become, he hated grilling her like that
about her employers when she needed sleep, but he was here
in Chicago to find out what Rockford and his buddies were
planning, and she had insider knowledge. That was something
his handler had been right about, but Frank would never have
agreed to put a civilian in that kind of danger, let alone the
woman he loved.

When she'd relaxed against him, he'd held her until her
breathing became deep and regular. Once he was sure he
wouldn't wake her, he slipped off the sofa, rechecked the
house and sat in a chair across the room, watching her sleep.
He had his gun out, the sound amplifier in his ear so he could
stay attuned to any noises he might pick up to signal her
assailant had found her house.

He had made up his mind to stay the night to protect her,
but what about all the other nights? He was already violating
FBI undercover protocol being there. He couldn't risk coming
back, but he didn't want her staying in this house alone. She
was so small and fragile, even more so now that she was on
her own. How could he leave her and go back to the streets to

finish the job he'd started knowing there was someone out there wanting to harm her?

He heard a jingle off to his right and instinctively drew his gun and aimed it the mop running towards the sofa, ready to fire.

Frank lowered his Glock. It was only her dog.

Mr. M jumped up to a corner of the sofa and lay down at Genie's feet. Resting his head on his outstretched paws, he eyed Frank with pleading eyes. Frank tucked the gun back into his belt. Mr. M closed his eyes and went to sleep.

Frank was partially dozing when he felt his shirt pocket vibrate. It was the case agent. Frank went on full alert; standing, he left the living room so as not to awaken Genie.

"What'd you find out?"

"A guy came into St. Mary's about 30 minutes ago with a shattered scapula and broken clavicle saying he fell down his stairs. The doctor found bullet fragments in the wound. Your guy's Russian. No papers. No passport. Something's screwy here. The boss wants to handle this interrogation himself."

"Ask him if he can hold off until I get there. I want to be in the observation room, behind the mirror, assisting."

"You're the lead on this case now. It's your call."

***

Just before he left, Frank handed me a small, snub-nosed revolver he had pulled from his boot and told me to keep it with me for the night. I wanted Frank to be what stayed with me for the night, to tuck me into bed and lie beside me, but I had to settle with him reassuring me my stalker was in custody. Frank stood outside the back door to ensure I locked it and shoved a chair up under the doorknob. I shoved the gun under my bed in one of my dog-mangled slippers.

Sometime after four in the morning, I sat bolt upright in my bed. Something had startled me awake. I just didn't know what it was. I sat there trying to calm my rapid breathing and pounding heart.

217

My hearing was on overdrive, trying to pick up any strange, unfamiliar sound in the house, trying to determine what had awoken me. Mr. M whined in his little carrier beside the bed where I had caged him for the night.

Was it him who woke me for some reason?

I groped around in the darkened room for his carrier. The hall light showed at the crack under my bedroom door.

I hadn't left that light on.

Mr. M gave another pitiful low whimper when I found the latch to his case and opened it. He made a beeline out, leaped up onto my bed and bounded into my arms. His little body quivered while I stroked his fur to reassure him, surprised to find him so soft and cuddly.

When I heard a floorboard creak in the hall outside my bedroom door, I knew someone had gained entrance into the house. Mr. M burrowed under the covers while I hunted around for something other than that gun to use as a weapon.

I hadn't wanted to let Frank know I had never fired a gun. I had a fear of them. I vowed that gun was not going to come out from its spot under the bed—ever.

The bedside lamp was a better makeshift weapon. I gripped its base with both hands and headed towards the light shining under the door. I stopped with my ear to the door, listening. Hearing no noise, I turned the knob as quietly as I could and opened the door a sliver to peer out.

Seeing no one about, I slipped noiselessly out into the brightly lit hallway to check things out. My nightgown billowed around me from the night air coming in from the open window at the end of the hall. I shivered from the chilled air hitting my bare legs and naked feet.

A scraping, clattering noise came from the vicinity of the bathroom. It was the sound the water pipes always made when they were turned off. At least my intruder was a clean one.

Knowing I had only minutes to overtake the villain before he overtook me, I welded the lamp one handed, put my hand on the bathroom doorknob and yanked hard. The door came partially open before I felt it pulled back from the other side.

Whoever was in there had probably escaped Frank in the parking garage and was now there to get me. I wasn't going easily. I wrenched on the door with all my might, fueled by adrenaline.

The door flung open wide.

I screamed.

Keiko screamed louder.

Keiko!

I dropped the lamp and threw my arms around her red and white pajama-clad body.

"What are you doing back?" I asked her.

She made a huge frowny face at the wooden lamp lying on the floor but hugged me just as tightly as I hugged her.

"That Man-D woman crazy," she told me when things had settled down, and we had both stopped screaming. "I stay with you. Too much bull spit there."

I laughed until my sides hurt, but I also felt the need to cry from relief. If my intruder was Keiko, that meant that Frank probably did have the right man in custody. I hoped and prayed that was true.

When I told Keiko the men I had been working for were criminals planning a catastrophe, but no one had been able to figure out what the catastrophe will be yet, her eyes got big.

"You spy, Missy Imogreen? Like father? Only for good guys?"

I assured her it was nothing like that for me, but a little seed had started to take root in my mind. *If I could save a city, could that one good dead cancel out the bad actions of my father?*

***

Frank was still steamed about Genie being placed in danger for the sake of a few investigative pictures, so it was a good thing his handler was not in the Chicago FBI headquarters when Frank got there. He entered via the garage and came up the service elevator to avoid running into anyone who might question his strange appearance in the building at night.

The minute he entered the observation room and saw the guy through the one-way mirror, Frank recognized him as the guy who'd been stalking Genie. His left shoulder was bandaged, his left arm in a sling.

Frank grabbed the microphone to the side of the observation window, clicked it on and spoke into it.

"That's the perp."

The message went to the earpiece of the man sitting across the table from the perpetrator. The interrogator's facial expression didn't change, but he picked up the pen sitting in front of him. The signal that he'd heard Frank.

"What happened to your shoulder?" the interrogator asked.

"I fall. Down stairs." The accent was unmistakably Russian.

"That's a lot of damage for a fall down the stairs."

"Long stairs." The man continued a stony stare at the agent.

Frank clicked on the microphone again and said, "His blood has to be all over that parking garage wall."

"What would you say if I told you we can get your DNA from the blood in the parking garage where we think you were last night?"

There was a slight flicker of the eyes. "I say you lie."

"Someone's lying here for sure," Frank said into the microphone. "Ask him why he was after Imogene Warren."

The interrogator picked up the pen from the table again and dropped it, a signal he heard, but did not appreciate Frank's suggestion.

"I've seen him scout out the area where she works and follow her to the parking garage for the past three nights," Frank hissed into the microphone. He wanted to walk into the room and pound the answers out of the man, but instead got up and walked around, rubbing his neck to cool his anger over the slowness of the interview.

"You've been seen casing the McClintock building. What's your interest in that building and the business section of downtown Chicago?" the interviewer asked.

"Is this not a free country?" The smirk on the man's face caused even his interviewer to clench the pen in his fist. After seeing the micro smile that turned the corners of the man's mouth up a little, the interviewer loosened his grip on the pen, set it down and gave it a twirl so it spun around on the table in front of him. It was a signal to Frank it was his turn to provide questions to the suspect.

***

I was startled when my cell phone rang. I hadn't expected Mr. Twerk to be so speedy at getting the service reinstated.

It was Frank calling me from the FBI headquarters.

"You okay?"

"Yeah. I'm doing fine. How are you doing?"

"Better now that you're out of that building, and your stalker has been caught. I want you to promise me you won't return to that job."

"But I can get you inside information," I pointed out.

"We'll find some other way to get that. It's not worth risking your life. Promise me you won't go back to work."

"I promise I won't go back there to work."

"Good."

Despite Frank's wanting me to abandon my job, I went back to the magazine office early the next morning with my USB bracelet. I wasn't going to go there to work; I was going there to spy. I hoped that tiny lie wouldn't drive a wedge between Frank and me when he discovered it.

With all the late nights Rocko, Randy and Mr. Pilfer had been working, I knew I'd have the place to myself if I could get there early enough. I could get into the computer system, get some info as to what they were up to, and get out of there before anyone was the wiser.

I also knew neither Rocko or Mr. Pilfer thought me to be anything other than a silly girl who crocheted. Neither of them had been after me last night. My assailant was tall, thin and according to Frank, Russian.

I used the McClintock's side door to get in earlier than usual and to avoid contact with Frank. I didn't want to give him a chance to stop me. If I was wrong about them robbing the jewelry store and Frank was right about them planning to bomb the city, a lot of innocent people's lives were at risk. I took Mr. M with me so I wouldn't be alone in the building so early in the morning.

I was surprised to see Rē already at the reception desk as I walked past. I had taken my raincoat off at the building entrance and covered the carrier with it to keep Mr. M quiet. Mr. M whined so loud when I passed the reception desk, I had to get Rē to pet him to shut him up.

"You're getting an early jump on the day," she said to Mr. M.

"Yeah and so are you," I said.

"Only because the building is closing early on account of it being Thanksgiving tomorrow. All the businesses in this area will be closed until Monday. Most of the businesses in this building have closed already."

"Oh." I hadn't wanted to think about Thanksgiving. With my aunt dead, the situation with my father, and Mandy being with Martin, I had thought Thanksgiving would be a downer, but now that Keiko was back, Thanksgiving sounded like fun.

When I got down to our office, the door lock to the back room was still flipped to the open spot, so I was able to open the door to Mr. Pilfer's office and get on to his computer with no trouble. He didn't have anything password protected. That could be because there was almost nothing of interest on his computer. I loaded as many of the files as I thought important on my USB bracelet and then got ready to leave. I decided to forego taking additional pictures of the back room.

Mr. M, however, had other ideas. He ran into the back work area before I could stop him. *Darn that dog.* So much for never going into their work area again.

It was dark and desolate in the back room when I pushed the door open wider. My fingers trailed along the wall.

Why couldn't I ever find that light switch?

I fumbled more than a pimple faced 17-year-old boy on a date with the high school prom queen. No switch. No light. I turned my phone flashlight app on so its weak light would allow me to me advance slowly into the gloom.

"Here, boy. Here, boy." I croaked.

The light illuminated only a few feet in front of me. I advanced past the crates of bleach and a few cardboard boxes covered in plastic and duct tape. The smell of bleach was stronger than ever.

I croaked a little louder. "Mr. Mister." I pulled a beef stick from my purse, and while it wasn't as aromatic as a sausage, I hoped the smell was strong enough for his K-9 nose to sense it over the smell of the bleach and get him to come to me.

I heard a whimper coming from beyond a row of boxes in the far corner. He was as far into the room as he could get and deeper in the gloom than I cared to travel.

I called again, "Here, boy. Here, boy."

He whimpered back in response.

It was not like him to turn down a treat.

I couldn't bear the thought of that puffy dog being caught on a piece of machinery or stuck in a bucket of printer's ink, so I shined my light to the floor. The light from my phone was weak, barely illuminating a small swath in front of me. The floor was littered with debris and tools. I had to shuffle walk to get through the mess on the floor without tripping. I kept on going hoping I was on a direct path to the whimpers, hoping my uncharged cell phone battery wouldn't give out and leave me stranded in the dark.

When two beady black eyes reflected red in the weakening light from my phone, relief ran through me. I ran forward to pick Mr. M up. I was almost to him when I stepped in something sticky. I moved my phone light to the floor and saw I'd stepped into what appeared to be a maroon puddle of paint.

The puddle extended all the way to Mr. Pilfer's unseeing, dead eyes and his bashed in head.

My phone light cut out. A strangled scream escaped me before I was able to stifle it.

I shook the phone and a weak light issued forth as I knelt down to examine the body that lay face down, sprawled out on the floor, arms and legs at unnatural angles, head and neck off to one side. The white hair encircling the head like a halo was stained red with a trail streaming down the side to the floor.

Poor Mr. Pilfer.

I felt something hit my legs with force. The light I held fell to the floor. As it skittered away from me, it gave up the glow, and I was plunged into darkness again. I managed to find the phone and switch the light back on. It gave only a faint glow, the battery almost dead.

Noise from the maintenance room had me instinctively grabbing up Mr. M as I headed back towards the reception room door. I ran, headless of the obstacles in my way and I stumbled over a box. As I plunged headlong to the floor, I gave into the fall, rolling so Mr. M wasn't crushed under me. My phone skittered away from me again and the darkness re-swallowed us.

I felt around. All I could find were those little pieces of strange papers, stacked and bundled, where they lay scattered by my fall.

When I heard Rocko's voice from the maintenance room ask, "Is that you Randy?" I stayed down on all fours.

Crawling frantically towards the sliver of light under the reception room door, I hugged Mr. M to my chest. His little body trembled as I three-legged crab walked towards the dim glow.

In my terror, I kept crashing into things that clattered to

the floor. When I finally reach my desk, I grabbed the edge of the desk to stand. Of all the times I'd tried to find that red button and couldn't, now I didn't want to push it and did, inadvertently. I had summoned Rocko from the depths of his grave digging.

I glanced around the reception area hoping to find something to use for our defense. I wished I hadn't given up knitting, at least I'd have my needles to fend off a murderer.

I picked up the phone to dial 9-1-1. This was an emergency if ever there was one. I no sooner picked up the received when a beefy finger pressed down on the little pop-up button to obliterate the dial tone. To obliterate me.

Rocko took a firm hold on my wrist. He must have caught sight of me coming out from the back area. He threw the phone and it ripped from the wall.

Mr. M squirmed and whimpered in my free arm. He was struggling, his little teeth clacking together so fiercely I had to release him to keep from being bitten. He dropped down to the floor and ran out the office door as Randy walked in.

"Hey!" Randy yelled at Mr. M's retreating backside. "When did we get another one? Can I keep this one?"

"Forget about the dog," Rocko told him. "We have other concerns right now." His grip on my wrist tightened painfully.

I was pleased Mr. M was running as fast as his little legs could take him. At least he'd be safe if he could get as far as Rē's desk.

"What were you doing in the back?" Rocko asked me. I could feel his hot putrid breath blast my face.

"NNNNothing. I was just looking for white out. I'm all out." I glanced down at the blood stains smeared across my shirt from holding Mr. M to my chest. Rocko glanced down, and his grip tightened so much I feared he'd snap all the bones in my wrist.

"You're out all right." Rocko dragged me towards the open back room door.

"Help," I said trying to attract attention while I still was in the reception area with the outer door open. Except I couldn't find my voice; my shout came out like a whisper.

Rocko laughed. Randy followed Rocko into the backroom as he dragged me along. Rocko pressed a recessed button near the door, and the lights came on. The place was a mess with stacks of greenbacks everywhere from where I stumbled over and then crawled through the tipped over box of money.

That confirmed it for me. They were the dognappers, and this was their ransom money.

Rocko didn't respond to Randy's repeated questions of, "What you gonna do with her?"

When Rocko saw my phone near Mr. Pilfer's dead body, I didn't need to hear Rocko's response to know I was the next corpse on his list.

"I won't be telling anyone about this," I told him as he picked up my phone. It was still on and the privacy lock open. He slammed me into a nearby chair and tried to access the last calls I had placed before my service was shut off. I thought about all the calls I'd made to the FBI about my missing money and cringed. I attempted to get out of the chair, only to get slammed back by Rocko.

I don't know how much he saw before my phone gave up the ghost, the battery completely dead. Randy flinched when Rocko threw my cell against the wall and it shattered.

Rocko dragged me out of the chair and backhanded me across the face. I saw Randy's shocked face as stars glittered in my field of vision.

"Stay put or I'll have to knock you out," Rocko growled.

"What you doing with Miss Genie?" Randy screamed, advancing towards us.

***

Activity in the business section of downtown Chicago was winding down in anticipation of the Thanksgiving Holiday with only a few businesses operating on Wednesday. Frank was waiting to hear back from his handler on a way to get into the building's basement undetected. He was glad that he was able to warn Genie to stay way. When he got the call about the building entrances, he was disappointed to learn that the basement wasn't up to occupancy codes, the elevators and the one main stairwell bt the elevators were the only way in.

Frank was ordered to stand down until a plan of action had been decided upon. With most of the downtown business section closing, Homeland Security felt the threat of a bomb going off was unlikely at that time. They were planning a search warrant raid on Sunday, just before the businesses reopened.

Frank wasn't as sure that nothing would happen before Monday. Rockford didn't always play according to sane rules. Frank returned to the outside of the building and began walking around to stretch his legs and think on how to best approach Boggs and Rockford's operation. He walked around the corner just in time to see Genie and her dog enter the building through a side door.

His anger flared. She hadn't heeded his advice to stay away. *What did she hope to accomplish by going back? What was she thinking? Did she really think she could get in, get evidence and get out without getting caught*? Rocko had killed once and undoubtedly would do so again.

Frank wanted to follow her—just to be sure no one else did, but he decided to stay outside to wait for Rockford's arrival—unaware that all three men had spent the night in the tunnel under the building finishing up their plans for the "Grand Opening."

When Frank saw Genie's little white dog run out of the building minutes later, he felt this was his answer; he could get Genie away from there when she came out to get her dog.

As was his custom, the white fluff ran straight to Frank, who was surprised when Mr. Mister jumped into his arms at a full run with a force that knocked Frank's hat off his head and caused him to stumble backward.

"Thanks, little fella. Your running out has made it easier for me to get Genie out of there without blowing this investigation."

Mr. Mister began yip barking at Frank.

"Hey, settle down. She'll be out to get you in a sec and take you to your favorite flower pot, and then I'll make her take you home."

Mr. Mister wriggled free, leaving something wet and sticky on Frank's sleeve. Frank examined the red spot; it looked and felt like blood.

Mr. Mister continued his flight across the street. He passed the Federal Reserve Bank planters and disappeared around a bend, still running.

No Genie followed from the building.

Was the blood the dog's or Genie's?

There was no hesitation on Frank's part. Without thought to his assignment, his order to stand down or the possible implications to the investigation, Frank ran into the McClintock building to find Imogene.

CHAPTER 29

"Don't do this, Randy. Please," I begged him as his huge hand clasped my shaking wrists together.

"I have to do what Rocko says. Ma said so." He had a sorrowful look to his eyes, and his hands were shaking almost as much as mine. "I don't want to. I got to."

His face scrunched up as he looked around the office area. "I don't got anymore rope up here." Then his face smoothed back out and he pulled one of the skeins of yarn out of my bag. He began winding it around and around my wrists.

I pulled at some unknown logic inside my head. "Remember what Bobby the Puppet says in his story books? Find a way to do what is right. There is always a way to do what is right. Is it right to kill me?"

"No. It's not, but Rocko says I gotta take care of you." He started winding the yarn around my ankles. Individual yarn strands might be easily broken, but not when there are several layers wrapped dozens of times. I knew it was hopeless to struggle against that much yarn.

When he picked me up and slung me over his shoulder, I tried to fight him by pounding on his back with my bound hands. It was no use. My hands and feet were bound in 4-ply yarn that was cutting into my flesh as I struggled.

I was going to be the next Lake Michigan drowning article

in the paper.

I began to cry because I knew I'd never see Frank, Gordon, my sister, or Keiko again.

"Don't cry," Randy said to me setting me down on my chair that he placed in the storage closet for me to sit on.

"You can twirl in your chair in here. I'm not going to put you in the tunnel like that man that was mean to the little dog he had in the box. Rocko said it's not like I really kilt that man. It was just when I got back to cut him loose he was dead from the water."

"You killed Mr. Flynn?"

"No," Randy shouted at me. "When you drowneded it's not like a real death; you turn into a merman if you're a boy or mermaid if you're a girl."

Randy took his handkerchief out of his pocket and wiped it on his pants.

"Is that what happened to the man with the tattoo on his face? He drowned because you put him in the water?"

"I didn't put him in the water. The water got to him later. That man went to swim with the fishes like Mr. Boggs said. I'll bet he's happy now. It's fun to swim." The handkerchief was tied around my mouth, and I start to gag from the smell of dirt and sweat and whatever else was on his handkerchief.

"Would you like to be a mermaid?" Randy asked me.

He couldn't hear my muffled cries of 'no' through the gag, so I vigorously shook my head no. He checked the knot at the back of my head and tied it a little tighter.

"I got to get rid of you like Rocko says, 'Ceptin I can't put you down there. You're afraid of water. The rainwater will fill the tunnel soon. Did you know that tunnel keeps the streets from flooding?" Randy said, seemingly proud that he knew how the deep tunnel worked.

"My brother worked in that tunnel. He knows lots of stuff about it. He says the tunnel will make us rich."

I watched as Randy opened my bag and removed the other skein of yarn I'd been using to make the blanket double thick.

He began winding me to the chair using the second skein. My breathing was labored, and every breath brought me the smell and taste of dirt. I wished I'd told him I was afraid of dirty handkerchiefs.

He stepped back to survey his handy work. "There. Now I've taken care of you just like Rocko said. And you cain't squeal to the police so he won't kilt you like he did Mr. Boggs.

"Now Rocko says I gotta go help him move the boxes, 'cause Boggs cain't do it now. And I gotta do what Rocko says. My momma said so."

***

Once inside the building, Frank patted the inner pocket on his coat to make sure his Glock was still there. He was dressed in a neoprene vest under his jacket and the scarf Genie made him was under his shirt to help shield him from the cold and the rain, but it was his Glock that gave him the greatest feeling of protection while living on the streets.

Like before, the pink haired girl immediately recognized his description of Imogene. "You've asked about the girl who sneaks the dog in the building before, and I told you to leave her alone."

"I have to find her. It's a matter of life or death. Do you know what office she works in?"

"Sure, but I ain't going to tell you. I saw what you did to her the other day."

Frank wanted to kick his handler's teeth in for lying to him about what Imogene was doing in the McClintock Office building. He had to get to Imogene but didn't know where in the building she was. If Frank weren't undercover he'd have his badge and some credibility, would be able to prove he was more than just a street bum looking to find a nice lady with a dog.

What would convince this girl to tell him where Imogene is?

"She happens to be a girl I was dating a while back. She

didn't recognize me since I've been down on my luck. She made me this scarf." Frank pulled out the end of the scarf that Genie made him.

"Hey!" Recognition lit Rē's eyes. "She's got a little piece of knitting just like that. I've seen her rub it up to her cheek when no one's looking."

Frank exhaled. He was finally getting somewhere. "It's very important that I find her. I think she might be in danger."

"Well... the building is supposed to be closing early today, but since I saw her come in and since she works in an office that accepts customers, it'd probably be okay if I told ya where she works."

***

Try as I might I couldn't get my heart to slow its tripping beat. I was gagging on my gag, trying not to throw up. That would probably have caused me to choke. I couldn't let myself cry either. Crying always gave me a stuffy nose. I couldn't breathe well with a gag and a stuffy nose.

I had to do my best to remain calm and wait for someone to rescue me. My therapist's advice for staying calm is to find your happy place; go to a time when you were happy and focus on that, so I concentrated on a particularly memorable spaghetti dinner with Frank. I could taste the sauce, feel the heat of the blush that came over me as he told me what he would like to do for desert.

My memories of Frank were so real I thought I could hear his voice calling to me.

"Genie. Genie where are you?"

It was not a memory; he was in the reception area. He'd come to rescue me.

I'm in here. In the closet.

I tried to stand, to shout, to warn him. Rocko and Randy were moving the boxes out of the back room into the tunnel. They would hear him call out for me and come back.

No. No. Go away.

232

Too late. I heard Randy say in his childlike singsong voice. "Are you here to find the pretty lady that brings me the Bobby the Puppet Boy stories?"

I heard Frank say, "Yes. Is she here?"

"She's back here."

Tears stung my eyes as I heard a heavy "whump" and someone fall to the floor. I had a sinking feeling the fallee was Frank. When no one came to let me out of the closet, I knew it had been Frank.

If I'd had any sense, I would have slipped that gun Frank gave me out of my slipper and learned how to use it. If I had that gun maybe Frank wouldn't be in knocked out cold with me tied to a chair, helpless in the closet.

Then I got a hold of my pity and flung it away. I needed to get free of that chair, that closet and find a way to help Frank—with or without a gun.

I scooted my chair over to the shelving units to find something to help get me free of my bonds. Spray cans and paper towels aren't much help against a dirty gag and yarn bindings.

There was a part of the shelf that hadn't been screwed together properly so a bit of the metal shelf stuck out several inches. I thought it might be sharp, but it was too high above my shoulders to be of much bond cutting help.

I tried to stand up and succeeded in standing with the chair wrapped to my backside, but I still couldn't get my wrists up to the sticky-out part of the shelf.

I rested my head against the shelf and began to cry when I heard Rocko's voice boom from Mr. Pilfer's office saying, "Good job, knocking him out, Randy. We're through with moving the boxes so take the rope off the dolly and tie him up with that before he comes to. We'll put him in the tunnel and let the water take care of him—like Flynn."

"You want him to be a merman, too?" Randy asked.

"Sure kid. Now hurry up. With Boggs out of the way, we need to finish up and get through the tunnel before the bulkheads open up and that tunnel floods with water again."

I jerked my head back up at the thought of Frank in a tunnel filling with water—like Flynn. My gag caught on the shelf part that jutted out. I moved my head up and down and managed to get the gag pulled off.

I breathed a deep breath, grateful that God and fate were on my side, even if fate wasn't backing me up one hundred percent.

I had the gag off, but I couldn't yell. I had no idea of where Randy and Rocko were. I thought of Mr. M and hoped he and his little sharp teeth had gotten out of harm's way.

Sharp teeth. I wished I'd had some. Then I remembered something I used to do when I was in a hurry to break my yarn so I could finish off a project.

The yarn I was tied up in was four-ply strong, but each ply could be bitten through separately if pulled apart from the other plys. I'd easily done that many times when I was too lazy to search for my scissors.

I strived with everything I had to get my hands to my mouth.

I charged into the maintenance room with a can of ant spray prepared to take on an army to save Frank. I was too late. They were all gone from there by the time I'd gotten free.

The plywood was off to the side of the room. In their haste, Rocko and Randy hadn't bothered to slide it back over the hole that lead down into the tunnel.

That hand-dug access to the tunnel was where the office dirt I'd dealt with came from. It was also the source of the ghostly "Ring around the Rosie" singing I'd heard as Randy dug at the dirt.

I stared down into the hole lit with an eerie glow from the emergency lights that were fastened along the length of the chain and steel-runged ladder.

It looked a long way down.

Had Frank survived them pushing him down to the

tunnel?

There was only one way to find out. I put one foot on the top metal rung, reached down and gripped the cold chain link sides of the ladder and closed my eyes against the dizziness that threatened to overwhelm me.

Ten steps down, the ladder rotated around a small metal platform and took up again on the other side. It went like that for several yards before I reached the bottom and could keep my eyes open.

I found Frank unconscious, slumped against the curve of the tunnel, not far from the ladder. He'd been tied to a horizontal pipe that ran up the side of the tunnel and then veered off laterally into the darkness to the left.

Water swirled in and had begun to fill the part of the tunnel where we were.

"Frank," I shouted, slapping his face trying to get him fully awake.

He moaned and started to come to as the cold water that began to fill the tunnel hit his legs. He struggled to stand. I helped him up as the ropes slid up the pipe they were fastened to.

"Genie. You're alive." There was distinct pleasure in his voice.

"Obviously," I said as I went behind him to try and figure out how to untie the ropes that bound his hands to the pipe. The ropes were super thick. My teeth weren't going to work this time.

The water continued to rise as I struggled to loosen the knots that held Frank's hands fast to the piping. The water was lapping at my knees as I broke every fingernail grabbing and pulling at the rope. It didn't loosen even a fraction. The rope was too thick and tied too tight for me to work it loose with just my hands.

A rat swam by in the dim glow of the tap light. I choked on bile, but the stifled screamed still managed to echo through our section of the tunnel. I prayed I hadn't alerted anyone to my presence. A few more rats swam away from us, stirring up a host of floating debris.

The water continued to advance rapidly.

"Can you find the end of the rope?" Frank asked. "Maybe you can force it back through the knot."

"I've tried. It's so tight I can't get it to go through."

The water had risen up to my waist and had covered Frank's bonds. It was impossible for me to see the knots anymore. I could feel them, but couldn't see how they were tied together.

I felt sheer panic set in, but I pushed it aside.

"Genie, do you have anything to cut the rope with?" Frank asked me.

I shook my head, then realizing he probably couldn't see me from my position behind him. I said, "No. I'm sorry. The bonds are so tight I can't seem to loosen them. "

I started to cry when the water reached my ribcage. Gauging by how fast the water was rising, I knew I wouldn't be able to climb the ladder, find something sharp enough to cut the rope, and be back in time.

"It's all right, Genie. It'll be all right. Don't cry," Frank said. I tried to stop crying, even as I kept up pulling at the ropes.

"Kiss me."

"What?" I stopped pulling and crying.

I didn't think I heard him right. People only spontaneously make love in the midst of danger in sappy romance novels.

"Kiss me," he said again.

When I hesitated. He said, "Now." Loud. Forceful.

I returned to working on the ropes.

When he said, "Please." Soft and pleading. I came around to face him.

Through my tears, I found his face with my hands, found his lips and pressed my lips to them.

The water had advanced to the top of my shoulders when he pulled his head back from the kiss.

"Now go!" He demanded. "Now!" He shouted at me.

Loud. Forceful.

I kept shaking my head, crying "No."

"You've got to go get help." Softer. Cajoling. Pleading. "The bulkheads will be triggered to open when the tunnel is completely filled. Go get help. Please go."

The building was deserted. The phone in the office disabled. I knew there was no way I could climb that ladder, find help and get back there in time to rescue him. I'd be coming back to a dead body.

If only I had that knife I always packed in my lunch bag or my yarn scissors.

The debris from the bottom of the tunnel was floating at my eye level, and I was having a hard time keeping the current from floating me away from Frank. Frank was powerless to stop me from holding on to his arms and shoulders to stay with him, but he kept yelling at me to go. I ransacked my brain for a solution.

Then, I bowed my head and closed my eyes.

Frank's shouting, the tunnel, the rats, the debris and everything around me receded as I prayed for a miracle.

Something hard, pushed by the current, clunked against my chin. I opened my eyes, back to reality.

Frank was still tied tight. I could once again hear his pleading with me to climb the ladder and save myself.

I was not about to leave him, this man I loved to the depth of my soul. I was not leaving him to the ravages of that tunnel.

"NO," I sobbed at him. "I can't leave you like this."

The bottle bumped my head again. In my anger and frustration, I grabbed that whiskey bottle and smashed it violently against the pipe that was holding Frank a prisoner. The pipe that was to be his death.

The pipe was unmoved by my wrath. The bottle shattered, and pieces of glass splashed everywhere, leaving me hanging on to the jagged remains that had put a small cut on my hand.

I tested the sharpness of the broken edge against my

finger, and when I felt it cut me, I dived down under the water. I felt my way along the length of the pipe until I reached Frank's wrists. I sawed at the rope feverishly with the broken edge of the bottle.

When my lungs felt like they were going to burst, I was forced to leave my work and come to the surface of the water for air.

When I surfaced and found the water was up past Frank's nose and mouth, I dived back down into the murky water with renewed urgency.

I could feel Frank struggling in the water.

Was he struggling for air? Was this it?

If he died, I wanted to die, too.

I immediately stopped those thoughts. I couldn't let the thought of him dying paralyze me into inaction.

Don't think about that. Focus. Focus. Focus. Forget that as you cut the rope, you are cutting the flesh of his wrist and turning the water red. Forget that your lungs are bursting. Focus. Focus. Focus. Keep trying.

I couldn't do it. There was one more strand to cut when self-preservation forced me to surface again for air.

Frank's head was totally beneath the water, his hair floating like one of Neptune's servants.

Determined not to let the water claim his soul, I dived back down and slashed wildly at the last rope strand, slicing his wrist open in the process.

Frank and I both burst to the surface of the water at the same time. While I was filling my lungs with dank, tunnel air, Frank was coughing up water. When I heard him take in precious air in big gulps between coughs, I knew he'd be okay.

Freed, we both fought the current of the water still entering the tunnel as it carried us farther and farther from the ladder. The tap light positioned near the bottom of the ladder was soon covered with water and flickering out.

Frank swam along the tunnel side, a firm grip on my shirt so we stayed together and our heads were as close to the top of the tunnel as possible to breathe the air trapped there.

Frank found the rungs of the ladder and pushed me up ahead of him. I didn't argue his choice of women first as we climbed out of the tunnel of death.

I lay weak and shivering on the floor of the mechanical room, but Frank was up on his feet after only a brief respite. He was holding the edges of his cut wrist together as blood dripped to the floor.

"Tell me about what they were moving through the tunnel," he said standing, pulling out his gun, then realizing it wouldn't work, he shoved it in the back waistband of his jeans.

"I don't know what was in the boxes," I got up to look for something to stop his bleeding. "They were wrapped in plastic and duct taped to stay dry."

"Why did they have to stay dry? To move them through the tunnel? Why the tunnel? Why not out the front door? Why was it so important to put them down in the tunnel?"

"I don't know. I only know they purchased 25 emergency lights. That must have been enough to get them where they wanted to get to by way of the tunnel."

We both heard the sound of the water receding as the bulkheads opened to move the water to the next chamber of the tunnel—ten minutes too late to have saved Frank from downing.

I found the dirty handkerchief Randy had used as my gag and tightened it around Frank's wrist so he could go back down into the tunnel.

I hadn't wanted Frank to go back down into that horrifying tunnel after the water had receded, but he'd insisted it was his job to stop Rocko's plans—whatever they might be. Given the length and breadth of the tunnel that traveled through the business district and the populated areas of the city, I knew any plan that Rocko had was dangerous enough to not argue with Frank's decision.

239

CHAPTER 30

After Frank disappeared back into the tunnel, I got to the building reception desk as fast as I could.

"Glad to see that guy...Oh my God! What happened to you?"

I shoved a startled Rē out of the way and grabbed the phone from her desk. "I don't have time to explain."

As I was dialing an all too familiar number, everything started to make sense to me. The dognappings, the strange paper, the bleach, Rocko working for the city in the deep tunnel and stealing the tunnel maintenance plans. I knew the what, the when, the where and the why. I just needed to get someone there fast to help Frank.

"You got to get someone over to the Federal Reserve Bank on LaSalle Street," I screamed into the phone the minute someone answered.

I was shivering from my wet clothes and had to clench my teeth together to keep them from chattering into the phone. "One of your undercover agents is on his way there now and he's been injured."

I was almost hysterical, trying to remain calm and think of what to say to get the FBI operator to believe me—believe that I was not just another crackpot calling in a crank call.

"We don't have agents at the Federal Reserve Bank." The

240

disembodied voice told me.

"You have one now. Frank Bachman is headed there. I'm Imogene Warren. Agent Stevens has been working on my case. He knows me. Tell him Frank is in trouble."

"Agent Stevens is off duty for the holidays. Is there someone else who can assist you?"

"Yes. Anyone can assist me as long as they get someone over to the Federal Reserve Bank," I said trying to maintain my calm.

"The Federal Reserve Bank would be the Treasury Department's jurisdiction. Would you like for me to get that number for you?"

"No! Yes! No! It will be too late by then." I slammed the phone down.

"What's going on?" Rē asked me.

"No time to explain. I've got to help Frank."

Frank was going back into that tunnel to his death. I ran down the stairs back into the maintenance room, searching for a weapon, anything I could use. I grabbed a ballpoint pen from my desk drawer, slid my coat on over my wet clothes, and wrapped the unfinished afghan around my neck for added warmth.

I went back down to follow the tap lights in the tunnel. I had to. It was where Frank was.

By the time I got to the bottom of the ladder, the bulkhead that held the water in the tunnel had opened completely and the water was rapidly receding. Even so, the water still came up to lap at my waist. I managed to keep the afghan out of the water and around my shoulders; that afghan and coat were all I had between me and hypothermia.

Some of the lights Boggs and his men set up for their traversing the tunnel were still working, a blessing; the rats that scattered as I waded through the brackish water were not.

Whoever said, "They are as afraid of you as you are of them" the first time is a liar. Nothing could have been as afraid as I was.

241

***

Frank didn't have a working gun. All he had was the mop and a can of ant spray, and the element of surprise on his side. He just hoped it was enough to affect a positive outcome. It would be great if Genie was right about their plans to rob the jewelry store. If that was where the tunnel lights led he'd back off and let the Chicago police take care it. But, if she was wrong and they planned to detonate a bomb underneath the city, Frank was worried he was already too late to stop it.

CHAPTER 31

I moved through the tunnel, noticing that as it slopped upward I was going up to drier levels. I heard voices and this time it was not my imagination. I could see a faint light shining down from the tunnel ceiling up ahead. I continued to walk towards the light hoping this was not where I'd meet up with a dead Jorgji, my mother or my aunts.

My life didn't flash before my eyes, but I was to a point in the tunnel where the light was shining down on me. Above me was a circular hole in the roof of the tunnel. The tunnel floor was dry in this area with several empty cardboard boxes and plastic littering the tunnel floor. There was another metal chain-linked ladder snaking down through the open hole. The distance to reach the opening was about 10 feet.

I could hear scuffling and grunting coming from above me. One of the grunts was the timbre of Frank's voice. Knowing he was in a weakened state, I grabbed the chains on each side of the ladder and began climbing. By the time I got to the top and peeked out from the hole in the floor, Frank had Rocko face down on the floor, Franks' knee in his back keeping him down. Rocko was being tied up with the zigzag scarf I'd made for Frank.

Rocko was not making Frank's job easy. He was twisting, turning, and cursing, but Frank had the upper hand, so I hefted myself out of the opening with some extreme effort and sat down on the tile floor next to a crying Randy.

Randy looked up when he heard me. His dirty face was streaked with tears. He didn't look injured so I asked him why he was crying.

"Now I can't get the dog I wanted. A little short black one with a beard. I was gonna name him Scotty." He pulled the leather strip that he'd gotten from my desk drawer out from his pocket. The thing I had thought was a piece of jewelry that turned out to be a dog collar.

I shuddered. Not only was I cold from the water, but I was horrified that two men were dead because Randy wanted the dog he'd been promised.

Frank sat down hard on the floor after he finished securing Rocko. Blood was dribbling down from one corner of Frank's mouth. He wiped it away with the tail end of his wet shirt. Then he wiped at the blood on his wrist and frowned at me.

"I thought I told you to stay back and call the FBI office for help," he said to me.

"I tried. No one would listen. They didn't seem to believe me, so I came here in case you needed my help."

I looked around. The man who was almost twice Frank's size was flat on the floor, tied up, still letting Frank know what he thought of his parentage. The other man, Randy, was sobbing quietly into his shirtsleeve.

"I guess you didn't need me after all," I said as I pulled the afghan off from around my neck and tried to twist a corner of it around Frank's gashed and bleeding wrist without looking too closely at the blood that was pooling on the floor of the vault.

Frank lay flat on the floor, his chest heaving with effort. "Oh, I need you all right. Trust me. I need you. I just wanted to make sure you stayed alive for what I need you for."

The vault door behind me creaked open. Two policemen with guns drawn stepped in, followed closely by two men in security guard uniforms, followed by a tall man in a business suit. The suit peeked around the edge of the door before deciding it was safe to step inside.

The business suit kept saying "Oh, dear. Nothing like this has ever happened before." He pulled a handkerchief out of his pocket and wiped his forehead.

The older guard had sleep wrinkles on his cheeks; his hair was tousled like he had just awoken. The younger man was on full alert. When he saw Frank and me his hand grabbed the handle of his billy club; the other hand went towards his gun.

The police had shown up in response to Rē's report of a bank robbery at the Federal Reserve. They'd gotten the manager of the Chicago Reserve to open the building and the vault. Once they sorted out who was who, the police hauled Rocko and Randy out in handcuffs.

I was surprised at how quickly they believed our story that Frank was FBI. He didn't have identification, but they must have trusted the look of him or just believed his FBI arrogance.

The bank security men and the bank manager were awaiting the arrival of the Secret Service agent assigned to the bank. Frank and I were asked to stay and give a statement.

The older guard kept peering down at the hole in the vault floor, and scratching his head at the sight of the boxes, plastic and duck tape strewn around down there.

"It's a darn opening with a duplicate pattern of the floor tiles on one side. Exact match. Hatch opens from below the floor. Just like you'd see on a submarine. Must have taken days. How'd they do that without us hearing 'em?" he scratched his head again, asking the younger guard.

The younger man just shrugged his shoulders and looked off to the side.

Mr. Business Suit examined the piles of money sitting on the shelves of the vault with equal puzzlement. The younger guard was looking everywhere but at the money he was supposed to be guarding.

Frank was sitting very still on the vault floor still getting his wind back from his fight with Rocko.

"I just don't get it," the older guard kept repeating. "All the money is here safe and sound except for these two boxes they were hauling out." He motioned to the boxes sitting on the floor all taped up in plastic.

"Looks like you two caught these guys before they got away with much of anything." The younger guard stated.

The bank manager stopped his "Oh, Dearing" long enough to complete a check of the vault contents. He thanked Frank and me over and over again for our actions. "The money destined to go out to banks on Monday is all here. Thanks to you two."

"Look again," I said pointing to the stacks of $100 bills lining some of the shelves in the vault.

The reserve manager picked up a stack of the money, flipped through it in its banded state and said. "Feels and looks okay to me."

My claustrophobia, fear of uniforms and general paranoia had started to make me leery of everything. I was not happy with the way the younger guard kept avoiding the counterfeit money being examined by the manager. Mr. Young Guard was cautiously slipping closer and closer to towards the door of the vault. If that door closed and locked, with the reserve manager inside, our only way out of there was back through the tunnel.

I inched myself closer to the door as well.

"That money looks authentic because it's printed with authentic Treasury paper using a mixture of ink specially cooked up to closely match the real ink," I said keeping an eye on the guard now that the police were elsewhere booking Rocko and Randy. "These $100 bills started out as crisp, new five dollar bills, doggy money, as my friend, Keiko, would say."

I picked up one of the stacks of fake bills and took it over to the young guard and said, "Take a closer look. You'll see they're counterfeit."

Mr. Young Guard was near the door and continuing to edge his way out, but had to stop and take a hold of the bill when I thrust it at him. I saw the hand that grabbed the bill had a tattoo on the back of it. A tattoo resembling a horse.

It was then that I saw his nametag clearly. "Jones."

Jones would sell out his mother to pay his gambling debt, was what Rocko had said.

I was now sure Jones was planning on locking us all in the vault so he could make his escape.

I was not going back into that tunnel. No amount of money was worth that. I yanked Frank's gun out from the back waistband of his drenched trousers. I knew the gun was non-functional from being in the water, but I hoped Jones might not think of that for a short while.

"Hold it right there," I said to him, pointing the gun at the young guard's chest with a remarkably steady hand. A fear of tunnel diving must trump a fear of uniforms.

His hands shot up in the air at the sight of the gun pointed at his heart.

The older guard was being questioned by the police who left him on duty when they arrested the young guard. I wanted to get Frank to the hospital, but he insisted that if his wrists were bandaged he'd be okay. The bank manager went to find a first aid box for me to use and told us the Secret Service agent assigned to the Federal Reserve Bank of Chicago needed to interview Frank and me before he could let us leave.

The older guard found one lone clean, dry uniform for Frank and me to share. Frank and I were alone in the office we'd been instructed to wait in, when Frank began to strip out of his wet clothes.

I too was cold, but I was hoping for an opportunity to uphold my modesty or to find a better location. Seeing none, I stood behind an open office supply closet door and stripped out of my frigid clothes.

Behind the relative anonymity of the door, I heard Frank gave a short laugh at my efforts towards modesty. "Isn't anything I haven't seen before."

My face burned at the memory. Even with Frank safely on the other side of the door, I buttoned that guard uniform top over my naked body in record speed.

I stepped out from behind the door and found I couldn't avert my eyes from the sight of Frank, exhibition-style, snapping and zipping the too tight uniform trousers shut.

I looked up to Frank's face and our eyes locked. I blushed and was thankful for the guard's arrival with the first aid kit.

The guard immediately left to see what was keeping the Secret Service agent when I advised him that even with a first aid kit Frank would need to see a doctor soon.

I wound the gauze bandages from the kit around Frank's cut wrist as best I could. Before I could secure the last bit of tape, he pulled me up from my kneeling position to have me stand in front of where he was sitting on the top of the bank manager's desk.

"I blew it this time when I turned my back on that guy Randy. Good thing I had a Genie on my side. Thanks for saving me." He maneuvered me between his legs so he could hug me to his bare chest.

"Frank. We're in some bank executive's office waiting for a federal agent to show up." I squirmed to get free, but when I felt his response and knew he was enjoying my discomfort, I gave up and settled into his embrace.

"It's okay if we get close," he said to me, stroking my back with his uninjured hand. "We were almost drowned in cold water. We need to share body heat to get warm."

"Just let me get this bandage secured. You've lost a lot of blood." I managed to get the paper tape onto the end of the gauze before his hand gliding over my back and the heat radiating from his chest distracted me.

"It looks worse than it is," He mumbled moving his mouth against my neck. His beard tickled when he talked. That made my legs rubber. I tried to back away from the desk so I could look at his face, but his not-rubber-at-all legs came up and encircled my thighs, holding me lightly to him. Not an altogether unpleasant fit.

"For a good looking chic you sure get into some ugly situations." He took a hold of my hand and placed it over his heart, holding it there. Then he kissed me, slow, leisurely, sensually. I could sense his want, feel his heat, feel his heart beating wildly under my open hand.

My lips were tingling. Every part of my body was screaming for this more intimate contact, but I wanted answers. With force of will I managed to break away from his kiss so I could move my head and body back as far as I could to study his face.

"Why did you force me to kiss you in the tunnel?"

He scoffed. "I wasn't in a position to force anyone to do anything. I was tied up. Remember?" He held up his left hand to show me his bandaged wrist.

"You know what I mean. Why did you beg me to kiss you and then order me leave? You knew every second counted if you were to be gotten out of there. Why lose precious time by having me kiss you? Why?"

His hands softly captured both sides of my face. He looked straight into my eyes, absorbing my soul with a powerful intensity. "I knew there was no way to stop the water, not in time. I knew I had to get you out of there, or you'd drown, too. I wanted you to be safe. To leave. I thought you'd be more apt to go if you thought you could bring back help."

"I couldn't leave you. I saw how fast the water was rising. I knew leaving meant you'd drown for sure. I'd rather have drowned with you than leave you there. And, you still haven't answered me. Why would you risk your life for just a kiss? Why was a kiss so important at that moment?" I didn't blink or look away. The eyes don't lie. I wanted to see his eyes when he answered my question.

He studied me for a moment, and then closed his eyes, deep in thought or in pain, I couldn't tell which. "I knew I was going to drown. I was certain of it. When that happened, I wanted the last memory I had to be of your kiss."

The conference room door flung open. Mr. Old Guard announced, "Secret Service Agent is here."

When the agent strode into the room, I gasped and moved to step back from Frank's hold on me. Frank's arms tightened and he held me securely between his thighs. One arm slid down to possessively tighten on my waist as the other arm protectively hugged me even tighter to his bare chest.

"Well, Well. Isn't this cozy," said Secret Service Agent Garrett Edmond.

CHAPTER 32

Agent Stevens had gotten my call after all. It had just taken him a while to get clearance for the FBI to enter the Federal Reserve Bank. He showed up with Frank's badge and department issued gun just as I was being handcuffed by Garrett.

"Imogene Warren Dalmat you are under arrest for counterfeiting. Anything you say can and will be used against you in a court of law," Garrett said to me.

"You're a moron. The police already took the counterfeiters out of here." Frank told Garrett. The blood was beginning to soak through the makeshift bandaging job I'd done on Frank's wrist. Without looking down or even letting on that he was aware of the blood, Frank encircled his wrist with his uninjured hand and began to apply pressure on the cut. Other than that, Frank acted like nothing was wrong. I marveled that he could retain control of himself and the situation, even leaking blood.

When Frank held out his good hand to retrieve his gun, Agent Stevens looked at me, at Garrett, then back to Frank's blanched white face. Agent Stevens rubbed his chin, tightened his lips, and held Frank's gun out to him.

Frank, his face very pale and his stance unsteady, took the gun. He looked at me, with my hands pinned behind my back, my uniform shirt askew. Frank hefted the gun handle in his hand and glared at Garrett. I saw Frank hesitate a fraction before he shoved the Glock in the pocket of the borrowed trousers.

Garrett paid no attention to the glares from Frank. He turned back to his task of arresting me.

I winced when Garrett cinched the cuffs tighter on me pinching my skin and jerking my shoulder joints back, popping a top button loose on the shirt.

He continued my Miranda rights. "You have a right to an attorney. If you cannot afford one, one will be assigned to you."

"You're not only a moron; you're an asshole, too. Take those cuffs off her." Frank stood up from where he was sitting on the desk. He wavered a little in his stance. Agent Stevens stepped up to Frank's side to either back him up or catch him when he fell; I wasn't sure which.

"This isn't an FBI investigation. You don't have jurisdiction here." Garrett looked pointedly at Frank, making sure Frank understood the Secret Service didn't have to take orders from the FBI.

I was glad that Agent Stevens showed up with Frank's FBI identification and gun before Garrett slapped cuffs on Frank, too.

"Genie didn't have anything to do with those counterfeiters," Frank said as he returned to sitting on a corner of the desk.

He was weak. I could see it.

Garrett smirked at Frank. "And you'd know that how? As the SSA assigned to this area, I was alerted by the police that some of the $5 bills I'd arranged to have invisibly marked for them as ransom payment for the dognappings showed up at the McDeed's. I never gave that a second thought. Twenty thousand dollars is chump change. What did I care that some rich old dames paid money to get their precious pooches back? Then I saw her."

Garrett pointed at me, a look of disgust crossing his face.

"She had a bleached out Cloroxed bill. Used it to write down a lunch order. I started investigating further. I found out she was working for Boggs, one of the Treasury's past counterfeiting culprits. Then I found where she paid her utility bills with counterfeit one hundred dollar bills. She had to have known what her boss was up to. The security strip was in the wrong spot on every bill she used."

"She's innocent. No one but uptight Treasury agents care where the security strip is on a bill. She didn't have a clue what they were up to until today."

"Come off it." Garrett became so agitated with Frank's defense of me, his nostrils were beginning to flare and his eyes glaze. "Her whole "I'm clueless about everything" had to be an act. No one can be that stupid."

Frank had Garrett pinned up against the wall in a flash before anyone in the room saw it coming. "You'd better watch your mouth, asshole. Naive and stupid aren't the same thing."

I might have tried to intervene in my defense, but my hands were handcuffed behind my back, and the shirt I was wearing had partially come unbuttoned. Even buttoned it only came down just below my hooha, so I stayed back and delighted in watching Garrett get what was coming to him.

Garrett didn't look one bit scared as he gave Frank a "go ahead. I dare ya" look. It was a draw which was tougher. Score one for Garrett.

Frank held himself in check, or rather his weakened state did. The fight went out of him quickly. He released the arm he had placed across Garrett's neck and came over to stand next to me.

Frank said, looking daggers at Garrett, "Might I point out that she is the one who put their scheme altogether. She alone figured out these guys were taking the real money and replacing it with the counterfeit bills so it would take a while for the theft to be discovered. She risked her life to come here and help stop those guys."

Frank paused just long enough to refasten one of the top buttons of my borrowed shirt that had come undone from

253

when Garrett pulled my arms behind my back.

"She's the one who identified the security guard here as part of their scam. The security guard who got past your federal background checks." Frank casually draped an arm across my shoulders. From the weight of that arm, I knew he needed help to stay upright.

"She's also the one who saved your sorry ass from being made a laughing stock when the bank opens on Monday, and they find you allowed counterfeit money to be smuggled in to replace the real money that was stolen."

I braced myself more as Frank's arm weighted heavier on my shoulders.

"Is that true? You identified the guard as part of the heist? And you figured out they were making a switch?" Garrett asked me. The nostrils were still quivering in rage, but the blue of his eyes were returning to liquid.

I would have stepped up to confront him when I answered, but I'm pretty mousy. I was clumsy with my hands cuffed behind my back, and Frank's weight was getting heavier on my shoulders. That didn't allow for much negotiation.

"Yes. I was doing some research on the convict that drowned in Lake Michigan earlier. I recognized the guard had a hand tattoo that was as part of a prison bookie gang symbol."

The nostrils finally stopped quivering, but they were still flared, and my handcuffs remained on.

Frank gave up his façade of bravery, his arm weight lifted from me as he found a chair and sat down heavily in it.

"You really weren't in this with Boggs?" Garrett asked stepping up closer to me. His blue eyes remaining fixed on my face, more ice melting.

"No."

"You didn't know I worked for the Secret Service and was the agent assigned to this bank?"

"No! How could I?"

"I thought for sure you figured it out when I brought your credit card back and knew your full name and where you lived."

"You used your agent status to get access to my personal information? You investigated me?"

"When I saw you with that bleached out bill acting like it was just a piece of paper, I just lifted your credit card and ran it through the system to learn who you really were. When I found out you were Imogene Dalmat, the woman whose billions got stolen in a fraud scam, I figured you were looking to make some quick money to make up for what you lost."

"I did need money, but not that way."

"When I found out you were working for Boggs, I figured you weren't really interested in me; you were just playing me along so you could see how close the SS was to finding out about your counterfeiting scheme."

So all that anger at me had been about his bruised male ego?

"Me playing you? The way you kept showing up and hanging around me, talking about writing and asking me questions about my aunt, I thought you were hired by my aunt's publicity and publishing agents to string me along so you could steal her unpublished manuscripts."

"I only went on about writing and made up all that stuff about wanting to be a writer so I'd have an excuse to keep coming back to keep an eye on Boggs." Garrett spun me around. The cuffs released their squeeze on my wrists as he pulled them off me and turned me back around to face him. His eyes were back to their Mediterranean blue.

"And to keep seeing you," he added with a sly smile that showed his teeth a little beneath the mustache.

I rubbed my pinched wrists to get the circulation back in them and smiled back.

Frank, weak from loss of blood, passed out and slid from the chair to the floor in a heap.

CHAPTER 33

"You're enjoying this, aren't you?" Frank asked me from his hospital bed. I did probably have a smirk on my face as the nurse pulled the white bed sheets up under his arms, tightly tucked the edges of the sheets around him and adjusted the drip of his blood infusion set up before she left the room.

"Absolutely. The shoe's on the other foot, now."

Frank was in a gown while I was back in a set of my own dry clothing. I leaned back in the chair I'd pulled up close to the side of his hospital bed, content to sit by him as he had with me before.

"No. No shoe on either foot. See." He wiggled both feet free from under the tucked in covers and waved his bare toes at me. "They took my shoes and socks away to make sure I wouldn't leave before this thing is done." He jiggled his arm and the red tube from the blood bag jiggled with it.

This was the second bag I'd sat through. Usually, the sight of blood made me faint, but I had started to adjust.

A lady with a white lab coat popped in through the door. She sat her plastic tray filled with laboratory style tubes and packages on the edge of the bed and announced she was there to check Frank's blood levels.

I stifled a giggle when Frank's face blanched even whiter than it already was. "Not afraid of a little needle are you, Frank?"

"Shut up and kiss me."

"What?" Remembering the reason for the last time he demanded a kiss, his request took me off guard.

"It will distract me. Please?" Frank pleaded while the phlebotomist tied a band of rubber around his upper arm and started swabbing the inside bend of his elbow with alcohol.

I reached down and grabbed Frank's big toe from where it lay exposed from the covers. "Not until you tell me about you and Samantha."

That got his full attention. Eyes wide, mouth open.

"How'd you know about...Ouch."

I never knew if he yelled out from my squeezing his toe or from the needle, he refused to say which.

The sight of Frank's blood filling the clear vial unnerved me. Blood going into Frank I was fine with. Blood coming from him, I was not. I returned my gaze to Frank's face and tried not to think about the blood. It was so easy to love him, scruffy beard, mop of hair and all, but I had to be sure of where I stood. I didn't want to start another relationship with a second woman in the wings.

"It doesn't matter how I know. I just know. You and Samantha." I made an index and second fingers intertwined sign where the lab tech couldn't see my reference.

"There is no 'me and Sam.' Not anymore. It didn't work out. That was over a while ago. We're just friends now." He visibly relaxed when the lab lady withdrew the needle and covered the spot with a cotton ball and band-aid.

I know she couldn't help but hear Frank's explanation to me, but she said nothing as she gathered up her belongings.

I waited for her to leave before asking, "Then why did you have Samantha represent me when I was charged with murder if you were 'just friends'? Were you longing to see her again?" I tucked his foot back under the covers. It wasn't the Victorian era, but he'd been rushed here in borrowed, too tight trousers. The sight of his naked foot reminded me he was probably naked in his hospital gown under the bed sheets.

"Because I believed in your innocence even though the

case against you was rock solid. You needed a lawyer. Sam worked hard and sacrificed a lot to be the best damn criminal defense lawyer in Michigan. I wanted you to have the best criminal defense lawyer around. I guess I loved you even then. I just didn't realize how much I loved you until later—like now. Do I get my kiss?"

Satisfied, I complied with his distraction request and happily kept him distracted until the nurse announced visiting hours were over.

CHAPTER 34

After being kicked out of the hospital, I went home and collapsed on to my bed. Every fiber of my being was wrung out. Knowing Frank was alive and safe at the hospital had settled my nerves enough that not even Mr. M jumping on my bed could keep me awake.

I opened my eyes later to darkness. Mr. M was shaking, and I could hear someone walking around in my room; the beam of a flashlight played along my dresser.

I'd been through too much, too soon to give in to fear this time. I rolled quietly over and felt along the edge of the bed to locate my slipper on the floor. I felt the cool, hard steel of the gun that was there, right where I'd left it.

I brought the gun up just before I turned on the bedside light.

My burglar shielded his eyes from the glare.

Martin!

I aimed the gun straight at him.

His hands shot up in the air. "Imogene, It's me, Martin."

"I know. That's why this gun is aimed at your head. What are you doing here going through my things? Are you robbing me?"

"I'm not robbing you, you silly twit. I'm only trying to get my sister's share out of those manuscripts. Why should you be the one to keep them? They are half hers. I looked everywhere in the house, except for that butler's place and your room. I couldn't get into his place so I thought I'd try your room."

"Those manuscripts are unfinished. They aren't worth a thing."

"Not according to Rosenthal and Gildenstein. They are confident a ghostwriter can finish them. There's not one, but two manuscripts. That's a fortune you've been sitting on."

"Mr. Rosenthal and Mr. Gildenstein put you up to this? You're working for them?"

"Don't play like you haven't already gone to Michigan to try and sell the manuscripts. They followed you there and back."

"They were the ones following me? I was selling my Bentley, not the manuscripts!"

"When you wouldn't deal with them, they remembered Mandy and I had been at the reading of the will and were disappointed to have not gotten anything, so they approached us. I told them I could get the manuscripts."

Mandy would have gone ballistic if I'd have shot Martin, so I had him arrested instead.

Frank and I told Janey how Rockford and Boggs had taken real 5-dollar bills obtained through the dog nappings and bleached them out so they could use the super printer to reprint them as $100 bills.

"Rockford used the stolen deep tunnel maintenance shaft plans to locate the spot that was directly under the floor of the Federal Reserve Vault. They extended the maintenance tunnel over and upwards and using non-vibrating drills they made a hole in the vault floor," I explained to an enraptured Janey while we waited for the baby to wake up for a visit.

"I understand why the vibration alarms didn't go off, but the vault must have had motion sensors," Janey stated.

"It did. On the outside." Frank grabbed a stick of cinnamon gum out of his pocket and began chewing. I felt a little flushed at the memories that smell evoked.

"If the digging was done in a maintenance shaft, why didn't any of the maintenance workers notice the dirt? Or the modifications to the tunnel?"

"Rockford knew the inspection routine, knew there wouldn't be any inspectors in there until after the Thanksgiving Holiday. He made sure Randy brought the dirt back to the McClintock building and stored it in one of the rooms off his office area so no one would be the wiser," Frank explained. "No one except for Genie," he added. He placed an arm around my shoulders and gave me a gentle squeeze.

Johnny whimpered, and Janey stood up to get him.

I jumped up. "Please, let me."

I picked Johnny out of his little bed and placed him up against Frank's chest. I then secured one of Frank's hands under the back of Johnny's head and the other on his bottom.

"You have to hold him like this, so his head doesn't wobble," I told Frank.

Frank got an awkward look on his face like he was holding a time bomb.

"He won't break," I reassured him. Johnny squirmed.

"I know, but I can't see him if he's up on my chest. How about this?" Frank laid Johnny down in his lap, cradled with an arm on each side, with his head in Frank's hand. Frank leaned over to get closer to Johnny and started making goofy, baby talk sounds to him.

Johnny was watching Frank's mouth move intently, trying to imitate Frank's mouth with his mouth.

"Don't talk to him in baby talk; he needs to hear adult talk so he can learn to say something other than goo goo." Janey stepped out from the kitchen doorway where she was cleaning away the remains of our lunch.

Frank turned his head towards the kitchen and stuck his tongue out at Janey, which Johnny immediately imitated. We all laughed. Janey returned to the kitchen. Frank refocused his attention back to Johnny.

"Hello, little man. I'm your Uncle Frank. I'm the one

who's going to teach you how to shoot a gun, drive fast sports cars, and lay beautiful women."

"Not that kind of adult talk." Janey came in and whapped the back of Frank's head with the flat of her hand.

He laughed and said, "See how your mother treats me? Aren't you glad you're not a twin?" Johnny watched Frank's face in rapt attention.

"Wanna help me in the kitchen for a bit?" Janey said to me.

I reluctantly left Frank and his nephew in the living room. I tried to focus on what Janey was asking me to do, but I kept glancing back to observe Frank and the baby. I'd almost lost him, and I wanted to make sure he was still there—Frank, the baby couldn't go anywhere yet.

After one long session of watching Frank blow soft raspberries on Johnny's tummy, I turned to find Janey studying me.

"Nothing sexier than the man you're in love with fussing over a baby, is there?"

I couldn't believe she just read my mind. I gave her a questioning look.

"Hey. It's written all over your face every time you look at my brother. It was double just now."

"Oh, am I that obvious?"

"Yeah. You're that obvious. It's that obvious on him, too. He's crazy in love with you."

"I believe you're right." I smiled. "When he saw I was in danger from an unknown enemy, he took on an armed Russian agent in a parking garage to protect me. Back in the tunnel, when the water was pouring in, Frank was willing to drown to keep me from drowning. I don't know how many more enemies I'll be facing because of what my father did. The thought of losing Frank during another dangerous assignment or of his being killed in my place terrifies me."

"You've got it bad," she said, shaking her head at me. "I'm sure that Russian agent won't be after you again, but you're going to have to find a way to deal with the fact that

Frank is an undercover FBI agent, a highly dangerous job. It's what he does. It's what he loves, and I don't see that changing—ever."

"I don't know if my fears will allow me to deal with it. How did your husband come to terms with your being an FBI agent?"

"He hasn't. He goes to sea for long stretches at a time, so he never hears about the day-to-day risks I face, and I don't tell him." Her gaze turned from me to the living room. "Now that we have Jonathan, I must admit...I've been giving a lot of thought to what that means for my career."

I wondered, too. It would be hard to leave a baby every day to chase after criminals, but it would be just as hard to see the one you loved chase dangerous criminals.

The memory of Frank in that dark tunnel tied to a pipe with water coursing over his head entered unbidden into my mind. I shuddered. *When would the memories fade and the constant fear stop?*

The next night Frank and I had a long talk over the spaghetti dinner I fixed him. The breadsticks were pre-made and the sauce from a jar I'd bought at the local supermarket, but I'd grated the cheese, heated the sauce in a pan and the breadsticks in the oven and poured the sauce on top of the pasta all by myself. Keiko told me spaghetti was an easy meal, and she was right. The spaghetti strings weren't as stringy as they should be and the bread sticks were scorched on the bottom, but I didn't hear one complaint from Frank—just the opposite.

"Carbon is good for you. Helps settle the stomach. El dente is good for you, too," he said when I apologized for the meal failures. "Gives your mouth a workout."

I wanted to give his mouth a workout in other ways, but I first needed to approach the subject of us and why I wanted him to come to the house for dinner rather than go out.

After I'd come home from Janey's, I'd gotten a call from the Department of Defense. They'd identified the Russian agent who came after me in the parking garage. He was part of an elite clandestine group formed by the Russian military.

The DOD called to put me on alert. I was told to be cautious because that Russian agent most certainly was not working alone. My father hadn't left the plans to the stealth missile with me, but if the Russian government had reason to think he had, they might come after me again to get the plans.

The DOD wasn't warning me strictly for my safety.

"Do you know where your father is?" the DOD director had asked me.

"No. I have no idea of where he is." I told him. It wasn't exactly a lie. At that moment, he could have been anywhere. Anywhere in the world.

"Well, if he attempts to contact you, we strongly urge you to come forward and tell us. If the Russians learn you know of his whereabouts, you'll be in danger. We can help protect you."

"Thank you for your offer, but I doubt I'll be talking to my father. I want nothing to do with him."

"Forewarned is forearmed. Be sure and contact us if you hear from him."

I was glad they didn't ask me if I had ideas about where he had gone because I had lots of ideas. None of them good.

After that call, I had the security code on the house reset and signed up for those self-defense classes Rē suggested. I didn't intend to return Frank's pistol, so I had hoped he wouldn't ask for it back.

After I explained the situation to Keiko and swore her to secrecy, I advised her to find residence elsewhere—out of harm's way. She didn't want to leave me alone, but understood I couldn't be worried about her and me both.

I didn't know how I was going to convince Frank to stay out of harm's way. I knew I couldn't tell him about the call from the DOD. He'd be inclined to want to protect me, and I must admit as good as that sounded to me, I couldn't deliberately put him in danger.

We finished the meal and the dessert and still I hadn't said what I'd set out to say. Every time I looked into his eyes, I was lost in emotion, unable to speak.

"You set a mean dessert table," Frank teased grabbing up the cinnamon candies from the bowl I sat in front of him at the table. I had wanted to make sugar cookies with the little red heart candies on top, but I underestimated the amount of time it took to boil the spaghetti, so I ran out of time. As a last ditch attempt at a desert, I put the candy hearts in fancy crystal dessert bowls instead.

"Thanks."

After a long lull in the small talk, we both said at the same time. "There's something I've been meaning to talk to you about."

We both laughed at the same time and said: "You go first."

Then again in unison, "No, you go first."

He stood up and pulled me up to him, and kissed me tenderly.

There was no passion in the kiss, just a lot of love and longing came through. He pulled me in closer, wrapped his arms around me and sighed. I wrapped back.

Mr. M yipped and pranced around us in circles.

"I think he needs to go out. Until I can get the yard fenced in, I go out with him so he won't be dognapped. Would you like to go with me?" I asked Frank.

"I'd love to go with you."

Outside, we watched Mr. M frolic in the snow fluff. I hadn't found the courage all through dinner to tell Frank I didn't want to be with him. I loved him so deeply, so completely it was a cruel irony that I couldn't lie to him and say I didn't.

I took Frank's gloved hand and pulled it up to my lips to kiss the exposed skin between the leather edges of the coat and glove. The angry purple bruises from the rope had mellowed to green and yellow. The deep abrasions from where I'd cut him were healing over into scars. Scars we would both carry with us for the rest of our lives.

"You know I love you." I decided on truthfulness.

"I love you, too." He laced his gloved fingers through mine.

We walked together, fingers intertwined, through the garden behind my house, arms slowly swaying together in stride, comfortable in who we were, what we were, both lost to our thoughts.

"Even with love, it will never work," he said at last, breaking our contemplations. I knew he was referring to him and me. Together.

"No. I can see that," I responded, a sigh hung heavy in my chest; I refused to let it escape. I was keeping my tears in check as well. I wasn't going to do that to him; saddle him with guilt over something that neither of us could control.

"My line of work is extremely dangerous. It puts everyone close to me in danger as well," he said, trying to soften the rejection, trying to explain.

I had a similar worry when it came to my father's enemies finding me and Frank getting in their way, but I couldn't put voice to those fears. They were too distant to mean anything at that moment. All that mattered was we had those few last moments together.

"I love you," he said again. "When your dog came out of the building without you... When I thought they'd hurt you...I lost all reason. You could have been killed because I behaved foolishly." He stopped and turned to face me.

I stopped to face him, also. I saw him swallow painfully hard. I felt the same intense pain; the pain I saw in his eyes.

"My life is filled with danger. That risk can carry over to the people I love. Hurt the people I love. Hurt you. I'd do anything to protect you. To keep you safe." His eyes closed. "Even if that means letting you go."

I thought about my current circumstances, and a sigh escaped me. He was right. I couldn't live a peaceful life knowing he was always in danger. I would die a thousand deaths if that threat came from me, from who I was, from what my father was.

"I agree. This can't continue," I said, relieved that he had given me an out, without my having to lie to him.

He opened his eyes and looked at me, stroking my face with his ungloved hand. We stayed that way for several long moments before we turned back to walk a few more steps up the path through the now dead rose garden.

I stopped to admire a single red rose that had survived the beginning of winter. Frank stopped beside me. The rose's dark red petals were dusted with small flakes of snow. The other flowers on the rose bush were brown and dead—just this one bright spot of color remained.

"Better to end it now, while we still can," he said as he stood stock still, unable to turn to face me again, breathing out puffs of vapor-laden breath beside me.

I looked down at the flower that had suddenly captured my full attention. A few seconds passed as we stared in companionable silence at the deep maroon that stood out in vivid relief against the monochrome landscape.

A lone tear escaped me. It dropped unimpeded onto the rose where it glistened on a petal for a brief moment before it fell and was swallowed up by the light layer of snow.

Not speaking, we both commenced walking again.

He began to gently swing the arm whose hand still held mine. I swung my arm in rhythm with his.

Snow started to drift down again. It clung to our hair and jackets as we set off in a slow and steady pace towards the back door of the house where Mr. M was playfully dancing around, enjoying the snow. He yipped delightedly when he saw us and ran around us in circles until we reached the back door and I let him in.

I stood outside the door, turning again to Frank, wishing I were a stronger person, but the memory of him lying pale and still in a hospital bed still burned painfully in my heart. I gazed longingly into the face that was forever etched in my memory.

My grip on his hand tightened.

His grip tightened back with equal intensity.

"You know you can always call if you need me," he said, pulling me in for a quick, tight hug before he released me and stepped back—studying my face. "Right?"

"Right," I reassured him. "And if you ever find yourself in over your head again, you know you can always call on me. Right?"

EASY CROCHET BABY BLANKET

Copyright by Celeste Bennett
Imogene's pattern notes are in [brackets].

The items made from this pattern can be offered for sale but the pattern itself may not be sold or distributed in any format or media without the copyright holder's written permission.

Difficulty: Easy.

Materials for Johnny's Baby Blanket:
6 ounces of baby soft yarn or sport weight yarn
8 ounces of coordinating color baby yarn or sport weight yarn
Size G/6/4.25mm crochet hook
Yarn needle
[Note: I had to make this blanket with sock yarns that I tied together. I hope your finances fair better than mine so you can use baby yarn.]

Materials for Frank's Blanket/Afghan
16 ounces Bernat Soft Boucle Yarn or other soft yarn
18 ounces of worsted weight yarn in white, cream or coordinating color
Size K/10 ½/6.50 mm crochet hook
Yarn needle
[Note: The super sized yarn packages they are sometimes a little thick so it may take more ounces then the Boucle to get the same yardage. Using a variegated yarn will give a color changing pattern to the blanket without having to change colors.]

Gauge: The actual gauge is unimportant. The blanket starting chain length determines the size of the blanket.[2]

Abbreviations and Stitches:
sc = single crochet

269

FO = finish off. Cut yarn leaving a long tail for weaving in the ends.
Ch = chain
Sl st = slip stitch

Instructions:
Hold the two strands of yarn together for the main body of the blanket. For the edging use two strands of the coordinating color or two strands of the Boucle held together.

Main body of the blanket/afghan: Ch 101. *[Note: this chain should be 3 feet long for a baby blanket[2]. If it is not 3 feet then adjust the number of chains so you have the correct length. Always have an even number of chains plus one or the pattern won't work up correctly.]*

Row 1: Work a sc in 2nd ch from hook, *ch 1, skip a ch and sc in next ch*. Repeat from * to * across to the last two chs. Sc in each of the last two chs. Ch 1. Turn. *[Note: You may wish to count the number of sc you have in this row so you have a reference number if the piece seems to be drifting off at the edges (i.e. getting narrower or wider) you can count and see if you missed a stitch or added a stitch somewhere and adjust.]*

Row 2: Work a sc in first sc, *ch 1, skip 2nd sc, work a sc in previous rows ch 1 space*. Repeat from * to * until you get to the last stitch. Work a sc in the last stitch. *[Note: you are working a sc in each chain space of the previous row with a chain placed between each sc. You need to always begin a row with a sc and end a row with a sc so the pattern works up correctly.]*

Subsequent Rows: Repeat Row 2 until the baby blanket is as long as it is wide. *[note: For Frank's blanket I worked until the blanket was the proper length for an Undercover FBI agent.]*
FO. Weave in ends

Edging: Divide the boucle that you have left into two equal balls *[Note: If you prefer, use the contrasting color].* Holding both strands together attach the yarn to any outside edge of the blanket.

Round 1: Work sc evenly around the edge of the blanket placing 3 sc in each corner. Sl st to beginning sc. Ch 1. *[Note: since the boucle doubled may be less thick then the boucle worked with another worsted weight yarn you will need to check every so often to make sure the edging is laying flat. If the edging is wavy pull it out and use fewer stitches along the edge. If the edging is puckering pull it out and work more sc stitches along the edge. If you tend to put too many single crochets along an edge, skip every 6th or 7th stitch.]*

Round 2: Repeat the first round for a wider edge on the blanket. If you'd like a thin edge skip this round.

Optional finish: If you would like a ropy type edge, work a backwards single crochet around the edge of the blanket being careful to keep the edging flat. Join with sl st to first sc. *[Note: A backwards single crochet is where you work a single crochet from left to right rather than right to left. You may need to skip every 10 stitches to avoid the edge waving.]*

Every effort has been made to ensure this pattern is complete, error free and easy to follow. If you have questions, please contact the author at celeste.s.bennett@gmail.com.

"Murder at Yarn Mansion"

The Third Yarn Genie Mystery
Due for release November of 2017

CHAPTER ONE

After all I had been through, I had yet to experience a night as dark and cold as the night I packed to leave my mansion. Laughter and champagne corks popping wafted up to me from the dining room below. If I hadn't been so distraught, I would have found it funny that a knitting agoraphobic like me was more frightened to stay in my home than to leave it. I stifled a sob, squared my shoulders, and swallowed hard. No one attending the party downstairs was going to see me leave my home in tears. That's because I was going to sneak down the back stairs and out through the kitchen.

I didn't have a clear destination in mind; I only knew I couldn't stay there.

I pulled all my yarns away from their hiding spots around my bedroom suite: the linen closet, the bathroom, the walk-ins, purses and shopping bags I had secreted behind my winter coats. Once all the yarns were on my bed, I got my suitcases out.

The reds, blues, pinks, lavenders, yellows, golds, greens, and every color of yarns imaginable were spilling over the sides of the bed and onto the floor. There wasn't enough room in my small Chevy to take all my precious yarns with me so I had to decide which ones would make the cut and which ones wouldn't. I picked up a skein of bulky green twist yarn. It screamed winter hat at me, but I shushed it and laid it back on the pile. I already had a winter hat. I ran my hands over the six balls of soft angora, but in the end I ignored its pleading to be made into a sweater and moved on.

The purple strands of chenille I had picked up were starting to get wet. I hate it when I cry over yarn, but I couldn't stand the thought of leaving any of them behind.

The laughter and tinkling glasses from downstairs were getting annoying, so I got up to close my bedroom suite door, only to find my half-sister, Mandy, standing there with a glass of champagne in her hand, watching me. Mandy is also my cousin, thanks to an affair my father had with my mother's sister. Mandy had swept her light brown hair up into a mass of green- and red-colored curling swatches. She had green eye shadow over one eye and red over the other. Her golden-threaded black dress barely reached her knees. Her upper lip was red. The bottom lip, pursing out in the pout, was painted green.

"I thought you were going to come down and join the party to celebrate," she said, as I watched in fascination while the green and red lips separated and pulled together with each word.

"What do I have to celebrate? The fact that you've moved your lunatic murdering brother into my house?"

"He's not a lunatic; he's not murdered anyone. It's been proven that he didn't attempt to kill you—no matter what you think." She looked over at my bed and raised her one green eyebrow. "This 'yarn mansion' is not just yours now. If you didn't want me to live here, you shouldn't have added my name to the deed."

I grabbed up the nearest skein of sport yarn and began to fiddle with the strands, avoiding her gaze. "You're my sister. I put your name on the deed because Aunt Tilly wanted us both to share in the inheritance she left. And, I wanted you to live with me so we could make up for lost time. I just didn't realize you'd move Martin in with you."

"You expected me to just leave my brother out in the cold? He's your cousin. He's family. You treat your yarns better than you do him. You're insisting he live in the basement is just preposterous. There are plenty of empty bedroom suites in this house. There's even that apartment on the third floor that isn't being used."

I couldn't get into all the reasons why Aunt Tilly treated her butler so lavishly, there wasn't time, so I only said, "Gordon has a life lease on that apartment, and there is nothing legally I can do about it, and I don't want to talk about Gordon, Martin or you. I want you to leave."

"All right. I'll leave your room. It's a mess anyway."

"Not just the room. I'd prefer you leave the house. It would be the decent thing for you to do since you lied in court to get your half-brother exonerated of attempting to kill me."

"I only spoke the truth. Martin wasn't trying to murder you. You was always a high-strung, nervous little thing who could never take a joke. You got all these phobias that get the better of you."

She was right about the phobias, but her courtroom testimony made it seem like I'd spent my inherited billions on shrinks when in reality the bigamist I'd married was the one who had stolen all my money and then hid it in foreign bank accounts.

Mandy pointed at the suitcase I'd shoved a few articles of clothing in before I'd gathered the yarns. "Are you planning a holiday vacation?"

"Of a sort," I responded.

"Good for you. You need to go somewhere warm and get some color in your face. You've been way too pale since that FBI creep dumped you."

"He didn't dump me. Frank and I agreed it was better for both of us to go our separate ways."

"Un-huh. If that was so good for you, then why have you been crying and moping around the house ever since you two called it quits?"

I shrugged and turned away from her so she couldn't see that her words upset me to the point of tears.

ABOUT THE DOGS

Just like Imogene, at a difficult time in my life, I found myself the unwilling owner of a dog, a Scottish Terrier. Beasley was in dire need of a place to stay for a few days until a forever home could be found for her. I was undergoing daily radiation treatments for breast cancer that left no time for the care of a dog, but I took Beasley in intending to quickly find her a good home with a family member or a friend. Little did I know that her forever home was destined to be with me as one person after another didn't find Beasley a good fit for them.

Beasley refuses to play with any of the toys I give her. She prefers to chase squirrels and rabbits. She is untrained and stubborn to a fault, but she is also incredibly loyal and loving. I credit my quick recovery from radiation treatments to Beasley's constant desire to be outside. She ensured I got plenty of fresh air. I saw every sunrise and every sunset, and all the wonders in between as I struggled to overcome the exhaustion brought on by my fight with cancer.

I wanted to salute her stalwart companionship by including her in this story. However, at 20 pounds, she was too big to be hidden under a crocheted afghan, and being a Scottie, she almost never barks—things the dog in the story needed to do. When I saw a picture of my hair stylist's adorable white Pomeranian, Dreampuff; I knew a Pomeranian was the perfect fit for this story. Thank you, Jason Franks, for showing me pictures of your pup.

A NOTE FROM THE AUTHOR

I am delighted you made it all the way through to the end of *Hooked Into Murder,* book two in the Yarn Genie Mystery Series. I hope you enjoyed reading it as much as I enjoyed putting the story of Imogene and Frank into print. If you did find this novel an enjoyable read, please consider leaving an on-line review of the book.

All books go through several edits for content and grammar, but if you catch a spelling error or grammatical mistake, I would appreciate it if you would let the publisher know at islandcitypublishing@gmail.com.

Please note that while I strive to make the story realistic, everything in this book is a work of fiction. The places used may be based on real locations, but the use of them and the events surrounding them are purely fiction and should not be construed as factual or accurate.

40567035R00153

Made in the USA
Lexington, KY
30 May 2019